M000284168

THE
ROSE
OF
Florence

First published by Romaunce Books in 2023
Suite 2, Top Floor, 7 Dyer Street, Cirencester, Gloucestershire, GL7 2PF

Copyright © Angela M Sims

Angela M Sims has asserted her right under the Copyright Designs and Patents
Act 1988 to be identified as the author of this work.

All rights reserved.

No part of this publication may be reproduced, stored in a retrieval system, or transmitted in any form or
by any means, without the prior permission in writing of the publisher, nor be otherwise circulated in any
form of binding or cover other than that in which it is published and without a similar condition including
this condition being imposed on the subsequent purchaser

A catalogue record for this book is available from the British Library

The Rose of Florence
Hardback ISBN 978-1-7391173-0-6

Cover design and content by Ray Lipscombe
Printed and bound in Great Britain

Romaunce Books™ is a registered trademark

THE
ROSE
OF
Florence

Angela M Sims

Contents

ACKNOWLEDGEMENTS

The Rose of Florence

It's difficult to know where to start when thanking those who have helped me to create The Rose of Florence, my first novel. Far from being a solitary activity, writing requires the support and guidance of many people, especially when you are new to the craft.

Firstly, I have to thank my husband, Keith. Not only has he sacrificed himself by accompanying me on many trips to Florence (such a hardship!), but he has also supported me every inch of the way, whether that be by tactfully ignoring the number of research books I've bought, encouraging me to write when the urge takes me or simply by making numerous cups of tea. Every step of the way, he has encouraged me from day one, and I am so very lucky to have him.

Once my story started to develop, a few close friends and family helped by sense-checking my writing, looking for elusive typos and inconsistencies, of which there were many. So, my thanks to Anji, Helen and Carys for their time and patience.

A little further down the line, I found support and encouragement in the Cariad Chapter of the Romantic Novelists' Association. While I hate to pick out individuals from this group of lovely people, it would be wrong of me not to highlight the help I received from Sue, Sandra and Jan. You helped me to believe that I could do this. As part of the RNA's New Writers' Scheme, my manuscript was reviewed by the wonderful Katherine Mezzacappa. Her advice and guidance, taken from her extensive experience was just what I needed to polish the story, making it what it is today. Thank you, my guru!

Thank you to Catherine, who edited the manuscript, working tirelessly behind the scenes.

Last, but by no means least, thank you to Antonia at Romaunce Books, who had the confidence to take on this fledgling author and publish The Rose of Florence, releasing it to the world.

So, while my name is on the cover of this book, it is the combination of love, help, support and guidance from many people that made it happen, and I am very grateful.

Angela M Sims
October 2022

FOREWORD

"L'appetito vien mangiando"

"The appetite comes while you are eating"
Italian proverb

A good story should be very like a good meal and should be just as satisfying. Each will have its own stages or courses, and each course should make you look forward to the next. Like guests at my dining table, I offer my story to you for your entertainment and enjoyment.

We start with the traditional Italian *aperitivo*, designed to whet the appetite, encouraging you on to the next course and the course after that. At each course, I offer a simple Tuscan recipe to represent each stage of the story. We finish the story with a *dolce* or dessert and a simple *digestivo*, which I hope will leave you figuratively patting your stomach in satisfaction.

Of course, you should accompany this with the wine of your choice!

Buon appetito!

APERITIVO

A summer drink or cocktail is the perfect way to start a meal. It is fresh and welcoming and encourages you to stay and taste more. A good aperitivo should not be all fruitiness and fizz, though. Pick up a large juicy olive for unexpected bitterness. The contrast will intrigue you. What will come next?

Aperol Spritz
Ice
100ml Aperol
200ml Prosecco
Slice of orange
Soda water, to top up if necessary

Place a generous handful of ice in a tall glass. Pour in the Aperol and the Prosecco. Add the sliced orange, and if required, top up with soda water. Enjoy while fresh and fizzy!

PROLOGUE

Fiesole, 1460

Summer in the Tuscan mountains. The haze of dry, dusty soil and the smell of thyme and rosemary hung heavily in the air. The sky above was approaching that magical mix between the gold of the setting sun and the first blue of the approaching night, giving the rooftops of the surrounding farms a fiery glow. A lone buzzard circled in search of an evening kill. Beneath its beady eye, a dormouse scuttled into the undergrowth and survived another day.

Fiesole, the small town on the hillside overlooking the bustling city of Florence, breathed a soft sigh as it began to rest in the early evening. The farmers and shepherds had returned home from the fields. Wealthy businessmen and noble families rested in their summer villas, enjoying the cool breeze from the mountains, so different from the hot, dry, foul air of the city. Wisps of smoke rose steadily from the chimneys of the farmhouses and villas alike, heralding the promise of the evening meal, and the aromas of cooking filled the air of the town. While the kitchens were busy, out in the town and surrounding farms, there was little sign of life on this lazy evening.

Just outside the town however, a cloud of dust rose from a small pathway. As the dusty trail got closer to the town, the sound of running footsteps grew louder until they reached the gates of a grand villa, a little way down the hill from the main town square.

In the kitchen of the villa, the cook was disturbed from his work by a frantic pounding on the door. With a sigh, he brushed his hands in his large apron and wearily rose to answer the summons. As he unlocked the door, it was flung open, and he looked down into the face of a young peasant boy. The cook knew him as the son of a local farmer, who often ran errands for the family and the staff, but he had never before seen the boy so agitated.

"Heavens, Tommaso! What on earth is wrong? You nearly knocked the door off its hinges."

"The young master!" the young boy almost shouted. "I need the young master. He needs to come now. Where is he?"

"The master is about to sit down for his evening dinner, young man. He doesn't want to be disturbed by the likes of you," said the cook, as he folded his arms over his ample stomach. "Now get along with you. You can speak with him tomorrow."

"No, no, no," said young Tommaso, his voice beginning to rise. "Tomorrow will be too late." With that, he pushed past the cook, ran through the kitchen and burst through the door leading to the family quarters.

"*Dio mio!*" said the cook, rubbing his forearm across his brow. "What was all that about? Something and nothing, I expect." And with a sigh, he picked up his knife and went back to chopping the vegetables for tomorrow's soup.

The villa was grand by the town's standards and envied as a summer residence by many in Florence and beyond. It had been built into the hillside just ten years earlier, to much acclaim. The loggia of the house led onto the terraces and provided the perfect position for admiring the gardens and the magnificent views across the valley and into Florence. Near the kitchen was a healthy herb and vegetable garden, but the other side was designed to display the flair of the garden designers and the skill of the villa's gardeners. These formal gardens were well-organised as they flowed down the hillside. Each terrace had its own lawn, and the winding pathway was lined with lemon trees, releasing their bright, citrus aroma. Splashes of colour were provided by terracotta pots filled with orange and red pelargoniums. The whole garden was a delight to the senses.

Sitting in the garden was a young man, insensible to the delights surrounding him. He gazed absently at the view before him. He knew how lucky he was to be allowed to stay here and study during the recent months. The family was very generous. He also knew that things would be difficult when he told his own family of the decision he had made. Much was expected of him, but in his own heart, he knew the path he had to take. This was not some flight of fancy that he had decided to follow on a whim, but a deep-seated absolute knowledge that it was the right thing, indeed the only thing, to do if his life was to have any meaning. He knew that his family would not share his conviction, and the knowledge that he was to cause such damage and hurt to his beloved parents broke his heart. He was torn from his thoughts by the sound of running footsteps along the gravel path behind him.

"Sir, sir, you must come!" gasped the young boy. "It's not good. It's really not good at all."

A little further down the hill stood a farmhouse. It was not a large farmhouse by any means, with just a small, enclosed yard at the back where chickens scratched the ground, pecking at seeds. Through a small gate and just beyond the fence, a neat vegetable garden led to a few trees with a healthy crop of olives just beginning to ripen. The farm stood in a pleasant position on the hillside, just a little way from Fiesole, where the sun nurtured the crops grown there. The house was small but well cared for, the terracotta roof absorbing the summer sun, and windows open to allow the mountain breeze to flow through. On this tranquil evening, the door also stood open, and through it flew a piercing scream.

Inside the house, in the single room which was used for living, sleeping and cooking, the screams came again. On the bed in the centre of the room lay a young woman, clutching the bed sheets, writhing in pain and bathed in sweat from her labour.

The older woman next to her looked worried as she bathed the young woman's forehead with a cooling cloth. "*Stai calma, cara mia.* Be calm, my love," she soothed. "I am here, and your baby is almost with us."

Under her breath, the older woman whispered a prayer to the Virgin Mary to protect this young girl and her baby. This birth was more difficult than any of the dozens that she had attended before, made more difficult for her because the mother in labour was her own daughter. A short while later, after the screams had died away, the older woman gently handed a soft bundle to its mother. "You have a beautiful daughter, *una bellissima figlia,*" she said, with a smile, trying to hide the fear that grew inside her. As she looked at the growing red stain on the bedsheets, she knew she could do no more. She looked up into the eyes of the new mother, and their gaze remained still and peaceful for many moments.

"Mamma…" said the young mother.

"Hush, *cara mia.* Rest now," she replied, even as she watched the colour drain from the face in front of her.

"No, Mamma. I know I have to go. I have no regrets. I have known love unlike anything I could have hoped for, and this love will live on in my little girl. She is the reason for my life. Promise me that you will take care of her, Mamma. Promise me…"

As the older woman released the lifeless hand, she thought her heart would break.

In the heavy silence of the following minutes, the only sound to be heard was the gentle snuffling of the tiny new born creature tucked up in a makeshift cradle in the corner of the room.

Outside, a young peasant boy and a well-dressed young man ran up the path to the farm as if the devil was on their heels. They both skidded to a stop as they entered the farmhouse through the open door and were hit by the silence. The two faces turned to the bed, but it was the young man who reached the bed first in just two strides.

"No!" he cried. "No, this cannot be. I don't believe it. Wake up, Clara. Wake up! We have so much to plan. We have so many things to do together. Clara! Clara!"

A gentle hand on his shoulder pulled him away from Clara's pale, limp body. "Hush now, child. There was nothing I could do. Sometimes, the good Lord sees fit to take those we love, and we must not question His reasons."

The young man buried his head in the older woman's shoulder and sobbed tears that he felt would never end.

When the tide eventually subsided, the woman pulled away and said, "We both loved Clara with all our hearts, but there is a new life to love now. Your daughter is sleeping in the cradle. See! She truly is a God-given gift."

He turned and took a tentative step toward the cradle. He stood and gazed at the baby, who slept peacefully, unaware of the emotions surrounding her in this small room. A few moments later, he gently stroked her cheek and touched the small pink birth mark behind her ear before turning and striding from the house.

The woman, drained and heartbroken, sat down, took the sobbing peasant boy onto her lap, closed her eyes and sighed deeply.

ANTIPASTI

*The antipasti is an exciting course, because it is open to all possibilities,
and so it is with a story. What will be served today? Where will it take
me?*

*To accompany slices of salami, prosciutto and mozzarella, I am
offering a sauce which complements thin slices of crispy, toasted
focaccia. It contains fresh, wholesome ingredients but has an
unexpected kick.*

Davanzati Sauce

*1lb ripe, red tomatoes • ½ cup extra virgin olive oil
4 cloves garlic • 1 tablespoon chopped fresh parsley
1 dried chilli pepper • Pinch salt*

*Peel the tomatoes by cutting a cross in the skin and placing in a bowl
of boiling water for 10–15 mins. The skins should easily come away
from the flesh.*

- *Chop tomatoes, discarding the hard core.*
- *In a saucepan, gently heat the olive oil, finely chopped
  garlic and chilli pepper.*
- *Add the chopped tomatoes.*
- *Cook on high heat for about 15 mins.*
- *Season with salt.*
- *Serve warm with thin slices of toasted focaccia.*

Recipe reproduced with kind permission from Nonna Viela and the
family of the Davanzati Hotel, Via Porta Rossa, Florence.

Florence

February 1478

Map of Florence

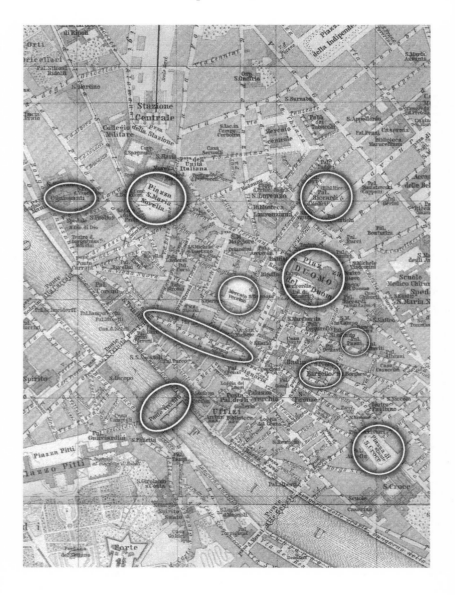

CHAPTER 1

Monday before Lent - morning

The morning dawned with early spring sunshine but with a brisk chill in the air. The narrow streets had been washed clean by recent spring rains, and the city was preparing itself to meet the sombre season of Lent this Wednesday. Some had been shopping in preparation for last-minute feasting, as there were still a few days left of Carnival season. Others were getting ahead in their quest to avoid the horrors of purgatory, by walking sombrely to church, head bowed. On the surface, all seemed calm and contented.

La Volpe stood on the bank of the River Arno, which runs through the centre of the city, his city. He leaned against the wall, his back to the river, which was teeming with the detritus of the butchers' shops which lined the main bridge. He had become immune to the stench, which pervaded the air and seeped along the side streets. He stood in a good position: it was a busy part of the riverbank, full of traders, shoppers, fishermen, and plenty of characters of questionable repute. He could see all the activity along the riverbank and the main road that ran away from the river and towards the city's great *Duomo*, the cathedral of Santa Maria del Fiore.

He was unremarkable in his appearance, which helped to make him anonymous in a crowd and therefore very good at his job. The only features that a passer-by might have noticed were his darting, ever watchful eyes and the fox's tail, which hung from his belt. He was pleased with the addition of the tail to his appearance, as he believed it added to his mystery and gave him a dangerous edge. Who was to know that the fox had died of old age, rather than by his own hand? Even so, he was good at what he did and was paid well for his skills.

As usual, he was waiting to meet his latest employer, the next person who was willing to pay for his services. Was it his imagination, or was the demand for his work picking up lately? Who was he to complain?

He spotted the man easily. Some were very good at being invisible in a crowd, but others made too much of an effort and became too obvious. He smiled to himself as he approached the man. This would be an easy job.

In a quiet, respectable neighbourhood, overlooking a small piazza on *Via Porta Rossa*, not ten minutes' walk from the River Arno, stood Palazzo Rosini, the home of the Rosini family. The Rosini were a wealthy family of textile merchants, not of noble birth but of honest and honourable standing, well respected by those who knew and conducted business with them. Signor Francesco Rosini lived in the Palazzo with his wife, Cristina. Their son and daughter-in-law, Niccolò and Tessa, and their young grandson, Gino, also lived in the family home. They shared this home with Nonna Isabetta, elderly nursemaid and now more a member of the family than staff.

On the top floor of the Palazzo, as in most rich Italian homes, was the kitchen, where the clash of the pots and pans, and the hustle and bustle of staff could be found. Far from being chaotic, the whole orchestration was carefully controlled and conducted by Eleonora, the cook. There were five members of staff in the household, and they were as much a family as the family they served. There was little hierarchy between them, but in the kitchen, there was no doubt who was in charge.

Eleonora was a short woman of indeterminate age, with strong arms from kneading bread and a soft bosom for comforting those in distress. She was a kindly soul with a gentle heart, except on banquet days, and this was a banquet day. Anyone with a certain sense of self-preservation either jumped to her command or stayed well out of her way. The banquet was to be held that evening, and preparations had been going on for days, but the final push was always fraught with last minute jobs and errands. Eleonora was always afraid that one small error would ruin the whole banquet. She did not believe there had been errors last time, but the evening had gone horribly wrong. So, she made sure that everyone concentrated on their duties carefully.

"Lucia!" called Eleonora across the kitchen. "How is my stew?"

"*Tutto bene*, Eleonora," Lucia replied. "It is all good. Your stew will be sensational, as always." Lucia was Eleonora's second-in-command in the kitchen and learning her craft well. A young girl of nineteen, she had been in the kitchen with Eleonora for around four years and was now quite skilled. The skills included much of the culinary magic that occurred in that kitchen, but also how to handle Eleonora on banquet days. As she stirred the pot above the open fire, Lucia pushed a strand of her long dark hair back under her cap.

The stew was but a small part of the banquet, although an important one. After all, Eleonora had a reputation to uphold. She was proud to be one of the very few women and yet one of the best domestic cooks in Florence, although she tried half-heartedly to hide it by waving off compliments with a blush. The only blushing to be seen in the kitchen today was as a result of heat and hard work. While most of her contemporaries would buy their bread from the bakeries in town (while catching up on the local gossip), Eleonora always insisted on baking her own bread. The Rosini were wealthy enough to buy the expensive white flour that Eleonora used to impress their guests and build her reputation. She was kneading a large mound of dough on the enormous wooden table at the centre of the kitchen. Her eyes were on the work in front of her, but she didn't miss someone trying to steal a taste of the stew.

"Antonio Matelli! Get your spoon out of that stew!"

Antonio jumped away from Lucia and the pot of stew, licked his lips, grinned at Lucia and wandered over to Eleonora, wrapping his arms around her. A good-looking young man with dark hair and smiling eyes, Antonio was well-liked in the household, did his duties well and enjoyed the attentions of the pretty Lucia.

"Ah, Eleonora, you know I can't resist your cooking. How has no man snapped you up? I'd marry you myself, but there are so many other demands on a man's time." He was used to using his charm to get him out of trouble.

Behind him, Lucia smiled, but Eleonora batted him away with floury hands.

"With so many demands on your time," she replied, "I'm amazed that you have time for this nonsense. Now get away with you! Have you and Matteo collected the fruit from the market yet? I don't want that Agnese from the Conti house to get the pick of the produce. When the Contis dine here tonight, they are going to get the best, but I wouldn't put it past that woman to buy up the good stuff out of spite."

"Eleonora, are these boys giving you trouble?" The soothing voice from the doorway came from Gianetta, a ladies' maid who also helped care for young Gino. Gianetta was just eighteen, but capable of ensuring the efficient running of the servant quarters and household events, while her youthful cheeriness spread a happy atmosphere wherever she went.

Eleonora huffed and went back to her kneading.

"I think you'll find I had nothing to do with it," piped up Matteo from the corner of the kitchen. Matteo was the most recent member of the group of servants, joining the Palazzo staff after a brief, unsuccessful period as an apprentice in a local artist's studio. It had not taken long for him to become a valued and loved member of staff, especially by Gianetta.

"I'm sure it was just a matter of time, Matteo," replied Gianetta, smiling back at him. "I see you sneaking tasters when you think no one is watching. Now, you know what Eleonora needs, so be off with you both. We still have much to do before this evening, and I have a list of jobs for you."

Antonio gave Eleonora another hug, which she shrugged off impatiently.

Matteo, tall, with long, unruly black hair and a twinkle in his bright blue eyes, bent down to kiss Gianetta on the cheek.

"*Ciao, Bellissima,*" he whispered.

Gianetta pushed him away with a smile and a wink.

"*Andiamo*, Matteo," called Antonio from the door. "Let's go." And with that, they left the kitchen and ran down the stairs.

Lucia had left the stew to its own devices and was now plucking one of the dozen pigeons which were to be roasted alongside a brace of pheasants, already prepared and sitting in their roasting dish. Her slight frame was sitting beside the fire, into which she threw the feathers. "It's very exciting, isn't it?" she said with a faraway look in her eyes. "So many important people dining here."

Eleonora carried on pummelling her dough, and Gianetta took a stool next to Lucia, picking up the next pigeon to be plucked.

"You should be used to seeing the Signori de' Medici here," she said. "They dine here often."

"Oh, I know that, but it's always a treat to serve them, especially Signor Giuliano." She winked at Gianetta, who laughed.

"You're wicked, Lucia. I thought you only had eyes for our Antonio."

"Oh, I do," she replied, "but it doesn't hurt to keep your options open. Who else is coming tonight, Eleonora?"

Without pausing her kneading, Eleonora said, "I believe we are expecting Matteo's old employer, Signor Sandro. With him and Signor Lorenzo de' Medici here, we can expect a late finish. They always talk late into the night."

"Ooh, did you know that they are calling him Botticelli, the Little Barrel? Signor Sandro, I mean. It's after his big round brother." Lucia paused in her work as she laughed, but Eleonora was quick to respond.

"There will be no use of that name in this house. We always have the greatest respect for our guests."

"I know, Eleonora. I wouldn't dare…but it is quite funny." And she giggled to herself again.

"I heard you mention the Contis, Eleonora. Are they bringing their son too?" Lucia had a mischievous look in her eye.

"Yes, I believe Signor Cesare will be joining us."

"You had better be careful, Gianetta," said Lucia. "He has taken a great liking to you."

"Don't you worry about me," replied Gianetta, firmly. "I can handle him."

Eleonora had finished her kneading and set aside the dough to rest. "Enough gossiping, Lucia," she said, brushing her floury hands in her apron. "Wash your hands and take Nonna Isabetta her lunch tray.

There is cherry sop in the bowl in the cold room and fetch some bread from the cupboard. Take a small cup of wine too."

"Oh, may the Lord bless her," said Lucia with a smile. "Poor Nonna. She's not as bright as she once was. I don't understand half of what she says."

"Oh, don't you worry," said Eleonora, wisely. "Nonna Isabetta is still as sharp as a knife. She misses nothing."

Lucia gathered the bread and sop, filled a cup with wine and completed the tray with a single iris from the bunches in the corner of the cold room, which were waiting to be made into displays for the dining room. "Nonna loves the colour of irises." Lucia smiled as she left the kitchen with the tray, the heavy door closing behind her.

In the meantime, Gianetta had finished plucking the pigeons and placed them neatly on the tray ready for Eleonora's magic touch of herbs, before roasting later. "Eleonora, come and rest for five minutes," said Gianetta. "We are on time with our preparations, so we can take a minute for a drink."

Eleonora nodded and sat wearily on her chair by the fire, while Gianetta poured two cups of herbal restorative from the jug in the cold room. Eleonora, known for her skills in the kitchen, was also skilled in her use of herbs for all ailments. Her father had been an apothecary, and as a young girl, Eleonora had been a watchful and receptive student. This draught included chamomile, vanilla and honey, although she used many recipes, depending on the season and what was growing in the herb garden.

"I know Signor Francesco loves this drink when he is busy or when he doesn't sleep, but I'm sure he won't mind sharing it with us today," said Gianetta, handing a cup to Eleonora, taking a sip of her own and sitting on the stool opposite her. "You know it will all be fine, don't you, Eleonora? Everything will come together as it always does. The family and their guests will eat and drink their fill, and you will again be celebrated as the best cook in town! *La prima cuoca!*"

"Oh, I don't know about that," she said, trying to hide a proud smile, but then her face changed, and she began to frown. "This is such an important dinner. I really have to keep an eye on every single detail today…after what happened last time," she said quietly, almost to herself.

"Do you mean Signor Lorenzo getting sick?" asked Gianetta. "You know what those Medici are like. They love fine food and wine. He probably drank far too much of Signor Francesco's best Vernaccia."

Eleonora shook her head. "They do love fine food and wine, as you said, Gianetta, but they never over-indulge. They are neither drunkards nor gluttons. They are fine gentlemen. No, this was something else." Her frown grew deeper, as she thought back to the dinner held at the Palazzo on the last Saturday before Christmas, just two months ago.

It had been a cold evening. It rarely snows in Florence, but there had been a whisper of it in the air that night. All the fires in the Palazzo had been lit; the rooms decorated with winter greenery, brought in from the marketplace. The cosy atmosphere was one of cheery anticipation ahead of one of the Church's biggest celebrations, the Birth of the Christ-child. As usual, the kitchen had been a hive of activity for some days, and Eleonora had surpassed herself with the sumptuous spread. It had been an intimate affair, with only Signori Lorenzo and Giuliano as guests of the family, but the evening had been a great success. Such was the closeness of the two families that by the end of the evening, Rosini and Medici were singing a mixture of devout Christmas hymns and bawdy tavern songs, which made Donna Cristina blush and Nonna Isabetta chuckle to herself. As the evening came to a close, the guests rose to leave. Lorenzo, however, clutched the back of one the dining chairs, complaining that his heart was pounding and holding a hand to his chest. While gasping for breath, he lurched towards the corner of the room and promptly vomited into a large decorative pitcher. He became so unwell that he had to be helped home by Antonio and Matteo. He remained unwell for some days but eventually recovered completely, and the incident was all but forgotten.

It was still fresh in Eleonora's mind, though, and not because of the injury to her pride. No, what bothered Eleonora was a memory of her father's apothecary shop. One night, a woman in great distress had pounded on the door of their home in Pistoia, waking the family. Eleonora's father had been preparing a potion for the woman's husband for some weeks. It was designed to treat his frequent headaches and palpitations and had been working well. However, on this occasion, it transpired that the woman's husband had mistakenly taken the whole concoction and was now in a dreadful state. His palpitations were worse than ever, and he was delirious and vomiting. Eleonora remembered being a young girl watching in distress as her father broke the news to the poor woman that there was no antidote to this poisoning, and all they could do was to pray to the Virgin Mary to take care of him. Sadly, later that day, the woman's husband died.

As Eleonora recounted this story, Gianetta was captivated. "The same ailments as Signor Lorenzo," she whispered.

Eleonora nodded.

"What was in the concoction?" asked Gianetta.

"The main ingredient was a flower," she replied quietly. "Some call them fairy fingers or throatwort. I believe the English call them foxgloves. They are rare here in winter, but I remember that Donna Cristina had ordered some from the hothouses for the display that night. After Signor Lorenzo became so ill, I kept thinking of that poor woman and her husband, and I wondered. I just wondered…" she tailed off.

"But you can't think that it was deliberate, Eleonora?" said Gianetta, shocked. "Who would do that? It must have been an accident."

"It can't have been a simple accident. The flower display was far away from the *credenza* where the cold food was presented, and even if it were just a flower petal, dropping into a salad, it wouldn't have been enough to cause such a serious reaction. No, there must have been quite a significant amount put into Signor Lorenzo's food or drink."

"But how? And how did he survive when the man your father treated died? And why try to poison Signor Lorenzo, anyway?" Gianetta was mystified.

"How?" replied Eleonora. "That's fairly easy. Any part of the plant and even the water from the vase is poisonous. The display was in the room for most of the day, and anyone could have got what they needed. How did he survive? I can only assume that it is because he is young and healthy. The man who died was old and already frail. His body probably did not have the strength to fight the poison. Why Signor Lorenzo? Well, that's a bigger question, but it's no secret that there are some people in Florence who would like to see the end of the Medici. Just look at that Pazzi family. They strut around Florence, proclaiming their nobility and boasting of their history of being in the Crusades, but what they really want is the Medici power over Florence. Signor Lorenzo is the head of the Medici family. What greater target?" She shook her head and sighed, but Gianetta wouldn't hear of it.

"I don't believe it. I don't pretend to understand the politics of men, but it has always been the same. There are always arguments and disagreements. One family is the rival of another, and that is always the case here in Florence, as it is in Pisa, as it is in Rome, but surely nobody would resort to murder in a family home...and at Christmas too!"

Eleonora smiled, leaned forward and took Gianetta's hands into her own. "Oh, my dear girl, you have much to learn. Sadly, the world is a wicked place, and a man's home is no longer the protection that it used to be. Those who wish to wield power in the *Signoria* will stop at nothing to achieve their ambition. A simple case of poisoning would mean nothing to them. You go out into the streets of Florence, and you will hear talk of uprising, revolt and unrest every day. You must have heard it."

Gianetta still looked doubtful.

"Dear Gianetta. Dear, dear Gianetta. You are young; you are in love. Do not deny it. I have eyes in my head, and I see you and Matteo together, the way you look at each other. The whole world is bright and full of promise for you, and that's as it should be, but don't let that blind you to what is going on around you. What is bubbling under the surface in Florence will affect us all eventually, and it is better that we are prepared and know who our friends and allies are."

"Ah, Eleonora." Gianetta smiled, blushing. "You miss nothing, do you? It is true. Matteo and I love each other, but whatever is going on in Florentine politics will never affect that. I still don't believe it. Who in this household would do such a thing?"

As Lucia returned to the kitchen, Gianetta jumped up to help her with the heavy door, and Eleonora whispered to herself, "Who indeed?"

Lucia was laughing, as she recounted her visit to Nonna Isabetta's chambers. "Apparently, cherry sop is only for babes or the elderly with no teeth, and would it really be so difficult to have some real meat at lunchtime? Oh, and as much as I'm good at my job, she would much rather have her tray brought to her by that charming young Antonio."

"You have competition for Antonio's affections, Lucia." Eleonora laughed.

"I do! However, I did find another charming young man heading in our direction."

"Gino!" Eleonora held out her arms to welcome the little boy onto her lap.

"Eli!" he cried. At six years old, with dark hair and eyes like his father, he was already using his charms. He was the only one who could shorten the cook's name without fear. "What have you been cooking? Can I try? I'm so hungry!"

"Let's see what we can find. *Andiamo*!" She stood up and led Gino by the hand to the pantry, Gino's favourite place in the whole world.

CHAPTER 2

Later the same day

Dusk approached, and as the sun set, the Palazzo was ready to greet its guests. It was a dry evening, and the central courtyard was warm and welcoming. Dozens of candles and lanterns were lit in the alcoves and on the stairways, and the aroma of many hours of cooking gently wafted through the open corridors and balconies and into the rooms. Above the courtyard, on the first floor, the dining room stood with its large doors open like embracing arms. All comfort, from food and warmth to wine and friendship, was to be found in this room, starting with the roaring fire in the enormous fireplace at the end of the room. Eyes are always drawn to a flame, and this fire sent great, hypnotic flames licking the back of the fireplace and up the chimney. A generous pile of logs in the basket alongside the grate would ensure that the early spring chill would not spoil this evening's merriment.

Donna Cristina walked slowly around the room, inspecting every detail and finding it impeccable, as always. The centre of the room was dominated by the vast dining table, set with twelve places. Each place setting included the best silverware from the Palazzo, plates, knives and spoons and silk napkins. Cristina admired the shine on each piece of cutlery. Was this Matteo's handiwork or Antonio's? She reached out to straighten a knife but pulled her hand back, afraid of spoiling the gleam caught from the bright candles. The hand-crafted drinking goblets of finest Murano glass were a gift from a Venetian family, grateful for the safe delivery of the best quality brocades bought for their daughter's wedding dowry bundle. The table's centrepiece was a sugar sculpture, one of the newest fashions to adorn Italian tables, and it brought a smile to Cristina's lips. Her husband always knew how to create a talking point. The sugar required to make such works of art was rare, and the practice was not widely known, but Signor Francesco's business contacts had enabled him to locate and purchase these ingredients. There were also enough local artists who were keen to try this new medium for sculpting. This sculpture was of a vase of roses, decorated with cochineal colouring to create red roses in honour of the Rosini family emblem. The decoration had caused great commotion when it was delivered, as it was the first of its kind to be seen in the Rosini circle of friends. Signor Francesco, a lover of all arts and new innovations, was very proud of it, and it would surely be a great topic of conversation in the evening to come. The enormous candelabra either side of the sculpture ensured that it was lit to best advantage, while also allowing the guests plenty of light to see and enjoy their food.

Opposite the doors, behind the table were three long windows, which, when open, would normally allow in enough light and air for long summer evening banquets. The windows of this Palazzo were glazed, as befitted the home of a successful businessman. The panes were made up of small circles of glass, and thus the windows were heavily leaded, stealing some light but providing warmth during the cold winter evenings. At this time of year, with the sun already set, they were closed and covered with heavy curtains of red velvet, trimmed with golden silk. Silk was the most expensive textile available in Italy, but in recent years, Florence had become one of the new centres for silk weaving, and while still expensive, it was becoming more popular among the rich and noble families.

While he was usually a modest man, Signor Francesco was more than happy to display his success by showing his wares in the dining room. These curtains had, with the aid of several jugs of good Vernaccia wine, led to several lucrative contracts for the supply of high-quality textiles to wealthy local families. Business was not a part of this evening's festivities, but the golden silk reflecting the flickering flames, added to the warmth of the welcome.

Cristina ran a hand over the fabric, savouring the sheen of the delicate silk and the luxurious warmth of the velvet. Above her, the high ceiling was adorned with a beautiful fresco. Francesco's patronage of the arts and his friendship with Lorenzo de' Medici ensured that he had access to many of the best artists' workshops. This fresco had been completed by a talented apprentice from the workshop of Ghirlandaio, one of the largest in Florence. Gazing at it for any length of time would have you believe that you were in a summer garden, with blue sky, gentle clouds and lush foliage. No doubt the apprentice who had completed this work under the master's tutelage was destined for great things.

Behind the doors, opposite the great, curtained windows stood the family *credenza*, an enormous piece of furniture, handed down from Fabrizio, Francesco's father. A highly decorated sideboard, it was usually used to display the family's collection of maiolica plates, but this evening, the surface was covered with enormous platters of food.

Dishes that did not need to be served hot from the kitchen were already sitting and waiting for the guests, and Cristina looked at each dish with admiration and not a little hunger. There were stuffed eggs, nuts spiced with cinnamon and nutmeg and *ciambelle*, fried bread rings flavoured according to Eleonora's preference with fennel. Alongside these were also slices of bresaola made from veal; prosciutto from Eleonora's favourite *macelleria*; figs in honey; loaves of fresh focaccia; soft mozzarella from a local farm, and bowls of fresh pesto sauce. Cristina closed her eyes and inhaled the aromas deeply. Jugs of wine stood to attention at the back of the *credenza*; a Vernaccia white and a deep, rich red Chianti made with the prized sangiovese grapes from Francesco's favourite vineyard in the Tuscan hills.

On a separate small table, next to the doors, stood a large bowl of water with delicate rose petals floating on the surface. This allowed the guests to wash their hands, as was the custom before eating. While some dishes could be eaten with spoons, many foods still required the diner to use their hands, and cleanliness at the dining table was a matter of routine for rich and poor alike. The dining room was perfect. Cristina always savoured these quiet moments before a banquet, when she could appreciate the work of her staff and anticipate a pleasant evening ahead.

Reluctantly leaving the room, she made her way to the courtyard on the ground floor to await their guests. The sound of distant voices below the dining room indicated that they had indeed begun to arrive and were being welcomed by the hosts and their staff.

Antonio in his finest formal livery greeted the male guests with a welcoming smile, taking their heavy cloaks, while Gianetta helped Donna Maria Conti with her winter cloak.

The Conti family were familiar visitors to Palazzo Rosini, since Donna Maria and Donna Cristina were childhood friends. Signor Piero Conti came from a respected, noble family and had inherited properties, wealth and land between Florence and Milan. Unlike many of the other landowning *signori*, Signor Piero was considered a fair and just landlord and was popular with his tenants. The Contis married later in life and were shocked and delighted when Donna Maria gave birth to a son at an age when most women were past the ability to carry and safely deliver a child.

Cesare, now in his early twenties, was greatly cherished by his parents and had a privileged upbringing, with the promise of a large inheritance when the time came. However, as is often the case when such good fortune has not been hard won, Cesare was not keen to do much work, enjoying his father's wealth as young men of the nobility often do, by indulging in leisure pastimes rather than learning to be productive. His mother indulged him, and his father had convinced himself that Cesare would soon grow up to be an asset to the family, but was beginning to wonder when that would happen. Even so, Cesare was charming company and was always welcomed by the Rosini family.

As Donna Cristina descended the stairs to the courtyard, Cesare was being greeted by her own son, Niccolò.

Cesare had always looked up to Niccolò as an older brother, and in fairness, Niccolò had consistently had patience with the capricious young man, trying to instil a sense of responsibility into him. Despite their differences in age and outlook, they remained great friends. This evening, they were dressed in their finest outfits, determined to make the most of this last social event before Lent. Both wore high-necked doublets in the latest fashion, Niccolò in velvet of midnight black, edged in gold silk thread, and Cesare in deep red. Their matching velvet hose and contrasting silk sleeves bore testament to the quality of Signor Francesco's textiles and the skill of the local seamstresses.

"How goes it, young Conti?" asked Niccolò, with his arm around the young man's shoulder. "Are you still terrorising the animals of the forest with your bow and arrow or do the young ladies of Florence need to be worried about a different kind of arrow?" He laughed.

"Niccolò, please!" exclaimed Donna Cristina.

"Apologies, Mamma. You know how I like to tease the boy. I will now be on my very best behaviour." As he bowed extravagantly, Donna Cristina smiled at her son and moved to greet her old friend, Donna Maria.

"*Buona sera, amica.*" Cristina linked arms with her old friend. "Ah, sons! Such a joy, but so incorrigible, even when they are married with a family of their own! Tell me, has Cesare chosen a wife yet?"

The women gossiped, while behind them, Signori Francesco and Piero clasped hands and enquired after each other's businesses.

Piero asked, "Is your shadow joining us this evening?"

Francesco threw back his head and laughed loudly. "No, Luigi won't be joining us tonight. He is in his quarters as he has some work on our latest contracts to deal with. Such is the joy of having a personal assistant. They can take care of the dull side of the business. And as you know, he is not one to enjoy these social events."

Cesare leaned in towards Niccolò as Antonio opened the great door to their next guest. "Ah, here he is, Maestro Sandro himself," whispered Cesare. "Do you know they are calling him Botticelli, the Little Barrel? It's after his older and larger brother, who is…well, barrel-shaped!"

"Yes," muttered Niccolò. "I'd heard that too, but if you want to keep my mother's favour, you'd better refer to him as Maestro Sandro!" And with that, he strode forward with his hand extended to greet their new guest.

Maestro Alessandro Filipepi was a painter in his early thirties and considered to be a rising star in Florentine artistic circles. He shook Niccolò's hand, and his light curly hair shook with the movement. He looked around at the assembled guests with deep, thoughtful eyes, which were ever watchful for beauty of all kinds. A serious character, he preferred his own thoughts and musings, but as an artist relying on the patronage of those who could pay for his skills, he was not averse to the occasional social evening, especially when the company included the de' Medici brothers, Lorenzo and Giuliano. Lorenzo was a very wealthy man and could ensure the financial security of any artist that he favoured. Giuliano was very beautiful, and while the maestro did not entertain romantic ideas in his direction, he did harbour hopes to capture him in his paintings one day.

Unnoticed by the gathering in the courtyard, two floors up, curious eyes peered over the open balcony.

"Who is that with Maestro Sandro, Eleonora?" whispered Lucia. "I can't quite see his face."

"That's Signor Marco Vespucci. It's good to see him out with friends again."

Lucia sighed. "So sad to lose such a beautiful wife. Consumption is a cruel thing."

"Yes, it's been two years since Simonetta died, and he seems happy enough with his new wife, but he does look as though some of the life has left him."

As Signor Vespucci handed his great cloak to Antonio, he smiled pleasantly at his hosts and companions but did indeed seem rather lost.

"Marco, *amico*," exclaimed Francesco. "*Come stai*? How are you? And how is your dear wife? I'm so sorry that she couldn't be with us tonight, but I know she is visiting her mother, and family must always come first, eh?" Francesco and Marco continued with their conversation until there was another great knock on the wooden doors. "Aha!" cried Francesco. "At last! Those Medici boys do like to make an entrance!"

The enormous doors swung open and in strode Lorenzo and

Giuliano de' Medici. The aura around the brothers was palpable, as is often the case with people of power. Lorenzo, the elder brother and head of the Medici bank, was in all but name the ruler of Florence, due to his political allies in the Florentine *Signoria*, the city's government.

In the balcony above, Lucia stood on tiptoes to get a better look at their guests. "He's not what you would call handsome, is he, Eleonora?"

"No, not with that Medici nose! There is something about him, though…" Eleonora had met Lorenzo de' Medici on a number of occasions and was always struck by the inner energy that emanated from him.

He was tall and rather powerfully built, but not elegant. With heavy-lidded eyes, a prominent lower jaw and the large nose of the Medici family, he could be called ugly, but he was known to be enormously charismatic. Women found him sexually attractive, although by this time, he had been married to Clarice Orsini for nine years. Men flocked to his side, eager to be noticed by and associated with this powerful man.

"I think I know what you mean," said Lucia, her head tilted to one side, as she tried to make sense of this contradiction of a man.

"I have cooked for him many times," said Eleonora, "and every night was a late night. Sometimes, he's flamboyant and entertaining. Sometimes, he will sit and talk about poetry and philosophy for hours."

"What's philosophy?" asked Lucia.

"A very good question," said a voice behind her. The two women turned round to see Luigi also peering over the balcony. "It seems that all men have their own philosophical views, and they need to argue about it constantly."

"Well, whatever it is, and however powerful he may be, when he comes through these doors, he is just Signor Lorenzo, Signor

Francesco's friend," concluded Eleonora.

Transferring her attention, Lucia looked at the other brother. Giuliano, four years Lorenzo's junior, was physically a stark contrast.

He was good-looking and elegant. A great sportsman, he held a special place in the heart of the Florentine people, especially during jousting tournaments, where he excelled. Giuliano liked to think of himself as a ladies' man, but in truth he could not be described as a heartless womaniser, more that he fell in love deeply and often.

Looking between Giuliano and Marco Vespucci, Lucia wondered, "Do you think the rumours are true? That he was having an affair with Signora Simonetta before she died?"

Eleonora huffed. "Always gossip with you, Lucia! You should be careful. It's a dangerous pastime."

Not to be deterred, she continued, "Well, do you? Plenty of people think so."

"Because he proclaimed her Florence's greatest beauty at the jousting tournament years ago? Every man in that tournament proclaimed someone a great beauty, whether it be their wives, mothers or the fishmonger's daughter. Were they all having affairs?" Eleonora was having none of it.

"But the banner...the one where she was painted as that Greek goddess...?"

Luigi stepped in to calm the situation. "Maestro Sandro painted the banner as a favour to the Medici and Vespucci families. It didn't do his reputation any harm either. It got him noticed, and he's been doing well for himself ever since."

With that conversation at an end, they all turned back to the balcony to take a last look at the gathering below, before returning to their duties, Luigi back to his papers, and Eleonora and Lucia back to the kitchen. They didn't notice the loose stone dust at their feet.

"*Miei amici*, my friends!" Donna Cristina stood on the stairway. "Before we go upstairs to dine, I have someone who would like to greet you." Beside her, her young grandson, Gino, stood proudly, looking out at his family and their guests. His mother, Tessa stood quietly behind him. Cristina made way for them.

Tessa, a pretty, plump girl went to stand by her husband, Niccolò, who put his arm around her, affectionately. "He has been excited about seeing everyone all day," she whispered. The proud parents watched as Gino went to each guest, bowing, shaking their hand and generally charming everyone. When it looked as though he was there to stay, Tessa called to him. "Gino! Our guests are getting hungry. We must leave them, and it is time you were in bed."

Gino looked crestfallen, but he replied, "*Sì,* Mamma." As he made his way up the stairs, holding Tessa's hand, he turned and waved. "*Buona notte, tutti!*"

"*Buona notte, giovanotto!*" came the replies.

Cristina invited her family and guests up to the dining room.

Gianetta and Antonio had already left the courtyard, so that they were on hand to serve the guests as they arrived.

Matteo remained behind to make sure that all the guests' cloaks were hanging neatly and away from the fire, so that they didn't smell of smoke by the end of the evening. He hadn't noticed a figure standing quietly behind him until he heard a slight cough. Turning round, he almost bumped straight into Cesare Conti. He had been half expecting this but had hoped to avoid a direct conversation with him.

"Signor Conti," he said, with a small bow. "Can I help you?"

"Oh, I think you have already helped me enough, don't you?" The young man's piercing green eyes looked directly at Matteo. Then, as if the sun had come out, Cesare broke into a beaming smile and put his arm around Matteo.

"I just wanted to thank you...for last week. What a coincidence that you should be passing, just as I was leaving that place."

"I have to pass it occasionally when I am running errands for Eleonora. What goes on there is no concern of mine, *ser*." Matteo was uncomfortable and hoped that was the end of the conversation. He made to move towards the stairs, but Cesare's grip tightened.

"We are grown men...er..."

"Matteo, *ser*."

"We are grown men, Matteo. Women serve a purpose from time to time. Indeed, some are very beautiful, but some of us also have other needs, which must be satisfied. Sadly, the city looks on some of those needs as vices, the "Florentine vice", I believe some call it." He shook his head, sadly. "Whatever the rights or wrongs of the situation, I could have been arrested that day. You could have turned me in to the guard, and the life I have now would have been over. But you didn't, and I wondered why."

"It's none of my business, *ser*. As I said, I pass that place often, and who I see going in or coming out is no concern of mine."

Cesare raised an eyebrow. "I suspect you hold many secrets, Matteo." He paused, as if deciding his next words carefully. Then he shone his beaming smile at Matteo. "Thank you, Matteo. Your discretion is noted and appreciated. I..." He paused, "...won't forget it." With a last glance, Cesare turned on his heel and bounded up the stairs to the dining room.

Matteo heaved a sigh of relief but was left feeling that it was not the end of the matter. He made a mental note to take a different route next time Eleonora sent him out.

CHAPTER 3

A s each guest entered the dining room, they washed their hands in the rose water bowl, drying them on a white cotton towel held by Gianetta.

Antonio was also standing by to hand the guests a goblet of wine as they made their way to their places.

"Nonna!" cried Lorenzo.

Nonna Isabetta was already at her place at table, being too infirm to make it down the stairs to the ground floor to greet the guests.

Lorenzo made straight for the diminutive woman and gave her a warm greeting, kissing her on both cheeks.

"*Giovane* Lorenzo! Young Lorenzo!" said a small voice. "Are you ruling the world, yet?"

"Not quite, Nonna, but I am working on it," replied Lorenzo, with a bark of laughter.

"*Bene.* Just make sure you keep those Pisan dogs under control!"

The guests laughed at Nonna's frank outburst but knew that she had reached an age where she was entitled to express opinions, tactless or indiscreet as they may be. Nonna, who was rather mischievous, also knew this and took full advantage whenever the opportunity arose. A small woman who could no longer move around with the energy she showed when looking after Francesco as a boy, she was nonetheless still a force to be reckoned with. While she gave the impression of being in her own little world, her eyes and ears missed nothing. Anyone who underestimated Nonna Isabetta soon learned to regret it.

"Pisa is an ongoing nightmare for me, Nonna," said Lorenzo.

"I hear you're still keeping the Pope's nephew, Salviati, from taking up his position as Archbishop in Pisa. How long is it now? Three years? You keep a close watch on him, *giovane*. That man is dangerous, especially when he's kept from all that lovely Pisan money. I wouldn't trust him as far as I could spit."

"You're right, of course, Nonna," he replied. "Don't you worry. Like a thorn in my shoe, I'm always aware of him."

Nonna grunted. "Well, are we eating this evening?" she asked, looking round at the guests and staff. "They only gave me a sop for lunch. How is a woman supposed to survive?"

"Tonight, Nonna," replied Francesco, "you will be able to eat your fill and dance until dawn should you so desire."

Nonna raised an eyebrow. "It's not that long ago when I would have done that, *giovane* Francesco. I could have danced longer than any of you." She smiled to herself, remembering some of the parties that were hosted by Fabrizio, Francesco's father.

As the guests took their seats with plates full of tasty selections from the *credenza*, and the conversation began to flow with the wine, Donna Cristina nodded to Gianetta, a signal that the dishes from the kitchen could now be brought in.

Gianetta hurried away, with Matteo in her wake, leaving Antonio to ensure that the guests' goblets never ran dry.

In the hot, busy kitchen, Eleonora was surprisingly calm. "We've done everything we can," she said, looking around with satisfaction at the platters waiting to be served. "The ingredients are good, and we have given them the best treatment. Lucia and I have taken care with every detail, and this dinner is as good as anything that could be offered by the Medici *cuoco* in their Palazzo, you mark my words." Eleonora could not be accused of false modesty, nor did she overestimate her own abilities. The dinner would indeed be as good as any found in the best palazzi in Florence. As she spoke, she set about carving the meat from the roasted pheasants. She fervently believed that the households that employed their own *trinciante,* or meat-carver, were simply pretentious. Without looking up from her work, she called to Lucia. "Lucia, change your apron and put on a new cap. Time to serve."

In the dining room, conversation had inevitably turned to art.

"It is our lifeblood," said Lorenzo. "We spend all our days working hard, whether it be in the bank, in business," he nodded to Francesco, "or in the market or on the farm, but what does it mean if we do not have the beauty of art? Look at your ceiling fresco. It is a cold night, but we could be dining on a summer afternoon. Look at your fine sugar sculpture, Francesco. The roses could almost be real. The skill of the artists who created these works is priceless. Very well, Sandro," as the artist looked up sharply, "maybe not price-less. Everything has a price. Our artists must be clothed and fed and allowed to bring us the wonders of God. That is why it is the duty of men like us to support the arts. We are, in fact, saving the souls of the common man! What say you, young Cesare?"

Young Cesare looked up from his goblet of wine. "I believe that I am in the presence of the wonder of God every time I look at a beautiful woman." He glanced up at Gianetta, who looked swiftly away from his intense gaze. "Every time I ride to the forest, every time I sup the wine from His vineyards. I don't need an artist to show me that."

Maestro Sandro looked as though he was fit to burst but decided that silence was more diplomatic in this company. He need not have worried, because Lorenzo was swift to counter his argument.

"Cesare, you speak true. God's wonder is all around us, but we are fortunate to be in such a position to experience it. How many of our average Florentines can ride a fine horse into the forests and appreciate what you see there? Or drink the fine wines that you are drinking right now? Think of the seamstress who put together your fine doublet (and it is a very fine doublet!). How much of God's glorious creation does she see in her dark workshop?"

Niccolò jumped in. "Cesare believes that the seamstress gets to see God's glory whenever he visits her for a fitting!" The mood lightened, and even Cesare and Maestro Sandro laughed.

Conversation paused as Gianetta, Matteo and Lucia arrived with dishes hot from the kitchen. It is said that a man first eats with his eyes and other senses before a morsel reaches his lips, and at this point, the company of guests began to feast on the work of Eleonora's kitchen. The soft, dark meat of the pigeons and pheasants glistened with the rich gravy as it was served. The guests helped themselves to platters of roasted vegetables, spicy nduja sausage and golden *arancini*, balls of rice flavoured with saffron. A large tureen of Eleonora's famous venison stew steamed in the centre of the table, ensuring that the guests could continue their evening without danger of going hungry. As was the custom, sweet dishes were served at the same time. As well as the platters of fruit, there was a large, golden *berlingozzo*, a ring-shaped cake whose recipe had travelled with Eleonora from her home in Pistoia. As if this was insufficient, Lucia also laid down a platter of *polenta y osei,* sweetened and shaped polenta finely decorated with birds made of pastry.

Nonna Isabetta clapped her hands. "Thank the Lord that we have our very own artist in the kitchen," she said, with her eyes gleaming, "and such an angel to bring it to us!"

Antonio caught her smiling up at him as he served and returned an awkward smile of his own.

On the far side of the room, Gianetta and Lucia caught each other's glance and stifled a giggle.

Matteo was circling the table, topping up the diners' goblets with wine. As he approached Niccolò, the jug in his hand began to tremble, and he poured an unsteady draught into the goblet. Niccolò waved him away impatiently, and Matteo retreated with a sigh of relief.

With the diners served and conversation resuming, the young servants left the room and gathered on the balcony outside the dining room.

Gianetta turned to Matteo. "What is it with you and Master Niccolò? There is always something amiss whenever you are near each other."

"I don't know, Gianetta," replied Matteo, shrugging his shoulders. "I don't think I've done anything wrong, but he always looks at me as though I have…or at least as though I am about to."

"It's true," said Lucia. "I have heard him snap at Matteo more than once. Master Niccolò is always polite and kind to us. It's very strange."

"I guess he just doesn't like me," said Matteo.

Gianetta frowned. She found this friction between the two men strange. She knew that, while she had a special place in her heart for Matteo, he was a likeable boy and worked hard. Signor Niccolò was usually a gentle sort and had always been kind to her. It was a conundrum that she found unsettling, but she pushed the thought to one side, remembering her duties. "Antonio, can you stay here to keep the guests' goblets full, help with any more serving and take care of the fire? They'll be fine for a while, but I'm sure they'll keep you busy."

ANGELA M SIMS

Agreeing, Antonio sat on the stool positioned near the viewing window, a small gap in the wall of the dining room which was made for just this purpose. Glancing through this window, he caught Cesare looking intently at him. He responded to Cesare's raised eyebrow with a small nod and a smile.

Gianetta, Matteo and Lucia returned to the kitchen, where Eleonora was scrubbing her kitchen clean.

Back in the dining room, the conversation had turned to the artistic pursuits of Maestro Sandro.

"I love our church of *Ognissanti* very much, Maestro, but I visit the church of *Santa Maria Novella* often," said Donna Cristina. "Your *Adoration of the Magi* is sublime. The colours are so vivid. Also, there are some familiar faces in the group paying homage to the Christ-child, are there not?"

"You are correct, *Madonna*." Maestro Sandro bowed modestly. "I am fortunate indeed to have the patronage of the Signori de' Medici here, and it is only fitting that I repay them by including them in my paintings."

"It is fortunate that you have the beautiful face of my brother to adorn your work," said Lorenzo, and Giuliano laughed.

"But such a shame that you had to include Lorenzo!" he replied. The brothers continued to tease each other.

"If I am not mistaken," said Francesco, "there is another familiar face in the work, eh Maestro?"

Maestro Sandro blushed and replied, "That is true, signor. I have included a small self-portrait in the corner. I, too, wished to honour the Christ-child. It is also a way of signing my work, and for that, I confess the sin of vanity upon seeing my image in such a venerable place."

A rustle at the end of the table indicated that Nonna Isabetta had been paying attention to the conversation and had decided that now was the appropriate time to make her contribution. "Well, I think that Joseph looks bored with all the goings-on. They have just travelled many miles, and Mary has just given birth to the baby Jesus. They don't need all that fuss. I would have sent them all away!" After a short silence, the table erupted with laughter.

"Well," said Francesco when they had all recovered. "I believe that your sponsor is the most fortunate man to be able to adorn his chapel with your work. Talking of which, how is my small commission coming along?"

"It's coming along nicely, signor," replied Maestro Sandro. "I hope to be able to deliver it to you soon after Easter."

"*Bene! Bene!*" said Francesco. "That's good. More wine, *amici*?"

Antonio appeared as if by magic to refill their goblets, and the dinner continued with food, wine and congenial conversation until late into the evening.

As the evening drew to a close, Nonna Isabetta retired to her chambers, having decided against dancing until dawn. Francesco and Cristina accompanied their guests to the courtyard, where Gianetta and Matteo were waiting with the guests' cloaks, ready to help them wrap up against the evening chill. There was laughter and back-slapping and hugs.

Then came a shout, and Giuliano was pushed so hard that he landed on his back. As he looked up, shocked and furious, wondering where the attack had come from, a large stone crashed to the floor on just the spot where he had been standing.

Gianetta, who had been helping Donna Maria, looked up. She saw the gap in the balustrade of the upper floor, where the large stone had fallen loose, but what was that? She was sure that she saw a figure retreat into the shadows, but it couldn't have been...could it?

Francesco, who had been the one to push Giuliano, leaned over to help him to his feet. "*Dio mio!*" he said, looking shocked. "Are you hurt?"

Giuliano jumped up, brushed himself down and said with bravado, "Me? Of course not! I've taken worse falls from my horse." But he glanced up to the balcony and then across at Lorenzo.

"Francesco, *grazie*," said Lorenzo, shaking the hand of his host. "Thank you for a wonderful evening. As always, the food and the company were splendid, and there is never a dull moment. Although," he said, glancing upwards, "you might want to spend a bit more of your money on maintaining your stonework." They both laughed heartily, but a little nervously, and with that, the guests left.

CHAPTER 4

Tuesday before Lent - morning

The following morning was just as sunny and cold as the day before. Lucia and Eleonora were already busy in the kitchen, preparing breakfast for the family. Antonio was clearing up the broken stone from the courtyard, while Matteo had left for the stone merchant's *bottega* to buy materials to repair the damage to the balustrade.

Gianetta was also out early, making her regular visit to the market for fresh fruit and vegetables. Eleonora was always insistent on an early visit for the freshest choice, but Gianetta didn't mind. In fact, she always enjoyed the early morning freshness of the narrow, cobbled streets of Florence and often took the longer route so that she could walk along *Via Por Santa Maria*, where the goldsmiths displayed their elaborate work. She loved to gaze at the glittering jewellery, admiring the craftsmanship that went into creating the intricate pieces. With such beauty on display, and with the sun on her face, she had all but forgotten the accident that had happened the night before, and continued to *Mercato Vecchio,* the Old Market, for her shopping.

With her purchases complete, Gianetta walked towards home past the church of *Santa Maria Novella*, stopping for a while in its open piazza to enjoy the space and fresh air. She continued toward the river along *Via Nuova di Ognissanti*, where Maestro Sandro had his workshop. Matteo had once worked for Maestro Sandro as an apprentice, and the other apprentices were still good friends to him, so she thought that she might pass by, just to shout a *"Buon giorno!"* to them. As she approached the open doors, she heard a familiar voice.

"…and then Signor Francesco jumped forward and pushed Signor Giuliano so hard that he fell flat on his back." Three faces were gazing at Matteo with their mouths open. The three men worked and lived in the workshop, where they learned their trade and earned their keep. Dino and Marco were young apprentices, new to their craft. Lapo was the most senior of the apprentices, helping to teach the younger ones the skills required by the Maestro. This morning, they sat around the main room, a spacious room with the double doors open to allow in air and light. They were surrounded by panels waiting to be prepared for painting, dust cloths, folded and used as seats, and wooden easels, stacked in a corner. It was a typical artists' workshop, such as could be found on many a street corner in Florence.

"No!" said the elder of the young men. "Why would he do that? He is such a gentleman. I don't believe that the anger in wine would ever take hold of Signor Francesco."

"Lapo, I assure you that he did, but it had nothing to do with the wine. *Ascoltatemi*, listen to me. Not a second later, an enormous stone from the balustrade of the balcony above came crashing down and missed Signor Giuliano by a hair's breadth. I speak true!" By now, his friends' eyes were popping, and they leaned forward, eager for more information.

"*Dio mio*," said Dino. "How on earth did that happen? Was he hurt?"

"He wasn't hurt, Dino, thanks be to God, but it was very close. The stone must have been loose, although I don't remember seeing it so."

"Are you sure it was an accident, Matteo?" asked Marco, quietly.

"Of course it was an accident, Marco. What else could it have been?"

"It's no secret that the Medici have their enemies in Florence. Who knows what might happen?" replied Marco with a shrug.

"Never," said Matteo, folding his arms. "Not in Palazzo Rosini. The Rosini are Medici supporters to the core, and they'll always be safe under our roof."

"Don't be so sure," said Marco. "The Pazzi families have supporters everywhere, and they will take any opportunity to strike at the Medici. Not just the Pazzi either. The Medici have other enemies too."

"Maybe out in the streets, but not in the home of friends," Matteo continued to protest.

"I would listen to Marco, Matteo." Gianetta had been listening at the door, but now came into the workshop and joined the conversation.

Matteo rushed to her, gave her a kiss on the cheek and took the shopping from her.

She made her way to a relatively clean pile of dust cloths, where she sat down gratefully.

"What do you mean, *cara*? Has the spring sun gone to your head?"

"What I mean, Matteo, is that I think Marco may be right. Eleonora told me yesterday that she believes Signor Lorenzo was deliberately poisoned when he became ill at that dinner before Christmas."

"No, surely that's just her imagination," said Matteo, shaking his head.

"I thought that too, but her story was quite convincing. Even so, I didn't really believe it until," she took a deep breath, "...until the accident last night. When I looked up to see where the stone had come from, I saw someone move away from the balustrade."

"What?" cried Matteo. "You saw what? Who? Who was it?"

"I don't know," said Gianetta, quietly. "At first, I thought it was a trick of the light, but no. I did see someone there, but I couldn't make out who it was. I think," she looked up at Matteo, "someone in the household wants to do harm to our Medici friends."

Matteo jumped up, his eyes flashing, angrily. "How did I not know this? I will pull the Palazzo apart until I find the dog who did this, and when I do…" He clenched his fists and his teeth and paced the floor.

"What is it to you anyway?" asked Marco, the youngest of the apprentices. "They control our lives from their privileged position, living in grand homes and eating the best food, while many Florentines go hungry. Why should we care what happens to any one of them?"

Before Matteo could reply, Lapo, a few years older than the others, answered for him. "The Medici and the Rosini have been very good to our Matteo. When he was just a young boy, his father brought him to Maestro Sandro to start his apprenticeship, just as your fathers did. We taught him all the techniques that you have learned, preparing wood panels for painting, taking care of the Maestro's brushes, keeping a clean work room and making basic sketches. We couldn't fault his hard work, but talent?" Looking at Matteo with a smile, he shook his head.

Matteo's anger cooled a little as he smiled at the memory and continued the story. "It's true. I never had the aptitude for this life. I always mixed the wrong thickness of gesso for the panels. I ruined more of the Maestro's brushes than I care to remember, and my sketches could have been done better by a child. The Maestro was very patient, but it was never to be. Signor Lorenzo often visits the workshop, as you know, and one day, he told the Maestro that Signor Francesco was looking for help in his household. He had seen me work but also could see that I was no artist, so suggested to the Maestro that I might be suitable. He agreed, and I left the next day for Palazzo Rosini. This was shortly before you started your apprenticeship, Marco.

"Since then, I have worked hard at a job that I love. Signor Francesco is good to me, and I am proud to work for him… and it was at Palazzo Rosini that I met my wonderful Gianetta." Sitting next to her, he put his arm around her, pulled her to him and kissed her on the cheek. "So, I have very good reason to be grateful to both the Rosini and Medici, and they will always have my loyalty."

Marco didn't appear to be impressed by the story, but Dino chipped in. "And Lapo and I will always be grateful to them for taking you away, so that we don't have to cover your mistakes!" He punched Matteo on the shoulder, and Matteo laughed.

"I wonder who it could be," said Gianetta, bringing the conversation back to the subject at hand. "I can't imagine anyone in the household capable of such a thing."

The group of friends went quiet as they each mulled over the question in their minds.

"Gianetta?" said Matteo, looking at her ashen face. "Gianetta, are you well? You look dreadful."

"I'm fine. Really… it's nothing to worry about. We had a busy day and late night, and all this talk of accidents that are not accidents…" Her voice tailed off.

"Come, *cara*. Let us get you home. I will see you boys soon. My regards to the Maestro." Matteo collected Gianetta's shopping, and they left the workshop arm in arm, with Gianetta recounting the conversation that she had had with Eleonora the day before.

The three gazed at the retreating couple: Matteo, tall and athletic with a shock of unruly, jet-black hair, and Gianetta, shorter than Matteo, but strong and shapely, with long, curly, dark hair, let loose while she was not at work. They made a handsome couple.

"He's living in a dream world," said Marco. "The people won't put up with Medici rule for much longer."

"There will be none of that talk here," boomed a voice from behind. Carlo, the foreman, older than the apprentices, appeared from the room at the back and had clearly heard the conversation. "The people of Florence know very well that the Medici make this city safe and prosperous. I will let that go this once, but if I hear any more such talk, you will be out on your ear, and you will be begging the Medici for scraps from their kitchen and shelter in their barn. Don't forget that their support for the Maestro's work pays your wages. Now be off! The Maestro's brushes need cleaning."

As Marco sloped away into the next room, muttering under his breath, and Dino and Lapo returned to their chores, Carlo shook his head and sighed. "Ah, the days of youth, when everything was black or white, good or bad."

"Where is she? Gianetta left hours ago. If I don't have my artichokes soon, they will never be prepared in time." Eleonora, as usual, was fretting about the next meal, waving her vegetable knife in the air as she spoke.

Lucia was weighing the flour for the daily bread, and Antonio, having finished clearing the courtyard, was washing his hands.

"She won't be long, Eleonora," said Lucia. "You know she always takes the time to select the best, and it's always worth waiting for."

"I think I hear footsteps now," said Antonio, and sure enough, the door opened, and Matteo led Gianetta through the door.

Gianetta was still pale.

"Eleonora," said Matteo. "Gianetta isn't well. Do you have any of that tonic that Signor Francesco likes?"

"Matteo, I'm fine!" protested Gianetta.

"Oh, *Mamma mia*, look at you. You are not fine! Come and sit down." Eleonora dropped her vegetable knife and went to Gianetta, leading her to the chair by the fire. "Lucia…"

"I'm already there," called Lucia from the cold room, where the restorative jug was kept. She brought out a large mug, and handed it to Gianetta, who drank, gratefully.

"Really," she said. "Such a fuss! It was a long day yesterday, and with the early morning, I'm tired, that's all…just like the rest of you." Changing the subject, she said, "Eleonora, Matteo was worried about last night's accident, and I told him the story you told me about the poison from your father's apothecary…"

"What story is that?" asked Antonio.

They all fell silent as they became aware of a presence at the door of the kitchen. Luigi, Signor Francesco's personal assistant, was standing quietly in the open doorway.

"Oh Luigi, I wish you wouldn't do that!" said Eleonora, with her hand to her throat. "You scared me witless."

Luigi was a short, grey-haired man with a superior air. He was always polite but with little warmth. His position in the household was neither as one of the family nor as part of the serving staff. He sat somewhere between the two. Nobody knew very much about him, but he had been with Signor Francesco for many years, was always very efficient and completely trusted by the family.

Eleonora always said that it was a shame he didn't open up enough to become part of the family of staff in Palazzo Rosini, that he was always…apart. However, he was still a member of the household and treated with respect.

"I have come with a message from Signor Francesco," he said, quietly. "Matteo, he would like to see you in his study within the hour."

"Me? What can he possibly want with me?"

Four curious faces looked at him, wondering the same.

"Well, if you don't get along, you will never know, but go and make yourself presentable first," said Eleonora, almost pushing him out of the door.

As Matteo rushed to his quarters, Luigi left the kitchen and returned to the study.

PRIMI PIATTI

By the time we reach the primi piatti (or first plate), the digestive juices are beginning to flow, and we are ready for something a bit more substantial. We want a little more to get our teeth into, but we don't want to overdo it just yet. So, something simple but full of flavour is called for.

What better than a Porcini and Truffle Risotto, using the prized truffles found in the forests of Tuscany?

Porcini and Truffle Risotto
(Serves 2)

1 onion, chopped finely • Olive oil
150g arborio rice • Salt and freshly ground black pepper
600ml vegetable stock • 1 glass dry white wine
A handful of dried porcini mushrooms, reconstituted
in 400ml boiling water • 30g Parmesan cheese, finely grated
Knob of butter • Shaved black truffle, to taste

Place the mushrooms in a jug and top with 400ml boiling water. Leave to soften for at least 10–15 minutes. Remove the mushrooms and roughly chop. Strain the mushroom water into the vegetable stock, leaving behind any grit from the mushrooms.

Gently fry the onion in the olive oil until soft but not brown. Add the arborio rice with salt and pepper. Fry together for 2-3 minutes, then add the glass of white wine. Stir and cook until alcohol has burned off.

Add the vegetable stock and mushroom water in small amounts (approx. 100ml), stirring all the time. Wait until the stock has been absorbed before adding the next 100ml. Repeat this until the rice is cooked. It should be soft but not gloopy!

Stir in the chopped porcini mushrooms, the Parmesan cheese and a small knob of butter.

Sprinkle with truffle shavings

CHAPTER 5

Later the same day

Francesco's study was on the first floor, not far from the dining room. As the hub of the family's business operations, it was always busy, but like Francesco, calm and dignified. It was a warm room, with a polished wooden floor and a few family portraits on the walls. The old furnishings matched the family *credenza* in the dining room. These included a highly decorated walnut desk with matching chairs, and a large *cassapanca* in the same pattern, which doubled as a storage area and a large bench for visitors and business acquaintances.

This morning, the curtains had been pulled aside to allow in the bright February sunlight, which shone across the desk. Francesco, greying now, but still a strong figure that belied his age, sat behind the desk. He leaned back in his chair, looking thoughtfully at his son, taller and darker than himself, following his mother's colouring.

"Niccolò, I'm not sure why you are so reluctant that we should be involved in the Easter Sunday celebrations with Lorenzo and Giuliano. To be asked to be part of the Medici retinue, as you well know, is an honour, even given our long friendship. It is the biggest celebration of the year, a perfect opportunity to show our support…and it won't hurt our business either."

Niccolò sighed and said, "Yes, I understand that, but this is a time to be rather more careful about public displays of loyalty. The Medici may run the city well, and most people may be quite content with the status quo, but the Medici enemies are getting bolder, you mark my words. We all know about the Pazzi family's envy of their power. Archbishop Salviati won't wait much longer to take up his post in Pisa, and I don't think we should underestimate Riario in Imola."

"Riario? He should be satisfied that he managed to gain Imola, when Lorenzo already had plans to buy it."

"That's part of the trouble, Papà. He enjoyed that victory, and he's now enjoying the power. I believe he wants more. He has his sights set on Florence, I'm sure of it. The grumblings are getting louder, and I really think we ought to stand back a little."

"*Mio figlio*. I appreciate your concern, my son, but I'm also a little surprised. I would have expected you to be just as delighted as me. Why such worry?"

"Papà, I… I think there will be trouble." He raised a hand to fend the question forming at Francesco's open mouth. "Don't ask me why I think that. I cannot answer you. I just…urge caution."

"Luigi!" Francesco looked across to the open doorway. "I didn't see you there. Did you deliver the message to Matteo?"

"Yes, *ser*," replied Luigi, with a slight bow of his head, glancing at Niccolò. "He has just returned from his morning errands and will be with you presently." Luigi walked across the room to his own more modest but equally busy desk in the corner of the study and proceeded to sort through some papers.

"That's another thing, Papà," continued Niccolò, frowning now. "Why that boy?"

Francesco laughed. "I don't know what you've got against Matteo, son, but he's a good boy. He's always worked well for me."

"Well, I just don't trust him."

"Whether you trust him or not, he has been invited by none other than Lorenzo himself, and we will not interfere with that invitation. He will be part of the retinue, and you will be civil to him." Francesco looked at Niccolò sternly.

Running footsteps along the corridor slowed to a more sedate pace until Matteo appeared at the door of the study. "Signor Francesco," he said, rather breathlessly. "You wanted to see me."

Francesco smiled at the boy. He had clearly just changed into clean clothes, as his shirt was still hanging loose, and an attempt to tame his wayward hair had failed. "Yes, come in, Matteo. Sit down." He pointed to one of the chairs near his desk.

Matteo looked uncomfortable, sitting on the edge of the chair and avoiding Niccolò's scowl. He looked nervously around the study, a room that he only visited when the fire needed tending, or the windows needed cleaning. He was relieved to see that the windows were indeed gleaming. He glanced at the *cassapanca* and the desk. They were fine, clean and shining. Didn't Gianetta polish them just yesterday? At least that was not why he'd been summoned.

Francesco watched him taking in the details of the study and finally said, "Don't worry, Matteo. You haven't done anything wrong. In fact, I have some good news for you."

If anything, Matteo looked even more worried, and Francesco covered a smile.

"We have been given a great honour, Matteo. Our family has been invited to attend Easter Sunday Mass at the *Duomo* with Lorenzo de' Medici and his family. He has but a modest retinue, and so we are greatly favoured to be among them."

"Erm…congratulations, Signor Francesco. I am very pleased for you, but…umm…"

"What does it have to do with you, eh? A fair question, and one to which I have a very exciting answer. Signor Lorenzo has also requested that you be part of the staff retinue, assisting the families with their preparations, attending Mass with the families and returning to their home, the *Palazzo Medici*, to help their staff with the banquet."

Matteo looked stunned. Luigi carried on working with his head down. Niccolò huffed and folded his arms.

Francesco continued. "It is a formal role, and you will have the Medici livery made for you. It will require you to be at your best, boy, but I have no doubt that he has chosen well. You will do the Rosini family proud, of that, I am sure."

Matteo was still unable to speak, and just looked at Francesco.

"Father, are you sure…" But Francesco held up his hand to Niccolò without taking his eyes from Matteo's face.

He nodded slowly. "Yes. I am sure."

"As you know, the Medici have a large household of staff, but one of their boys has broken his arm, and so they need a replacement for him. They can manage from day-to-day, but they need every man for Easter, as it is such an important event. Their family and household will be visible to the whole city, and they must make sure that everything is perfect. It is not as simple as attending Mass. It is almost a performance. Florence expects the spectacular, and the Medici will provide it!"

Matteo had recovered his composure somewhat and managed to respond. "Of course, Signor Francesco. You can count on me. I will be at my best. I will make you proud. You will have no need to worry on my account…"

"You're babbling, boy," said Niccolò.

Matteo snapped his mouth shut and looked down at his hands,

twisting in his lap. Normally quite confident in himself, he didn't know why he was always nervous in the presence of this man.

"Enough, Niccolò," said Francesco quietly, and then to Matteo, "I am sure Signor Lorenzo has chosen well, and that you will do your best. The seamstress will visit tomorrow to take your measurements for the new livery, and we will speak again about what will be required of you. Now, go about your duties. I'm sure Eleonora has need of you."

Matteo stood and bowed his head to Francesco, turned on his heel and made to leave the study, followed by the gaze of Niccolò and Luigi. He stopped at the door and turned back. "Thank you, *ser*," he said. "Thank you for trusting me with this honour. You will not regret it," and with another short bow, he was gone.

"What is your opinion of the boy, Luigi? You must see more of him than us. Can you reassure my son of his integrity?" asked Francesco.

Luigi looked nervously between father and son and cleared his throat. "Well, *ser*, I'm sure it's not my place to judge, but I have not seen him cause any trouble. He doesn't shirk his duties, even though he does seem to have an eye for Gianetta."

"There you have it, Papà. He cannot be trusted!"

"Gianetta, eh?" Francesco smiled. "He's a young man, and she's a pretty girl. Who can blame him? You see, Niccolò, there's nothing to be worried about."

"Let's hope that he's as reliable as everyone seems to think…for everyone's sake." Niccolò was not convinced.

Back in the kitchen, it was business as usual. Eleonora was directing operations and preparing the artichokes for the evening meal. "Lucia, are the lunch trays ready? I believe the gentlemen are eating in the study today. Donna Cristina, Donna Tessa and Nonna Isabetta will still be in their chambers, and I'm sure Gino will be here shortly!"

"They're nearly done, Eleonora. Gianetta and I are just finishing them now. We will wait until it is time to serve before pouring their drink. It is a good thing that you made more of your tonic. They will need it after last night."

"I always prepare plenty of tonic after one of their banquets. I know it will always be needed, but perhaps they need it more today, after such a shock." Eleonora shook her head and pressed her lips together. She was more than ever convinced that there was trouble in the house, and she worried about who was involved and where it would end.

"The young Medici was lucky. There is no doubt about that," said Antonio. "If Signor Francesco hadn't seen the stone coming, it would have killed him for sure."

The kitchen door opened slowly, and Matteo stood in the open doorway, pale and dumbfounded.

"*Eccolo!* Here he is!" said Eleonora, looking up from her work. "Matteo! Whatever is the matter? Come in, boy. Sit down. You look as pale as Gianetta was. *Che mattina!* What a morning! Lucia!"

"*Sì*, Eleonora!" replied Lucia, as she made her way to the cold room for the tonic.

Gianetta sat next to Matteo, holding his hands and looking concerned. "What is it, *tesoro*?" she asked. "Tell us. It can't be that bad."

Matteo finally found his tongue. "No," he said. "No, it's not that bad. In fact, it's quite…incredible."

His companions were huddled around him, as he drank the tonic that Lucia had pressed into his hands.

"Lent is coming," he said. "After Lent, is Easter."

"He's finally gone *pazzo*," whispered Antonio, tapping the side of his head.

"No. No, I haven't. *Ascoltatemi*, listen. We all know that Easter Sunday is a great celebration for the whole city, and that there is always a parade of the great families. Well, Signor Francesco and the family have been asked to join the Medici retinue, to accompany them to Mass and then back to *Palazzo Medici* for the Easter banquet."

"Oh, *che meraviglia!* How wonderful!" said Eleonora.

"No, that's not it. There's more."

"More?" said Gianetta. "What is it?"

"Signor Lorenzo de' Medici…himself…has asked for me to be part of his staff retinue."

After a pause that allowed the news to sink in, everyone spoke at once, offering congratulations and kisses and embraces.

Eleonora even wiped away a small tear of pride with the corner of her apron.

Only Antonio wasn't quite as enthusiastic, and asked quietly, "Did they say why they wanted you?"

"No, they didn't," replied Matteo. "I'm sorry, *mio amico*. I know you have been here longer than I have, and maybe they should have chosen you. I'm just replacing one of their own boys who broke his arm. Perhaps I just resemble him."

Antonio just shrugged and laughed. "No matter. It's good enough that one of us can enjoy a bit of Medici feasting." And he wrapped his arms around Matteo.

"Wait a minute! I won't be doing any feasting. I'll be serving the feast." Glancing at Eleonora, Matteo continued with a wink, "and I'll have to serve a second-rate feast too."

"Oh, be off with you. You know as well as I do that the Medici will spare no expense for such an occasion. I expect you to take note of everything you see, hear and smell…and if possible, taste. I'm always looking out for new ideas to try."

"You want me to be your spy, Eleonora? How treacherous. I'm not sure Signor Francesco would approve." He continued to tease her, but she was having none of it.

Next to the fire, Gianetta was sitting next to and holding hands with Lucia. Lucia was beaming, but Gianetta had tears in her eyes. "Oh Matteo, I'm so proud of you," she said. "They really have given you a great honour. Never mind Signor Giuliano. All the eyes will be on you. You will be magnificent in such a fine livery. I'm afraid, though."

"What are you afraid of, *mia cara*? That one of the noble ladies will snap me up as their plaything?"

Antonio laughed. "Maybe in your dreams, *amico*, but you can't flash those blue eyes at everyone and expect them to fall at your feet!"

"My eyes are just for Gianetta. No fine lady would be able to turn them in her direction."

Antonio rolled his eyes. Lucia sighed, and Eleonora smiled, glancing at Gianetta.

Gianetta also managed a small laugh. "Well, that may be part of it, it's true. Just make sure you keep your eyes on your duties!"

"And speaking of duties," Eleonora brought them all back to earth. "It's time you cleaned out the fireplace of the dining room, Matteo."

"You see, Gianetta? How could I leave such glamour?" Matteo spread his hands and with a wink, he left the kitchen for the dining room, where the large, dusty fireplace awaited his attention.

CHAPTER 6

Monday, 3rd week of Lent

A few weeks had passed. Carnival season, with all its excesses, was over, and Lent was all around. It was a time for reflection and repentance. Meals were simple, avoiding meat, cheese, eggs and wine. People dressed simply, and so did the churches. No adornments on wrists, necks or altars. There was no doubting the mood of the season, and it seemed to pervade the whole city.

In the marketplace, one young trader asked her mother, "Why is everyone so bad-tempered, Mamma? Nearly all the men I've served today have snapped at me."

Her mother smiled. "It's Lent, *cara mia*, and they've all been listening to those Dominicans preaching hellfire and forbidding carnal relations at home...or anywhere else!"

"Oh!" The young girl was slightly puzzled. "Is that why everyone looks forward to Easter so much?"

"Well, of course they are celebrating the Risen Christ...but I'm sure that's not all they are celebrating." Turning her attention to the next grumpy customer, she muttered under her breath. "At least I get a few more weeks of peace in my own bed!"

Back in the kitchen of Palazzo Rosini, Gianetta and Eleonora were at their weekly task of preparing herbal remedies to Eleonora's precise recipes. Sicknesses were still a fact of life, even during Lent, and Eleonora would always be prepared for whatever came along. While many Mammas and Nonnas were skilled in their use of herbs, both medicinal and culinary, Eleonora also had the added knowledge of her father's apothecary profession. This made her potions, tonics and restoratives prized by the household. These skills were usually passed down from one generation to the next, and Eleonora, not having any children of her own, was keen to share hers with Lucia and Gianetta. Like Eleonora with her father, the young girls proved to be keen students, and now they took turns to prepare the potions but always closely supervised by Eleonora. Her first lesson, and one she frequently repeated, was to stress that in the wrong quantities, the medicines that heal could become poisons that afflict or even kill. Such a mixture was the relieving potion for Nonna Isabetta's painful joints. Into the bowl went some musk mallow and, "Just a touch of hemlock. It's very effective, but even just a little too much can be so very dangerous," warned Eleonora.

"It definitely helps to ease Nonna when she is in pain," said Gianetta. "Although I'm glad that you are making this. I would be too afraid that I would get the quantity wrong."

"As long as you pay attention, you won't make a mistake. Just watch carefully. It's how I learned from my father." She topped up the bowl of chopped herbs with hot water, stirred it carefully, covered it with a cloth and set it aside to cool.

Gianetta nodded and returned to her task of preparing the digestive tonic of anise, angelica and mint in the same manner. Alongside her on the table were sprigs of feverfew and chamomile, ready to be made into the tonic that Eleonora recommended for headaches.

The jug containing the calming restorative tonic stood empty, as it had been used considerably in recent days. As Eleonora started to chop the leaves of lemon balm, chamomile and lavender, she turned her attention to Gianetta. "Tell me. How fares Mamma Sofia? I have not heard any news from your home of late. Is she well?"

"She is well," replied Gianetta. "Like Nonna Isabetta, she suffers with pain in her knees and hands, but she manages reasonably well. She can still take care of herself, and even takes in some sewing from the town. The gardens and olive trees are too much for her now, though. Luckily, Tommaso still lives nearby and is able to help with harvesting."

"I'd like to meet Tommaso. He seems like a good man."

"Oh, he is, Eleonora. He's always been like a big brother to me. Not having a father, it always meant a lot to me."

Eleonora looked at her sadly. She remembered how much her own father had meant to her and couldn't imagine what it must have been like to grow up without a father. "Do you know anything about him? Your father, I mean," asked Eleonora.

Gianetta shrugged. "Not much. Only what Mamma has told me. He was a kind man. Apparently, he loved my mother, but…" She shrugged again. "Who knows? Mamma didn't see him again after the day I was born."

They worked in silence for a few moments, until Gianetta continued. "Mamma and I had a wonderful life. I really did have a happy childhood. Mamma taught me to cook, to sew, to tend the garden, and there were children from the town that I played with. As I grew, though, Mamma began to slow down. I knew I had to leave home to work. Mamma simply couldn't manage without the money that I send her, but it was hard to go. Knowing that Tommaso would look out for her made it easier for me to come here. She seems to be quite happy with her own company and the occasional visit from friends and neighbours. I hope to visit her soon, though."

"Yes, you must. I'm sure we will be able to spare you for a few days after Easter. I'll make some tonic for her pain, and you must take some cakes too."

"Oh, that would be wonderful. Thank you, Eleonora. She will be delighted."

They both looked up when a stifled giggle came from just outside the door. Eleonora marched across the kitchen and opened the heavy kitchen door as if it were nothing. In tumbled Antonio and Lucia, rather ruffled and looking considerably flushed. Both tried to compose themselves, but Antonio was beaming widely, and Lucia was blushing as she tucked her hair into her cap.

"Exactly how long does it take to prepare Donna Cristina's bath, may I ask, Lucia? Or to set the fire in the dining room, Antonio? Did you have to travel to the forests of Rome for firewood? This is not the time or place for your frivolity. We have work to do. There is always work to do, and I won't have you shirking your duties. Antonio, go and wash your hands. Lucia, change your apron. There is soot all over it, and I don't need to ask where that came from."

"*Sì*, Eleonora!" They both spoke at once and went immediately to do as they were told, while Eleonora took the finished tonics to the cold room for storage.

As Lucia passed, Gianetta gave her a nudge and a wink. "It goes well with our handsome Antonio, then?"

Lucia blushed a deeper red, and her eyes sparkled. "Gianetta, it goes very well. Indeed, I believe he may ask to marry me. He is so very attentive and passionate."

Gianetta smiled at her friend. "I'm glad for you, *amica*, but take care. Sometimes, young men are not looking for a wife, just some amusement."

"Such serious wisdom from one so young, eh?"

"You know that I never knew my father. I know what can happen. I would hate for you to be in that position…or worse, that you would have to visit the wheel at the *Innocenti*."

"It will be fine, Gianetta. I'm sure Antonio is true. There will be no unwanted babies." And with another blushing smile, she left to change her apron, passing Matteo in the doorway.

"Ah! *Eccolo!* Here he is, Signor Matteo!" Antonio took the opportunity to change the subject of his and Lucia's indiscretion and shift attention elsewhere. "How goes it, *ser*?" He said, with a bow.

"You may arise, *giovane!*" Matteo joined in the teasing, looking haughtily down his nose at Antonio, and they laughed together.

Lucia came back into the kitchen wearing a clean apron, and asked, "Do you have your new livery, Matteo? What is it like? Tell us everything."

Matteo looked a little uncomfortable. "Umm…it's very like any other livery, I suppose. Tunic, hose, shoes…you know."

Lucia gave an exasperated sigh. "Matteo! What colour is it? Is it rich fabric? What style?"

Gianetta laughed. "You don't expect him to notice such things really, Lucia? Besides, he has only just been measured by the seamstress. She says it should be delivered during Holy Week…although it's not the most appropriate time to be trying on fancy garments."

"There you have it, Lucia," said Matteo, with his gentle, lop-sided smile. "You will have to wait, like everyone else, even though patience is not in your nature."

"Have you been with Signor Francesco?" asked Gianetta.

"Yes," he replied. "He's been telling me about my duties for the day, how I must behave, who must be called *Madonna*, who to avoid and what to look out for."

"What to look out for? What do you mean?"

"What Signor Francesco says, Antonio, is that I just need to keep my eyes open for any trouble and keep Signor Lorenzo in sight at all times. Of course, he is being cautious. After all, it will be Easter Sunday, and everyone will be in the mood for celebrating, not looking for a fight. In any case, I can manage any trouble that comes my way."

Eleonora returned from the cold room. "Trouble? What trouble?"

"There's no trouble. I was just explaining my duties for the Easter Sunday Mass. I have to be at *Palazzo Medici* early, dressed in the new livery, line up with their other staff and walk through the streets to the *Duomo*. We must be there in plenty of time, but we mustn't rush the parade. The people must get a good look at the Medici in their finery. After Mass, as you know, I will be returning to their Palazzo to help with the banquet.

"Signor Francesco just told me to keep a sharp eye out for any trouble that may come along. I'm sure he was just being over-cautious, though. There has never been any trouble with people going to Mass, not here in Florence."

"Well, let's hope you're right," said Eleonora. "I think you need to take it a little more seriously, though, Matteo. There are some crazy people about. Who knows what they will get into their heads?"

"I agree with Eleonora," said Gianetta. "You must be on your guard."

Antonio did not take it quite as seriously. "Our lucky Matteo? He will be fine. Stop worrying, ladies. One look from those blue eyes of his, and any assailant will be bowled over. He doesn't need a sword or dagger when he's got such an effective weapon. Besides, he's fast. Any trouble, and he can be out of there faster than the wind. I've seen him leaving a tavern when it's his turn to pay the bill."

They all laughed, and Matteo took the teasing in good humour.

Luigi had joined them during the conversation and was sitting at the great kitchen table, taking a drink.

"What say you, Luigi?" asked Antonio. "Do you agree that our Matteo here has luck and charm enough to fend off any attackers?"

"Charming, he may be," replied Luigi, nodding his head, "but invincible, he is not. I think you should listen to Eleonora, boy, and take care. I may not be a man of many words, but I am always listening to what is going on around me. I hear discussions in Signor Francesco's study and out in the marketplace. I do believe that the enemies of the Medici feel that their time is coming, and it is time that people took them seriously. Keep a watchful eye at all times. Luck and blue eyes will only take you so far. They certainly won't protect you from a determined Pazzi dagger." He paused, then concluded, "There are eyes and ears everywhere. We should all be mindful of what we are saying..." He looked up at Antonio "...and doing."

The kitchen was silent as Luigi spoke. This short speech was probably the most he had ever said, and the effect was mesmerising. Antonio shuffled uncomfortably.

Eleonora was the first to speak. "Thank you, Luigi. At least someone has the sense to advise caution. We remember what it is to feel the invincibility of youth but have lost too many loved ones, and we don't want to lose any more."

Matteo nodded seriously. "*Va bene*. It's fine. I understand, and I'm grateful for your concern. I really am. I promise to be careful. Lucia, I think the livery will be red velvet with gold trim..."

There was a nervous laugh from everyone, as they recognised Matteo's attempt to lift the mood.

Eleonora was still looking at Luigi.

He looked up and said, "Thank you for the drink. It was much appreciated. Now I must return to my duties, as do you, I am sure."

And with that, he left the kitchen as quietly as he had arrived.

"I wonder if we will ever really get to know our Luigi," Eleonora said.

CHAPTER 7

Later the same day

O n the *piano nobile*, the first floor, with the dining room and Signor Francesco's study, stood the *sala*, the main reception room where the family and their guests would gather. The *sala* in the Palazzo Rosini was a mirror-image of the dining room, situated on the opposite side of the building, above the main door and overlooking the thoroughfare of *Via Porta Rossa*. It boasted the same large, glazed windows and an enormous fireplace, which was roaring against the chill of the day. Like most homes, it did not have much furniture to clutter the space. A *credenza*, the twin of the piece in the dining room, held the display of family silverware, when it was not in use for banquets. In the corner of the room was a small spinet, belonging to Donna Cristina, who was an accomplished player and singer. She had hoped to teach Niccolò to play, but he had shown no aptitude for the skill. The walls of the *sala* displayed some of the paintings commissioned by Signor Francesco. He had an eye for talent amongst the Florentine artistic community, and like his friend Lorenzo, was keen to support them as they grew in their skill and reputation.

That afternoon, the family were gathered in relaxed companionship.

Donna Cristina was sitting near the window with her embroidery. Tessa and Gino sat together at the spinet, as Gino practised a simple tune, helped and encouraged by his mother. Niccolò was reading some business documents, and Nonna Isabetta was snoozing in her chair by the fire. Signor Francesco was looking at the space on the wall, where the eagerly awaited painting from Maestro Sandro would be placed.

"I do believe that this work will be the crowning glory of our collection. The man paints with the hand of God."

"Francesco, that's blasphemy! He is just a man – a man with a God-given talent, but still just a man."

"As you said, Cristina, his talent comes from God. When the best of God and man are combined, how can that be blasphemy? The Greek, Plato, says that there are three kinds of men: lovers of wisdom, lovers of honour and lovers of gain. I suggest that there is another kind of man: he who strives to share wisdom and honour for another's gain. Seeing beauty all around and being able to recreate it for your fellow man is wise and honourable, and don't we all gain from that?"

Nonna Isabetta woke briefly to ask, "Have you been dining with Lorenzo and his philosophical friends again, Francesco? You always talk nonsense when you have been in their company. God won't approve of all these modern ways."

"Nonna, we are living in an enlightened age. We are learning the wisdom of the ancient Greeks and seeing it in a new light, in God's light. How can He not approve?"

But Nonna had drifted back to sleep.

Niccolò looked up from his papers and put them on the small table in front of him. "Papà," he said. "I have to raise again the issue of the Easter Sunday parade with the Medici family."

Francesco sighed.

"You must acknowledge that there is trouble brewing for them."

Francesco gazed at the floor, nodding slowly.

"Tell me, Niccolò," said Cristina. "What is different about the situation now? The Medici have had their troubles for generations. What makes you so concerned now?"

"I don't pretend to understand the intricacies of politics, Mamma, but that's at the root of it all. Money...and power, and, I think, the Pope."

"The Pope has too much money and too many nephews, if that's what they really are!"

"Yes, Nonna. You may be right," replied Niccolò. "With Riario in Imola, looking enviously at Florence, and Salviati still desperate to take up his post as Archbishop of Pisa, the Pope has two nephews with reason to wish ill to the Medici. That's a very powerful backer, if they should wish to push into Florence."

"I thought Lorenzo was looking to purchase Imola," said Cristina.

"Yes," said Francesco. "That was the plan. Lorenzo had an agreement with the Duke of Milan to purchase it, strengthening the position of Florence on the trade route to Venice. I know he was very keen for that agreement to be fulfilled. I, too, was hoping to expand our business in the town. It would have been a great opportunity for us."

"That would have been the best outcome for Lorenzo and Florence," continued Niccolò, "but the Duke of Milan came to a different agreement with the Pope, selling it at a lower price in exchange for marrying his illegitimate daughter to Riario."

"*Bastarda!*"

"Nonna!" Francesco looked nervously across at Gino, but he hadn't heard and continued playing.

"So, Lorenzo has enemies," said Cristina, "and they may be powerful, but they are not within the walls of Florence. Surely, they can't present any immediate danger without an army to march on the city, and we would have heard about it if that was the case."

"We're not aware of an army, no, Mamma," said Niccolò, "but if they have allies within the city…"

"But who…?"

"The Pazzi!" said Francesco.

"I understand what you're saying." Cristina had put down her embroidery. "And I agree that it's a volatile situation, but there is no reason to believe that there is an imminent danger, is there?"

"I was doing business with the wool dyer near Santa Croce this morning. You know that they are having terrible trouble getting enough saffron crocuses from San Gimignano? Everyone appears to want yellow cloth at the moment." Francesco began to digress but returned to the point after seeing his wife's raised eyebrow. "Well, it seems that he has also heard rumours that the Medici enemies are getting restless."

"That old goat? He's a bigger gossip than anyone I've ever met!"

"Maybe so, but he has reliable customers. I do believe that he may be right."

"There you have it, Papà," said Niccolò. "Do you see why I'm concerned about being involved with the Medici so publicly?"

Before Francesco had chance to reply, Cristina added, "I also worry about what is going on in this house. The stone that nearly hit Giuliano could just as easily have hit you, Francesco. What if someone in this house is plotting something terrible?"

"Yes!" Niccolò stood up, getting animated now. "Yes! That is precisely my point, Papà, and yet you still insist on taking that boy with us to Mass on Easter Sunday. Who knows what he has planned?"

"Niccolò, *basta*! Enough!" Francesco raised his voice. "You know very well that Lorenzo asked for Matteo personally, and that is good enough for me. You have no evidence to suggest that he is anything other than completely loyal to us and to the Medici. He was even in the courtyard with us the night that the stone fell and couldn't have pushed it. In fact, you weren't there. You could have been the one to push the stone!"

Niccolò's dark eyes flashed angrily, but he bit his tongue.

"Francesco! Niccolò! Fighting amongst ourselves will not help us, or Lorenzo for that matter." Cristina now stood before them both, her authority in the family undiminished by her short stature. Nonna Isabetta was now wide awake and watching carefully. Gino had stopped playing and was looking at each of the adults in turn, worried and confused by the tension in the conversation. Tessa was trying to distract him, while also hiding her own concern.

"Now, if what you both say is true, then there is a danger, whether it be out in the streets of Florence or here in our own home. Francesco, you are my husband, and I support whatever decision you make, and if it is to attend the parade and Mass with Lorenzo and the family, then so be it. I agree that it is right we should be loyal to our friends. They have always been good friends to us, so I will also be in the parade with the women of the Medici household, showing my support for you and the Medici family."

Donna Cristina lifted her proud chin, trying to control the quivering bottom lip. Her dark eyes, which had been inherited by Niccolò, now fixed on her husband and son. "But I beg of you, please, please look after each other. Keep a sharp eye for anything unusual. Make sure that the guards are also watchful. You are my world, and I couldn't bear it if anything were to happen to either of you."

Tessa had now moved to be beside her husband, holding his hand and looking into his worried eyes, while Gino clutched at her skirts.

Francesco took Cristina in his arms and kissed the top of her head.

"I promise," he said. "We will take care of each other as we always do. I promise."

"We are twice armed if we fight with faith," said a small voice.

"Nonna!" said Francesco with a smile. "Are you quoting Plato?"

As they looked toward the fireplace, Nonna Isabetta was asleep once more.

CHAPTER 8

Holy Week – Maundy Thursday

L a Volpe stepped out from a side door of the Palazzo Pazzi onto the *Borgo degli Albizi*. He looked up and down the street, as he tucked the handwritten message away.

It was Maundy Thursday, the day before Good Friday. Good Friday was a very solemn day, commemorating the Crucifixion of Christ, and the streets would be empty but the churches full. Maundy Thursday, however, meant that the streets were still busy, as people prepared for the feasting to come on Easter Sunday. La Volpe approved of this. He did his best work in crowds, and today would be no different. This was a simple task, but he still prided himself on doing it well. He had reached the end of *Borgo degli Albizi* and looked left and right, up and down *Via del Proconsolo*. Which way? As he looked to the left, his eye caught the edge of the *Bargello*. He had crossed paths with the *podestà*, the magistrate, in that building once before and had no desire to repeat the experience. So, he turned right. The route was a little longer, but he had plenty of time. He walked amongst the traders, street entertainers and shoppers until he reached the end of the road. No longer a walkway, he now stood in a large piazza and his eyes were drawn upwards to the magnificent dome above the Cathedral of Santa Maria del Fiore, the *Duomo*. It was acknowledged that this miraculous construction in the centre of Florence was the biggest in the world, and nobody, not even La Volpe, could fail to look at it in awe and wonder. He stopped momentarily, gazing upwards, wondering what judgement awaited him when he eventually passed from this life, but then shook off the thought. He was, after all, only doing what was necessary to survive in a tough world.

He continued in the shadow of the great Cathedral, until he reached *Via del Calzaiuoli*, and with a backward glance at the great façade, he turned left into the busy street to lose himself among the crowd. After walking for a few minutes, he spotted *Via Porta Rossa* on his right. This was the street, and he was on time. Now all he had to do was find the right house. He'd been told to look for a crest containing a red rose but had no idea how far along it would be. This part of the job was always the most dangerous. Studying each house and walking slower than normal could easily attract attention, and he didn't want that attention. He needed to be invisible. His heart started to beat a little faster, and he became more acutely aware of his surroundings.

There! What's that? Is that a red rose? Yes, it is! He had found the place and looked up at the tall, fortified house. Another wealthy household. He smiled to himself. If these wealthy families ever managed to get on with each other, he would be out of work. He had no idea who was to receive the message that was safely tucked inside his tunic, just that they would be expecting him.

As instructed, he knocked quietly three times on the heavy door, the message now gripped in his hand. Within seconds, he heard the heavy bolt being drawn back, and the door slowly opened a fraction. He knew there was no chance of seeing the face of the person who opened the door, so he looked out for the hand, and there it was. La

Volpe had seen many hands in similar situations and had learned to tell a lot about their owners: male or female, hard or soft, young or old. He looked at this hand and made an accurate mental picture of its owner, but he made no judgement. He'd seen them all before. He pressed the message into the waiting palm and turned away. His job was completed, and the coins in his purse were now waiting to be handed over to the nearest tavern keeper. The face behind the door peered out but saw nothing except a fox's tail, as it disappeared into the narrow alleyway across the street.

The atmosphere inside Palazzo Rosini was of suppressed excitement with not a little apprehension.

In Donna Cristina's *camera*, or chambers, she was modelling her Easter Sunday outfit for Tessa and Nonna Isabetta. As much as Nonna protested that she was not interested in such things, she always had an opinion on fashion, as much as any other subject. Cristina was conscious of the fashion etiquette and had made sure that she did not match or clash with the colours to be worn by the Medici women, but complemented them without outshining them. However, as the wife of one of Florence's leading textile merchants, much was expected of her. It was a difficult balance, but she was well practised in the art of diplomacy.

Her seamstress had done well following her mistress's instructions, and the result was exquisite. As always, there would be three layers to her outfit, starting with a plain white silk chemise as a soft undergarment. The next layer, the *gamurra*, was a full-length dress of red velvet, in acknowledgement to her Rosini family. However, so as not to outshine the red and black of the Medici women, most of the red in her *gamurra* would be covered by the outer gown of gold silk brocade, the best that her husband could provide. The whole outfit was in the highest fashion, with wide sleeves and a full skirt, pinched to emphasise her still small waist. As a married woman, she would wear her dark hair up, and would adorn it with a *trinzale*, a sheer netting, beaded with pearls. Cristina was not an ostentatious woman, but always made sure to meet the expectations of the society in which she mixed. She blushed when she thought of Francesco's reaction when he first laid eyes on her in her new outfit, but she knew it was a complete success when Nonna nodded and said, "Most satisfactory."

"Thank you, Nonna," she said. "I do wish you would come with us, Tessa. Such a great event, and an opportunity for you to meet more of the ladies in society."

The two women had a warm relationship but differing outlooks on society. Tessa was essentially a private person and shied away from large public gatherings, preferring the company of her son and her books.

Cristina, however, shone in large gatherings and had learnt that her diplomatic role in Francesco's business was every bit as important as the dry details of each contract he negotiated. Knowing that one day Tessa would need to take on this role when Niccolò took over the business from his father, she continued to encourage her.

"Oh, Mamma," Tessa replied. "I understand that it's important. I really do, but I am not ready to be part of such a group. I wouldn't know what to say to everyone, and all the ladies will be so elegant, and I…" She looked down at herself, spread her hands and looked back at Cristina despairingly.

Cristina walked across the room to Tessa and held both her hands. "My dear," she said gently. "You are a beautiful woman. You worry that you are not as elegant as other ladies because you still bear the cushioning from childbirth. Let me tell you that most of those elegant ladies spend their time fussing over each morsel that they put in their mouths and gazing at themselves in their looking glass, and they are as cold as ice. You have given us a beautiful grandson. You are warm and kind. My son loves you so very much, and we are fortunate to have you in our lives. It is those ladies who should envy you."

Tessa had a tear in her eye as she nodded. "I am fortunate in the love that I have found here, and for my Gino. Niccolò deserves a wife who will support him publicly, and I will be that wife...but I have promised Gino that we would watch the parade, and then spend the day together in the park."

"I understand, my dear," said Cristina. "I will help you prepare for the next big event, and you will dazzle everyone."

"Yes," piped up Nonna. "They're not used to seeing proper child-bearing hips. You'll be a sensation!"

Cristina sighed as she saw all the new-found confidence drain from Tessa's face.

Downstairs in the study, Luigi was watchful as the unease between father and son lingered. Their disagreement over the public support for the Medici had been set aside as they worked together, but Luigi could still feel a conflict in the air. As Francesco and Niccolò worked, Luigi watched and wondered how the situation would evolve. One of them would most certainly be proven correct, and he tried to imagine what the study would look like in a few days' time, after the Easter Sunday parade and celebrations. He was still daydreaming when Niccolò looked up and caught his eye. With a nervous cough, he returned his attention to the papers on his desk.

Just along the corridor, Lucia was polishing the silver in the *sala*, as Antonio arrived with a basket of logs for the fire. Her heart jumped a beat as he brushed past her.

"What? No kiss for me today?" she asked.

Antonio was kneeling by the empty fireplace, refilling the log basket. "I have to get on with cleaning and laying the fire."

"That didn't stop you before," she teased. "I heard you come in last night. You were very late. You don't have another woman, do you?" Lucia was only half teasing now. She knelt beside him, putting her hands around his waist, but he shook her off.

"Lucia, stop. Life is not all fun and games, you know. We both have work to do."

Lucia caught her breath and sat back on her heels.

Antonio dropped his head and sighed. "I'm sorry I snapped at you. There is just so much going on. So many people don't see it or find it difficult to understand. Everyone is so protected within these big walls, but things in Florence are changing, and…I'm afraid."

"What are you afraid of?" she asked.

Antonio paused, deep in thought before he replied. "The future," he said, bluntly. "You're used to having a warm, safe roof over your head, with Eleonora feeding you. You must see that it won't last forever. There are strong forces at work in the city, and we have to make sure we're on the right side. Now Matteo is going to work with the Medici. Where will it end?"

"Matteo is just attending one event, because one of their boys is injured. He'll be back before the end of the day. Is that what's worrying you?"

"Well, let's hope he does come back," said Antonio, taking Lucia into his arms.

In the kitchen, Eleonora was rather at a loss. For the first time in many years, she was not required to prepare a grand Easter Sunday banquet. By now, she would normally be decorating grand cakes, collecting poultry from the market and planning dish after dish of celebratory food. Gianetta and Lucia had tried to convince her that it was an ideal opportunity to have a rest, which Eleonora had reluctantly agreed to do. In reality, she was finding the stillness difficult. Every inch of the kitchen had been scrubbed, and each pot and pan was gleaming. The store cupboard was fully stocked with a range of herbal tonics, cakes and pies, and today's bread was already baked. The pantry would make Gino's eyes pop with wonder when he visited later. There was nothing else for Eleonora to do, so she sat by the fire with Gianetta to catch up with the news from the market.

"Tell me, is that old rogue still trying to sell stale bread as freshly baked?" she asked.

Gianetta laughed. "Of course he is, but this morning he was trying to sell it to Agnese from the Conti house. He didn't get away with that. She gave him a piece of her sharp tongue. They had quite a crowd by the time she had finished with him!"

"I'd like to have seen that," said Eleonora, "but serves her right for not making her own bread. No excuse for that."

"Well, if nothing else, she provided the marketplace with today's entertainment. The baker did say something that worried me, though. He said that all the Medici supporters, including the Contis, would soon have an awakening, and the time would come when they would be begging him for his bread. Then, I'm sure I heard him saying something about Easter, but it was so quiet I couldn't be sure. Oh, Eleonora, I can't wait for Easter to be over, and then maybe I'll stop worrying about Matteo."

"Try not to worry too much, child. Matteo is a smart boy, and he will be able to sense trouble before it happens."

"That's true, but he also fancies himself as a bit of a hero, and I'd be afraid that he might do something silly."

Eleonora stood up and patted Gianetta on the shoulder. "Some tonic to drink," she said, walking to the store cupboard, then she looked back at Gianetta, who was twirling a strand of her hair through her fingers and gazing into the fire. "But," she said to herself, "not the raspberry leaf, I think. No, not the raspberry leaf."

CHAPTER 9

Holy Saturday

Two days later, and it was Holy Saturday, a day of vigil, of watching and waiting: a day of prayer and preparation. The whole of Florence seemed peaceful. The streets were empty, and the churches were being decorated with flowers, in readiness for the Easter celebrations. In homes across the city, food was being prepared for a feast. Kitchens in grand palazzi and humble homes alike were hectic, at odds with the quiet atmosphere in the city.

The only other person who was busy was La Volpe. He thought back to the recent job that had taken him to *Via Porta Rossa*. It had been well paid, and he had enjoyed the fruits of his labour by visiting his favourite tavern across the river. His mind lingered on the whore who had relieved him of his last few coins, and he smiled. "Worth every last *soldo*," he thought, and promised himself a return visit once these jobs were over. In truth, he had become extremely busy over the last few days, and while he was curious, he was not interested enough to try to find out what it was all about. He couldn't read the messages he was given to deliver, and even if he could, he wouldn't risk opening them. He had his reputation to consider, after all. No, he was content in his assumption that it was yet another intrigue between the wealthy families, another feud that would eventually either quietly die away or end up in a swordfight. Either way, it meant good business for him, and he would make the most of it while it lasted. He adjusted the fox's tail on his belt, checked that he had the messages safely in his tunic, and continued his passage through the streets of Florence, from Palazzo Pazzi to homes and boarding houses across the city. He had several calls to make before the bell of the *Palazzo della Signoria* sounded the curfew.

On the top floor of Palazzo Rosini were the servants' quarters. It was afternoon, and there was a short period of quiet before the evening meal was due to be served. In Gianetta's room, Matteo paraded around the small room in his new livery: a red velvet high-necked tunic with a pleated skirt and matching shoes, which was completed with black hose. The gold stitching was evidence that no expense would be spared for the parade, and Matteo felt very grand. The seamstress had delivered the clothes that very morning.

"It's a bit late," said Gianetta, with pins in the corner of her mouth. "You should have had this days ago. How am I supposed to make alterations at this late stage?"

"It's fine! Don't you think I look elegant?" said Matteo, with his hands on his hips, twirling around and watching the movement of the skirt.

"You'll be a laughing-stock if I don't do something with those sleeves. They're so long, you could trip over them."

"I'll just pull them up. Don't worry."

"You will not!" exclaimed Gianetta. "Now stand still and stretch out your arms, so that I can see where they should be."

Matteo walked across to where Gianetta sat on the bed impatiently.

He held his arms out towards her. As Gianetta removed the pins from her mouth, he made to tickle her behind her ear but just succeeded in making her jump. She let out a yelp, as the pin pricked her finger.

"*Ahia!* Matteo, *basta!*" Gianetta sucked the blood from her finger, angrily.

"I'm sorry, Gianetta," said Matteo. "I just meant to cheer you up."

"Cheer me up? Cheer me up? Are you serious?" Gianetta looked as if she were about explode.

Matteo, who knew what was coming, looked nervous. He'd been on the receiving end of one of Gianetta's outbursts before, and he had no desire to endure another.

"You are going to be parading with a family who have many enemies here in Florence. You have heard the rumours, that there is going to be trouble. You, yourself, could be in great danger, just by being near them, let alone associated with them." Her voice was rising with each passing syllable.

Matteo was holding his hands out and attempting to calm her, but Gianetta would not be pacified.

"You know how worried we all are, and yet you still insist on being part of this performance, without a second thought for us."

Hysteria was not in Gianetta's nature, but Matteo felt that she was getting close to it now.

He became stern. Sitting alongside her, he held her at arm's length and looked into her eyes.

"You know that I have been given a great honour in being asked. You also know that there is absolutely no chance of me letting down Signor Francesco or Signor Lorenzo. I know you are worried, but I will take every care to ensure that my Lords and I are safe. Now, I will not listen to any more of this nonsense!"

He wondered if he had gone too far. He was gentle and easy-going as a rule but felt he needed to stand his ground on this matter. As he looked at Gianetta, he saw that she was crying. He pulled her close in an instant. "Ah, *mia bellissima*, I know you are worried, but I promise I will take care."

"Oh Matteo, I can't possibly lose you. I couldn't manage without you. Not ever."

Matteo kissed the top of her head.

"Nor I you," he said. "Who would look after me the way you do? Who would pin my sleeves up, so that I didn't disgrace the family's honour?" He chuckled softly into her hair, but Gianetta pulled away from him. She took a deep breath.

"Matteo, the problem is…" She stood up and started pacing the small room. "Well, it's not a problem really…Matteo…" She stopped pacing and turned to look at him. "…I'm going to have a baby…"

Gianetta clasped her hands, as if in prayer, and looked at her feet, as Matteo slowly stood. After a moment of silence, she looked up into Matteo's eyes. She read in them all the emotions that she had been feeling for the last few weeks and wondered which emotion would eventually win out. When she saw how he truly felt, she thought she would faint with happiness and relief. Not a word passed between them, as he held her close and let the tears of joy flow freely.

"A baby!" he eventually said. "We are going to have a baby! *Che miracolo!"*

Gianetta laughed gently. "A God-given miracle indeed, Matteo, but it happens all the time. We are not unusual in that."

Matteo looked as though he had been slapped, as he moved away from her, his hand to his head. "Yes! God-given! What will Padre Cristoforo say? We are not even married!"

Gianetta whispered, "No. No, we're not."

"Gianetta?" Matteo held her face in his hands and looked into her dark eyes. "Will you marry me?"

Her eyes filled with tears, as she nodded and then buried her head in his chest as she held him close. They sat in silence on the bed in each other's arms, each with their own thoughts. Gianetta thought about her own family. She just had Mamma Sofia, but she had taught her everything about family life. There could be no better role model for her as she embarked on this new chapter of her life. She turned to look at Matteo, trying to read his mind.

Matteo's thoughts were following a similar pattern. He worried that he might not have what it takes to be a father. A father! He gulped at the enormity of it all. What did he know about being a father? He thought about his own father and smiled. He supposed that his father had had the same thoughts, but he had managed, hadn't he?

"Are you thinking about your father?" she asked.

He nodded, still smiling.

"Tell me about him," she asked, quietly.

He rested his head back, closed his eyes and told the story that he had heard countless times about his parents and the life they had lived together...

Matteo Cavallo had been born in Settignano, a small village to the northwest of Florence, known for its vineyards and olive groves, but also boasting a marble quarry owned by a man called Ludovico Buonarroti. Matteo's father was employed in this marble quarry. His job was to tend the animals used to transport the stone that had been quarried. Depending on the size of the block of marble, transportation could be either by donkey, horse-drawn cart or for larger pieces, carts pulled by oxen. There was a large stable of animals to care for, and it was an enjoyable job.

He had a special love for the horses in his care, and whenever he had time, would saddle up and take a ride into the forest. During one of these rides, he came across another rider. She was a beautiful woman, tall and slender and graceful on the back of her black thoroughbred.

"A magnificent specimen," he said out loud.

The woman smiled and asked, "Are you referring to my horse or me?"

He became flustered and mumbled something incomprehensible, until she stopped him.

"My name is Piera. To whom do I have the pleasure of speaking?"

"Dario, signorina. Dario Cavallo." He bowed his head, while reigning in his horse, who was impatient to ride further into the forest.

"Buongiorno, Dario," Piera replied. She looked carefully at the handsome, dark-haired man with piercing blue eyes. "It seems that our horses are not keen to stand and converse. Shall we ride together?"

Dario looked concerned, but Piera laughed. "Don't worry. If you show any sign of impropriety, I am a swift rider and can be back at my brother's house before you've had time to click your heels."

Side by side, they rode through the forest, talking all the way. He pointed out unusual flora and fauna. He knew the forest well, and she was keen to learn. He asked about Piera's horse, and they discussed the attributes of the horses they had ridden and the joy it gave them. Eventually, the dappled light from the trees gave way to bright sunlight as they emerged from the forest.

"Grazie, Dario," said Piera. "I have enjoyed our morning ride." She paused, looking down at her hands holding the reins and then continued, "I am currently staying in my brother's house, and I often take a ride at this time of day...should you find yourself in the same vicinity."

Over the following weeks, when Dario was able to escape from his work, they met and rode together, talking and enjoying each other's *company. Gradually, their love grew, and they spent every spare moment together in the shade of the forest trees. When Piera told him that she was to have a child, Dario was thrilled. There were to be hard times ahead, though.*

"My family will never accept us," she said. "My brother, Ludovico, will be furious."

"Lodovico? Ludovico Buonarotti?"

"Yes, that's my older brother. Do you know him?"

"I work for him...or rather, I used to work for him. He will have my job, if not my life! What are we to do?" he asked, desperately. "I will do anything for you, mi'amore."

"I cannot bear to be parted from you, Dario," she replied. "I must leave my family. Will we survive?" she pleaded.

Dario was removed from his job, as expected, and Piera left her family, although Dario's life was not in danger. She was a formidable woman when she set her mind to it. They found a small holding on the outskirts of Settignano, and settled there, where Piera gave birth to a healthy son, calling him Matteo. It was a poor but happy family life.

Piera learned to cook and sew and tend to the garden. Dario did odd jobs for the people of Settignano but was constantly worried about their low income. They lived hand to mouth on the vegetables that they grew and from produce that they could exchange for their services. Dario knew that they were barely surviving, but Piera never once complained.

One winter, when Matteo was about eight years old, people in the village started to get sick. The winter was harsh, and medicine and good food was scarce. People were beginning to die from this sickness. When Piera started to show signs of the fever, Dario was desperate. He travelled from house to house, pleading for help, but the villagers were unable to help themselves or anyone else. He tended to her night and day, trying to get her to drink some broth, but it was no use. Finally, on Christmas Eve, with Dario holding her hand and young Matteo resting his head on her shoulder, Piera slipped quietly away.

Gianetta wiped away a tear, as Matteo clutched her closer to him.

"I was so lucky to have my mother, even for a short time. Our baby will be just as lucky to have you for a mother, but me? A father!" He paused. "Papà…"

"It must have been so hard for him," she said, "but you've always spoken so fondly of him. What was he like?"

"He was such fun. We always played…in the forest, with the horses, by the river… He taught me to look after the horses, taught me how to fish, taught me which fruits I could pick in the forest and which were poisonous.

"After Mamma died, he was sad. We both were. For a very long time, nothing seemed to make sense. We just drifted from day to day. Eventually, our life became normal…a different normal. Our normal. We worked together; we went to Mass together. We even learned how to cook a meal together." Matteo smiled as he remembered some of the disasters they'd had. Eleonora would no doubt find it funny.

"I think we grew up together. One day, he came home from town very excited. He told me he had found me a position here in Florence, to be apprenticed to a great artist. I didn't want to go. I enjoyed my time with my father and just wanted to stay at home with life plodding along, just as it always had. Papà wouldn't hear of it. He said I needed to make a place for myself in the world, that I needed to be independent, to make something of my life. I didn't understand it at all. I'm afraid I was very difficult about it, and we argued a lot. In the end, he was my father, and I had to do as he said."

He stopped and looked at Gianetta's flat stomach, gingerly placing a hand where the tiny baby was growing. "I guess that's what fathers do, isn't it? Make difficult decisions for their children…"

Gianetta placed her hand over Matteo's. "You will be a wonderful father. Your Papà taught you well, and your heart is good. Our baby is lucky to have you."

They sat quietly together in peaceful companionship, savouring the quiet, absorbing the realisation that their life was about to change for good and simply feeling happy.

"We will marry before Pentecost, I promise. We can start to make the arrangements after this Easter Sunday event is finished. Pentecost…forty days after Easter…can you wait that long?"

"Of course, I can wait, Matteo. It is enough to know that we will be married and that we will be a family."

"I can see why you are so worried about this parade," said Matteo, "but don't give it another thought. Nobody would dare to challenge me now. I feel as tall as a tower and as strong as a horse." He stood up and flexed his muscles.

Gianetta didn't know whether to laugh or cry, so she did both. "Oh, Matteo, I love you so much, but please, no displays of heroism. I just want my Matteo home safe and sound."

"I promise, *cara*. I promise. I have responsibilities of my own now, and when have you ever known me to shirk my responsibilities?"

In a fit of excitement, he jumped up, lifting Gianetta off her feet and swung her round until they both collapsed in laughter.

Out in the street, as La Volpe passed the door with the red rose crest, he heard shouts and laughter from above. He looked up briefly but didn't pause. He had completed his work for the day, and the coins weighed heavy in his purse. Head down, he and his fox's tail headed for the bridge to take him across the river and to his favourite tavern.

CHAPTER 10

Easter Sunday morning

L
a Volpe's head throbbed as he reached for the door. He slowly pulled it open, and the blinding sunlight pierced his eyes. He groaned out loud. The tavern-keeper had left him asleep on the floor overnight. In fact, he could not have done much else, as La Volpe had been so drunk that he would have had to be carried out. This morning was payment time, though. Not in terms of coin. Those coins had disappeared the night before, into the tavern-keeper's pocket and the whore's purse. No, the payment was in pain. He checked himself for any injuries, but it seemed that the pain came from within. Perhaps it was bad wine, but he gave a short laugh. The wine was fine. It was the quantity of wine that was the problem. With his purse full of wages, he had seemed to attract many new friends, all of whom were very thirsty. He had been happy to play the genial host and share his brief wealth with these friends. Then the highlight of the evening, the trip up the stairs with his whore. What was her name? Maria? Marina? No matter. She was a very pleasant memory. He put his hand to his sore *cazzo* and hoped that what he felt was just a passing irritation.

"Here!" The voice behind him came from the tavern-keeper. "Some bread, *mio amico*. You look as though you need it."

"*Grazie, grazie*." He took the bread and put it in his pocket. He couldn't face it just at that moment; maybe later.

He checked himself over once more. Yes, his fox's tail was still attached to his belt, and yes, his purse was still empty. He sighed briefly but shrugged off any regret. He was sure to get more work soon. He left the tavern behind and made his way towards the river.

As he crossed the *Ponte Vecchio*, the oldest bridge in Florence, he noticed that although the butchers' shops were closed, the stench from the river was still strong and stomach-churning. He took a great gulp of air to try to quell the rise of bile that threatened to overwhelm him. As he fought with himself, he thought again about the closed butchers' shops. He was out early, but not that early. Then he remembered that it was Easter Sunday. No shops would be open today. Everyone would be at church or celebrating at home with their families. Ha! Some chance of that! Still, Easter Sunday was always a spectacle, with parades and crowds enjoying themselves. He'd make his way to the *Duomo*, the Cathedral, find a comfortable spot and watch the comings and goings of the great and the good. He cheered up at the thought of the entertainment ahead, took a bite of the bread from his pocket and set off for the *Duomo*, feeling considerably better.

Upstairs in Palazzo Rosini, Donna Cristina's chambers were bursting with energy and activity. The heavy wooden bed was littered with dressing gowns and towels, following her bath early that morning. Cristina was lucky to be one of the few ladies in Florence to have a bathroom within her chambers. It was a small side room, with a metal bath in the centre, but the water could be emptied straight into the drain, which would take it outside and away from the Palazzo. The walls of her bedroom were heavily decorated with a red and blue geometric pattern up to the level of the window. Above the window, the fresco depicted ornate architectural details with the coats of arms of Rosini ancestors. In the corner, was a fireplace, but it was not lit, as the morning already promised to be warm.

Cristina had said her morning prayers, specifically praying that the day would pass smoothly. Gianetta was tending to her gown, and Lucia was completing the finishing touches to Cristina's hair. Tessa was watching in fascination, while Gino jumped up and down on his grandmother's bed, enjoying the excitement.

"Oh *Madonna*, you look exquisite. Signor Francesco is going to be so proud of you. You will outshine any of the Medici women." Lucia continued to fuss with her hair and the clips holding the *trinzale* in place.

"Lucia," said Nonna from a chair in the corner, positioned so that she could see everything. "Donna Cristina could eclipse any woman in Florence...but she chooses not to."

"Thank you, Nonna," said Cristina. "I believe that was a compliment." She laughed and stood up to the admiring gazes of the women in the room. "My seamstress really has done a splendid job, hasn't she?"

"She has, *Madonna*," said Gianetta, "but Lucia is right. You will be beyond compare at the parade. I will be so proud to watch you pass by."

"Thank you, girls," said Cristina. "You are very kind. I wonder if the gentlemen are ready."

Along the corridor, in Signor Francesco's chambers, Niccolò was already dressed and sitting in a chair, watching Antonio fastening Francesco's doublet.

Francesco was the picture of calm, as though parading and

banqueting with the Medici in their Palazzo was an everyday affair, although Antonio's hands shook a little.

Matteo was also ready, dressed in the Medici livery, standing to attention by the doorway and trying to control his black, wayward hair. He looked rather nervous but was also twitching with excitement.

"Well, boy," said Niccolò. "It looks as though we are stuck with you for the day." He stood up and looked him in the eye. "Do as you have been instructed. Do our family proud. My father trusts you...so I trust you."

The two men looked at each other for a moment. Matteo swallowed and said, "Yes, *ser*."

"And tidy your hair!"

Matteo thought he saw a smile as Niccolò turned away from him but dismissed the thought.

"Where is Luigi, Papà?"

"I gave him the day off," replied Francesco, as he brushed invisible specks from his sleeves. "We have completed our business for now, and he is of no use to us in this department, so I gave him some time away. He will be back tomorrow morning."

"Luigi? A day off? I'm not sure I have ever known him take a day off," said Niccolò, surprised. "What do you think he will do with it? Does he have a family to spend it with? A wife and twelve children, perhaps?" Niccolò laughed at the thought, realising that he knew very little about the man he spent so many hours working with.

"Unlikely, I think," said Francesco. "Luigi is...well, let's say he is a very private man."

Niccolò nodded, absently, making a mental note to find out more about his father's personal assistant. Maybe tomorrow. Today, there were other pressing matters. "What about Nonna?" he asked. "Will she be at Mass too?"

"No." Francesco shook his head. "She disapproves of the pomp of the *Duomo*, so Tessa and Eleonora took her to the dawn Mass at *Chiesa di Ognissanti*. She'll have a goblet of wine with her lunch and will be snoozing before we hear the Communion bell! *Andiamo*, it's time we prepared to leave. The coach will be waiting for us."

In the courtyard, the whole family and staff had gathered, apart from Nonna, who had retired to her chambers after her early morning.

Francesco gazed at his wife and said, "Ah, *mia cara*. You are simply sublime. You look more beautiful today than the day I first met you, all those years ago." And he kissed her, tenderly. He looked round at the waiting staff members. "Thank you all for your hard work. Once you have closed the doors behind us, make sure you enjoy this special day. If you catch sight of us in the street, be sure to wave. It will be good to see a friendly face."

The great doors of the courtyard swung open to the street, where the coach and horses, sent by Lorenzo, waited to take the family and Matteo to the *Palazzo Medici*.

Gianetta stood next to Eleonora, biting her lip. She looked at Matteo and forced a smile for him. "You look so dashing," she said, "and your sleeves are the perfect length." She continued quietly, "May God be with you, *amore mio*."

He held both her shoulders and kissed her forehead. "I will be home before you have missed me," he promised.

The family climbed into the coach, with Matteo hopping up next to the driver. As they pulled off, he turned and mouthed to her. *"Ciao Bellissima!"*

"You told him, then?" said Eleonora, quietly with a smile.

Gianetta's head swung round quickly to look at Eleonora. "How did…?"

But of course, she knew. Eleonora always knew.

Earlier that morning, near the *Basilica di San Lorenzo* in the north of the city, Luigi had been getting ready for an important day. Rather a lonely soul, he lived alone in a single room dwelling in a boarding house where the tenants were only men. Locally, it was known to be a sodomite house, but the tenants in the house were older, and they were more discreet than some of the younger men who occasionally visited. The neighbourhood was largely accepting of the boarding house, as it was rare that they were visited by the Office of the Night, a body of men tasked to combat the common, but illegal, practice of sodomy in the city. Living in such a delicate and dangerous environment had made Luigi watchful. He was naturally an introspective man, a keen observer of his fellow man and would have made a very interesting dinner companion should he ever feel the need to share his thoughts, which he seldom did.

This morning, he was deep in thought. He was relieved when Signor Francesco told him not to present himself for work that day. He knew that he had a challenge ahead of him and not having to ask for the time made it easier for him and less likely to raise suspicion. He never asked for time off work.

Luigi had dressed carefully. While he was not in the habit of dressing elaborately, he was especially careful to dress in such a way that he could be almost invisible. Drab clothing that was clean but worn would make sure that he went unnoticed by anyone passing him in the street. It was a fine day, but he also wrapped a scarf around his neck, in case he needed to cover his face. Finally, he picked up the last item for the day ahead. The sharp knife, taken surreptitiously from the Palazzo kitchen, glinted in the narrow shaft of sunlight coming through his window. He looked at it intently, feeling the weight of it in his hand and clutching the handle, testing its grip. He felt his heart beginning to race, took a deep breath to calm himself and put the knife safely inside the pocket in his cloak.

As he left his room, closing the door quietly behind him, he bumped into one of his neighbours. A large man, with a cheery disposition and loud voice, he clapped him on the back and boomed, "Off to see the procession, eh?"

Luigi smiled and nodded. "Of course. Isn't everyone?"

"Indeed!" His voice dropped to a whisper that echoed along the corridor. "For myself, I am hoping to catch a glimpse of the pretty Giuliano. What say you? Ha!" With another hefty thwack on Luigi's back and a dramatic flourish of his cape, the man bounded down the stairs and out into the street.

After taking a moment to catch his breath, Luigi followed the man outside. Taking the direct route to the *Duomo* would not take him very long, but he had decided to take a longer, quieter route, skirting the *Piazza di Santa Maria Maggiore*, eventually arriving at the *Duomo* from the west. While he didn't want to bump into people he may know, he knew he had to stay watchful. Arriving at the *Duomo*, he noticed the crowds had begun to gather already. Assuming the appearance of one of the many sightseers, he mingled with the crowd, keeping a close watch on the people around him. Where would be the best vantage point? Where did he need to be when the trouble erupted, as he knew it would? The best place, he decided, would be in front of the great front doors of the *Duomo*. Perhaps near the Baptistry? He knew just the place. He made his way towards his chosen spot, only to find it taken. Sitting on the floor, munching a piece of bread, was a man with a fox's tail on his belt, looking distinctly worse for wear. Judging by the smell of stale wine, this would not be a pleasant place to wait, so he moved on to the south side. He spotted the perfect place.

On the corner of one of the side streets, opposite the south door of the *Duomo*, was a shop with a low windowsill.

"*Perfetto!*" he said to himself. "I can sit here and wait until I'm needed."

SECONDI PIATTI

Now we have reached the main course, the main event. Everything we have consumed so far has been leading up to this, so it's time to turn up the heat and sink our teeth into something a bit meatier.

It is said that Florence was a resting point for British pilgrims on their way to Rome. They loved the meat that they were served and would often chant for more. "Beef steak! Beef steak!" And so, it became known as Bistecca, and obviously, the very best version is now known as Bistecca alla Fiorentina.

Bistecca alla Fiorentina
(Serves 2)

- *1 porterhouse or T-bone steak, approx. 2-3kg*

- *Make sure to choose the best meat. Chianina is the best.*

- *It is necessary to have meat that has matured 25–28 days. This will ensure that it is tender.*

- *The steak should be at least 4cm thick.*

- *Take it out of the fridge around 1hr before you cook it.*

- *Cook on wood embers to give it the best flavour.*

- *The embers should be very hot in order to cook it well on the outside but remain rare inside.*

- *Cook each side for about 5 mins.*

- *Salt the meat once it is cooked. (Maldon salt is the best, but regular coarse salt is fine.)*

- *Rest the meat before serving on a sharing platter.*

Shared with kind permission from Piero and Lorenzo, Ristorante Totò, Borgo degli Apostoli, Florence.

CHAPTER 11

Easter Sunday morning

As the coach drew into the *Palazzo Medici* courtyard from *Via Larga*, Matteo looked around in wonder. The Palazzo was renowned in Florence as being a symbol of its most powerful family. The great, fortified stones that made up the exterior of the ground floor reflected the strength and solidity of the family, as was the intention. Cosimo, Lorenzo's grandfather, had originally hired Brunelleschi to design the building. This architect was famous for creating and completing the great cupola, the dome that topped the *Duomo*, the Cathedral. However, Brunelleschi had produced a very grandiose design for the Palazzo, and while he was extremely wealthy, Cosimo was, in essence, a modest man and wished to appear so to the people of Florence, and so, he had opted for this simpler design.

The exterior design may have been simple, but inside, the elaborate courtyard, staircases and the garden that Matteo could glimpse through the archway was like nothing he had ever seen before. The archways around the courtyard were held up with finely decorated columns, and above these were friezes of mythological figures that Matteo did not recognise. He recognised the Medici coat of arms, however, by the balls on a shield. He remembered shouting "*Palle! Palle!*" in support of Giuliano de' Medici at a jousting tournament some time before. As he smiled at the memory, his eye caught a statue in the centre of the courtyard. It appeared to be made of bronze, and was of a boy…but he looked like a girl… How strange! He spotted that the figure had a sword in his hand, and his foot on top of a decapitated head. It must be David. He had heard the story, of course, about David defeating the giant, Goliath. This must be what he was seeing, but he hadn't pictured David to look like a girl. Then, the driver beside him coughed, and he remembered his duties. He jumped down to open the coach door for Francesco, Cristina and Niccolò.

"Sorry, *ser*," he said, as Signor Francesco stepped down from the coach.

"Don't worry, boy," whispered Francesco. "It does take your breath away, rather, doesn't it?" He was also taking in every detail, although trying to look less awestruck than Matteo.

Donna Cristina was straightening her gown when a voice boomed from behind them.

"*Amici!* Friends! *Benvenuto!* Welcome to my home!" Lorenzo strode towards them, holding out his arms in welcome. He stopped short when he caught sight of Cristina. "*Che bella!* Francesco, you are a lucky man!"

"Oh, I know that very well, Lorenzo. How goes it this morning?"

"We are all ready," he replied. "All except Giuliano, who is indisposed. I don't ask what ails him. Our mother is trying to rouse him, and we just hope he makes it to Mass. Come! We shall go into the garden, while we wait for the ladies." He nodded toward Matteo. "Your young man can join my men by the staircase. They'll tell him what to do."

It was a short walk from *Palazzo Medici* to the *Duomo*. In truth, on any normal day, it would take less than five minutes, but of course, this was not a normal day. Crowds had gathered in the street in the bright sunshine. Some were making their way to Mass; some were there to enjoy the celebration of the Risen Christ, and maybe share some wine with friends and neighbours, and others just wanted to get a glimpse of Florence's most powerful family. Women from all levels of society stretched their necks to catch sight of the ladies' fine dresses, and all gasped at Cristina's sensational gown, but she kept her head bowed modestly.

Lucrezia Tornabuoni, Lorenzo's mother, walked alongside her, and whispered, "Do not feel uncomfortable, my dear. We are all part of the same parade, and for better or worse, today you are a Medici. Enjoy their admiration."

Cristina looked up at the formidable woman, smiled, lifted her chin and looked out at the crowd, beginning to enjoy the moment. It was indeed proving to be a very special day.

Matteo, who had been walking ahead of the family, stood at the top of the steps leading to the great door of the Cathedral with his new colleagues, as they waited for Medici and Rosini to finish their journey. The men alongside Matteo knew that they might be waiting some time. It was important that everybody saw the men who ruled them. In the crowd, Matteo spotted Tessa and Gino. Gino was jumping up and down, waving frantically. He smiled and gave a small wave. Was he allowed to do that? He wasn't sure. Finally, the two families arrived at the door. They paused to greet members of the clergy and other noble families, all the while conscious that from their elevated position, even more people could see them. One man, who Matteo thought he recognised, asked Lorenzo, "No Giuliano? I was hoping to see him today."

"He was detained, Jacopo," replied Lorenzo with a stiff politeness. "I believe he will be along shortly. In fact, I am told that two of his friends are bringing him here, as we speak."

"*Bene, bene.*" The other man nodded and made his way into the Cathedral.

Matteo heard Lorenzo mutter under his breath "Pazzi bastard!"

At Lorenzo's signal, they all entered the great Cathedral.

After the bright sunlight, it took a moment for Matteo's eyes to adjust to the subdued lighting inside. Indeed, not only did the light disappear but the sound too. From the joyous crowds outside, to the reverent silence within, it was as if all sensory perception had been shut off. Gradually, he became accustomed to the change in atmosphere. His breathing slowed, he bowed his head in a short prayer and then looked around him. The great nave was already busy with people, gathered for Mass. Every alcove was filled with candles, making the air thick and smoky. Incense was burning from censers around the altar, adding to the heady mix. Matteo and the other men slowly led the families past the crowds and up the long aisle to the benches nearest the altar. As they walked, Matteo scanned the congregation. He recognised many of the people as friends of the Medici family or notable men from local businesses. He faltered slightly when his eyes met the piercing green eyes of Cesare Conti, who smiled and inclined his head in Matteo's direction.

Sitting beside him, his parents, Signor and Signora Conti, took no notice of Matteo but craned their necks for a glimpse of the Medici and Rosini family members. They were proud to have some association with this important entourage and were looking forward to the banquet to follow. The parade reached the front benches nearest the altar, which had, of course, been kept free for them. The men took the benches to the left of the aisle, and the women, the benches to the right, Matteo and the other manservants sitting behind their masters.

Matteo looked around him and his gaze stopped at a fresco on the west wall, fascinated. It clearly depicted a scene from Florence, as he could see the dome of the Cathedral and the *Palazzo della Signoria* in the background. In the centre was a man dressed in red, holding a book. Above him were the moon and stars. All fairly similar to other pictures he had seen, until he looked behind the man's right shoulder. So many figures tortured, descending to Hell, or trudging around a circular mountain. Was this the nine circles of Hell that the famous poet Dante Alighieri wrote about? He had heard the stories of course, but never had he pictured it like this. Is this what Hell was really like? He wanted to get up and take a closer look but knew that he dare not.

In front of Matteo, Niccolò was looking upward.

Matteo followed his gaze and looked straight up into the middle of the magnificent dome that was the envy of the world. He swayed slightly from the vertiginous effects of such an enormous structure. "God must have truly guided the hand that created this," he thought to himself. "And Florence must be blessed to have men able to create such a wonder." He shook his head in disbelief and promised himself that he would bring Gianetta here and share it with her. The people of Florence rarely strayed from their own parish churches, and the closest to Palazzo Rosini was *Chiesa di Ognissanti*, a beautiful church but nothing on the scale of the *Duomo*.

Next to Niccolò, Francesco and Lorenzo were whispering together. Lorenzo looked to the back of the nave and returned to Francesco, nodding.

Matteo also turned to see what he was looking at, and at the back, near the door, stood Giuliano, accompanied by two men, presumably his friends. Matteo smiled to himself. "That was a lucky escape," he thought, assuming that a late night of revelry had prevented Giuliano from being on time for the most important event of the year.

At an invisible signal, a bell sounded the start of the Mass, and the congregation stood to greet the celebrants. A choir of young boys and men led the large procession up the aisle, their voices filling the nave and rising to heaven through the great dome. Behind them, another group of men swung large gold thuribles, dispensing more incense into the air. The priests and clergy, holding their missals, were the last in the procession, their elaborate vestments drawing more than one sideways glance from the more avaricious of the worshippers.

When those in the procession had found their places on the altar, the priest turned to the congregation. His booming voice greeted everyone present. *"In nomini patri, et Filii, et Spiritus Sancti."* He offered the blessing by making the sign of the cross to the faithful, which was mirrored by each one in their own blessing.

Matteo allowed himself to be absorbed into the familiar flow of the Mass, the Latin words washing over him, and the responses coming automatically to his lips. He had almost forgotten that he was surrounded by such a large congregation in an unfamiliar church.

Eventually, the priest came to the most solemn section of the Mass, the consecration of the bread and wine into the body and blood of Jesus Christ. Everyone bowed their heads in reverence as the bell rang.

At that moment, from the back of the church came a loud shout. *"Traditore!* Traitor!" and somebody screamed, and then many more people screamed.

Matteo turned to look at what was happening but couldn't see, as the congregation had risen and were starting to move towards the disturbance. However, he could see that it came from the area where Giuliano had been standing. It couldn't possibly be an attack. Nobody would dare such a thing on sacred ground, and in the middle of Mass too. Perhaps there had been an accident. He heard someone shouting again, and his eye caught sight of a knife, and…was that blood? Yes, it was!

The moments following the realisation that someone was indeed launching an attack on the Medici passed in slow motion for Matteo. He could feel a wave of panic spreading as the whole congregation tried to escape the nave. He heard some people crying that the dome was collapsing. A glance above him confirmed that the dome was intact, and no such disaster was imminent. Other more fatalistic members of the congregation were announcing the arrival of Judgement Day. It took but a second for Matteo to realise that this was simply an assassination attempt, sacrilegious as it was. His first thought was for Francesco and Niccolò, but they were still in front of him, safe but looking equally as confused as many of the crowd.

Lorenzo was trying to make his way to the back of the nave, to his brother, but the chaos in front of him made it impossible to pass.

His mother, Lucrezia Tornabuoni, however, had managed to run along the side aisle to her younger son, and her screams echoed around the great cavernous space, enough to tear the heart of any man.

It was at this point that Matteo realised that there was a closer threat. He heard swords and daggers being drawn; he saw blood, and the noise of men shouting was deafening. The bell from the altar, and the pleas from the priest were drowned. There were fist fights, sword fights and daggers all around. He turned to Lorenzo just as one of the other priests from the altar went at him with a dagger that had been concealed beneath his vestments.

Lorenzo clutched at his neck where the dagger had found its mark. Francesco rushed to help his friend, but Matteo's attention was immediately drawn to a man nearby. His hair and his eyes were wild, and in his hand, he clutched a long dagger, glinting in a sunbeam that pierced one of the high windows. The blade of the dagger was pointing straight at Francesco, who was oblivious to the threat bearing down on him. From that moment, all Matteo knew was chaos and terror. Shouts, blades, screams, blood, torn clothes, men hitting the floor, fists flying, and then the blackness closed in.

Out in the piazza and the streets beyond, chaos continued. Some were still proclaiming Judgement Day or the collapse of Brunelleschi's great dome, but the majority of people realised that something far more earthly had happened and rushed to escape the many swords and daggers that were still flying. Men and women rushed out of the great doors, their finery, so elaborate, so coveted, now torn, dirty and covered in blood. Their well-trained gentility and good manners were long forgotten as they pushed, shoved and trampled over bodies in their desperation to reach safety.

Lucrezia Tornabuoni's inconsolable screams could be heard across the piazza and down the surrounding streets.

Nobody noticed the man with the fox's tail, sleeping off his hangover in the doorway of the Baptistry.

CHAPTER 12

Easter Sunday – early afternoon

An hour later, Francesco, unhurt but frightened and shaken, was pacing his study. His head was pounding, and he was breathing heavily, running his hands through his hair and trying to make sense of what had just happened. Somehow, during the turmoil, he had been knocked unconscious. It could only have been for a few minutes, because when he came to, he could still hear the terrifying screams and shouts of deadly fighting all around him. He found himself on the floor, under a bench. Blood was splattered over the floor, over his clothes, over his hands. He turned his head and looked straight into the dead eyes of one of Lorenzo's men. At that moment, he knew he had to find his family. Cristina, Niccolò! Where were they? Were they safe?

He scrambled out from underneath the bench, stood up and was immediately knocked back down by a group of scuffling, scrambling, fighting men. The bloody skirmish passed by him, and he got to his feet again. Looking around, he saw a sea of faces, frozen in fear or fired with bloodlust. He pushed his way through the crowd, desperately looking for Niccolò's face. He saw nothing. He called his name, over and over, but his voice was drowned in the commotion. Perhaps he had gone to find Cristina. Fighting his way across the church, dodging flying fists and blades, he made a path to a group of women, who were sobbing hysterically. He recognised one or two of them.

"My wife! Have you seen my wife?" he asked. Getting no response, he took another by the shoulders. He knew this woman had been talking to Cristina before Mass and would know her.

"*Madonna*, I beg you! Tell me where did Cristina go? Where is my wife?" By this time, he was almost shaking her, which just had the effect of making the woman more hysterical. She seemed completely unaware of her torn bodice, exposing blood-stained breasts. Her elaborate black mantilla, a symbol of her feminine modesty, had been trampled underfoot and long forgotten. Francesco gave up and pushed her to one side, moving on. Again, he scuffled with groups of fighting men, stepping over injured men, bleeding copiously over the ornate floor tiles of Florence's grandest monument. The cavernous roof rang with the screams of hysterical women, bloody handprints covered the great pillars along the side aisles, and wherever Francesco looked, he met the cold, staring eyes of dead men, making the whole scene feel like one of Dante's nine circles of Hell. As he moved around the church, it soon became clear that he wasn't going to find his family, and he prayed that they had found their way out of this madness and to a haven of safety.

Outside the church, he shielded his eyes from the bright sunshine and looked around him. More pandemonium greeted him, more blood on the ground, more screams from the women and dying men. Then he spotted one of Lorenzo's men, leaning against the great *campanile*, alongside the main cathedral building. He was trying to catch his breath and wiping blood from his face, whether his own or another man's, it wasn't clear. Francesco ran to him and put his hand on his shoulder.

"Have you seen my family? Signor Niccolò? Donna Cristina? I need to find them. Please…tell me that you know where they are!" By this time, Francesco was desperate and on the verge of hysteria himself. The man looked up at him.

"Signor Rosini. I am glad to see you. What happened in there? What happened? I don't understand."

"I don't know. I really don't know. I just know that I must find my family."

"I'm sorry, *ser*. I haven't seen Signor Niccolò since the start of Mass, but I think Donna Cristina has escaped. I saw her with one of our household ladies' maids and one of my men."

"Where did they go? Which direction?" Francesco demanded.

The man shook his head. Francesco put his hand to head and sighed in frustration. What would they do? Where would they go?

"Home!" he said to himself. He thanked the man, wished him well and set off for his Palazzo.

He arrived at the Palazzo and immediately made for his study, where he knew his son would go. However, he was not at home, and neither was Cristina, so he paced, wondering what to do for the best. It was absolute bedlam in the streets, with men shouting for revenge or revolution, wielding knives and swords, so any chance of finding his family was very low. However, his wife and son were still missing. What sort of a man hid in his home when he had no idea where his family were, or indeed if they were alive or dead? Having made his mind up, he raced down the stairs. As he reached the courtyard, he heard a pounding on the door. Relief rushed over him, as he ran to the door. He unlatched the door, and opened it to find a group of bloody, ragged individuals, holding each other up. As he was about to close the door again, he caught sight of one of the women's gowns. He recognised the red velvet...the gold silk brocade...torn...dirty... bloody...

"Cristina!" As he rushed to her, she collapsed into his arms, sobbing. "Are you injured? Tell me, did they hurt you?"

As she was unable to speak, he looked at her companions, who looked just as dishevelled, shocked and blood-stained, although they appeared unhurt. He recognised one of Lorenzo's men.

"What happened, man?" he demanded.

"I don't know what happened in there, *ser*," he replied, "but I saw Signora Rosini trying to fight her way out of it all. She was so distressed, but I managed to bring her home."

Francesco nodded, gratefully. "Thank you, signor. *Grazie*. You have my eternal gratitude. Now go; get yourselves home and out of this madness."

As he closed the door behind their retreating figures, he swept Cristina into his arms and carried her up the stairs. As he made his way to the study, he saw Lucia returning from Nonna Isabetta's chambers, having delivered her tea.

"Lucia," he called. "Bring some hot water and clean towels. Donna Cristina needs help."

Lucia looked shocked at the sight of her mistress's blood-stained clothes and limp figure but bobbed a small curtsey and rushed to the kitchen.

In the kitchen, things were no more peaceful than in any other home in Florence that afternoon. Just before Francesco had arrived home, two more of Lorenzo's men had dragged a lifeless bundle of rags into the kitchen.

Eleonora persuaded them to stay, take a drink and something to eat. The bundle of rags, red and black with gold stitching, had opened enough to show a shock of blood-stained black hair.

Gianetta had covered her mouth to stifle a scream, but it was Eleonora who reached Matteo first. The men had lain him on a bench in the corner of the kitchen, where Eleonora now tentatively reached for the cloth that covered his head. As she pulled it back, she surveyed him with a practised eye, looking for signs of life and the extent of his injuries. She let out a loud sob.

"Gianetta! Oh, Gianetta! He's alive. Matteo is alive!" she cried.

Gianetta was at her side in an instant, trying to get close to Matteo.

"No, not yet, child," said Eleonora, holding up her hand. "Let me check his injuries. We do not want to damage him any further than he is. He is unconscious. Judging by the lump on his head, I'd say that was the reason, but I want to make sure we haven't missed anything else."

Gianetta moved back to give Eleonora room to work, and she watched her every move.

The older woman moved her hands gently around his head and neck, moved down his chest and abdomen and both arms, reached underneath him to check his back and eventually assessed both his legs. She sat back with a deep sigh and blessed herself with a sign of the cross.

"Thank the good Lord. He has quite a deep cut on his hand, but there are no other injuries to worry about. He will eventually wake up, but he will have such a headache. Oh, God is indeed good and merciful!"

Gianetta was now holding Matteo's hand and sobbing. "Oh Matteo! What did you get involved in? What happened out there?"

"We'll find out soon enough, no doubt," said Eleonora, "but for now, I'll make a witch-hazel poultice for that bruise on his head, while you clean him up. Lucia will be back from Nonna's chambers shortly, and she can help."

Lucia soon returned, but she entered the kitchen looking shocked and ashen faced.

"What's wrong, child? Come along!" said Eleonora, with some impatience. "We have work to do here. Gianetta needs help with Matteo. He will be well, but he needs our attention."

"It's Signor Francesco," whispered Lucia. "He's going to the study with Donna Cristina."

"They're supposed to be dining at *Palazzo Medici*. I don't have time to prepare anything now. I'm sure they'll understand, but they'll have to wait."

"She has been hurt, Eleonora. They asked me to bring hot water and clean towels...so much blood!" Her voice was rising, and she was on the verge of hysteria.

Eleonora put her hand to her throat, closed her eyes and whispered to herself, "I knew it. I knew something was going to happen."

By this time, Gianetta had recovered her composure and was buoyed by the relief that Matteo was safe. She got up and went to Lucia, holding both her hands in her own and said "Don't worry, Lucia. It will be fine. Can you help clean up Matteo? He's alive and will wake soon. Eleonora will be here with you. I will attend Donna Cristina."

Eleonora nodded, acknowledging that Gianetta was a steady hand in a crisis, which is just what was needed. She continued preparing the poultice, while Lucia went to Matteo and sat beside him on the bench.

Gianetta poured a bowl of hot water from the pot on the stove and started to gather clean towels.

"While you go to clean up Donna Cristina, I will prepare something for her injuries," said Eleonora. "If she has been cut, the wound will need to be cleaned to prevent poisoning and corruption."

After gathering all that she required, she sat down at the table, where Lorenzo's men were silently finishing their bowl of vegetable broth. They were not only silent but clearly anxious, and Eleonora soon picked up on this atmosphere.

"What is it?" she demanded. Setting aside her pestle and mortar, she crossed her arms and looked at each of the men in turn. "Tell me now, or may the blessed Virgin Mary help me..."

The men looked at each other, and the older of the two braced himself for the news he had to break. When he finished speaking, Eleonora stood slowly and said, "Come with me." The two men duly rose and followed her out of the room.

Sensing the disturbance, Nonna had managed to make her way from her chambers down to the study, even leaving behind her tea. She checked to see that Francesco and Cristina were not badly hurt, then sat in a chair in the corner to oversee proceedings and offer unsolicited advice. Tessa arrived soon after.

"Where is Gino?" asked Francesco, worried that Gino would be disturbed by his grandmother's appearance.

"He's asleep, Papà," replied Tessa. "He had so much excitement at the parade and in the park this morning, that he is worn out."

"*Bene.*" Francesco nodded.

Gianetta knocked and entered the room with a bowl of hot water and clean towels and set about cleaning up the blood from Cristina's face and chest. Luckily, it seemed that she had been unhurt by the experience, and the blood belonged to someone else. She was still in a haze, though.

"I think she is in shock, *ser*," said Gianetta to Francesco. "I will ask Eleonora to bring up one of her tonics and some broth. She will be fine, I am sure."

There was another knock at the study door, and Eleonora entered.

"We were about to call for you," said Francesco, then stopped as he caught sight of the two men behind her.

"These men, *ser*. They're Signor Lorenzo's men. They brought Matteo back to us."

Francesco bowed his head and thanked God. He looked up and asked, "What happened? Do you have news of what happened out there?"

"*Sì,* Signor," said the older of the two men. "We were with Signor Lorenzo when it happened. Then when it was all over, we found your man still alive, so brought him home."

Francesco held up a hand. "*Aspetta!* Wait a moment! Go back to the beginning, man. Tell me everything you know."

"It was a plot, *ser*," began the exhausted man. "A plot to kill Signor Lorenzo and Signor Giuliano."

Everyone in the room took a shocked intake of breath. Tessa put a hand to her mouth; Nonna bowed her head; Gianetta stopped washing her mistress's hands; Francesco said nothing, while Eleonora muttered, "I knew it. I knew something was going to happen."

"Did…" Francesco cleared his throat. "Did they succeed?"

"Signor Giuliano is dead, *ser*. They killed him right at the start of it all. It was the signal that started the attack. They stabbed him so many times, that…" Glancing up at the women in the room, he stopped himself. "He was stabbed, *ser*."

"And Lorenzo?"

"Signor Lorenzo is alive."

"Praise be to God," said Nonna, crossing herself.

"They injured him badly. They cut his neck, but it was a flesh wound. We managed to get him to the safety of the sacristy before they could finish the job. One of them was even a priest. They tried to beat the door down, but it held. We, that is, Signor Lorenzo's men, stayed to defend him, and eventually the attackers were outnumbered, and they fled.

"We began to try to identify the dead around us, and that is when we found your man. He was unconscious but still breathing, so that's when we brought him home."

The man faltered.

Tessa spoke in a quiet voice. "Did you identify any of the dead men?" she asked.

Without looking up, he replied, "Yes, *Madonna*. Yes, we did."

"Niccolò?" she whispered.

"I am sorry, *Signora*, but yes. He was one of the men we identified."

Cristina's cry came from the very depths of her soul and shook every inch of the Palazzo, as she stood, then collapsed to her knees.

Nonna was beside her in an instant, cradling her in her arms.

Francesco found the nearest chair and slumped into it, stunned. For the next ten minutes, the only sound was Cristina's soul-tearing grief and Nonna's soothing noises, as she rocked her like a babe.

Tessa was silent, but tears streamed down her face unchecked.

Gianetta cleaned up the spilt bowl of water as the tears spilled down her own face. At that moment, in that place, it seemed that all joy had left the world, and Gianetta offered a prayer for the souls that had been lost, while thanking God for sparing Matteo.

Lorenzo's men stood still, the younger one sobbing silently, as the wave of grief in the room crashed around them all.

Eventually, Francesco raised his head and asked them, "What happened? Did you see what happened to my boy?"

"No, *ser*," replied the older man. "We could see that he had a stab wound to his chest, but we didn't see it happen. I'm so sorry." He bowed his head as his own tears began to fall and silence returned to the room.

Francesco sat in his chair, staring blankly into the distance, his face pale and drawn.

Gianetta watched as his heart broke. Slowly, she stood and walked over to him and, kneeling by his side, took his hands in hers. She said nothing, but just watched him, wishing she could take his pain away.

Francesco, who had always liked the girl but had never really taken much notice of her, looked at her and smiled gratefully. Then a memory stirred, and he looked at her more closely. He thought it strange that at such a time, he could think of such things, but she reminded him of someone. "Who?" he thought. "Was it…? Yes, she looks just like her. How very odd."

Only Nonna, who was observing him very closely, could guess at his thoughts.

CHAPTER 13

Easter Monday

It was the day after Easter and a pall of grief had descended on Palazzo Rosini, while in the streets of Florence, there was still confusion and tension. Many of the culprits had been caught and summarily executed, and their bodies were left to hang outside the *Palazzo della Signoria* and the *Bargello*. Others were still being hunted down outside the city walls. No stone would be left unturned, and not one of the guilty men would be left unpunished.

The grieving Lorenzo de' Medici, supported by his colleagues in the *Signoria*, had decided that justice would be swift and merciless.

The kitchen of Palazzo Rosini was unusually subdued. Everyone carried on with their duties automatically, alone with their thoughts and worries. Nobody was keen to eat much, but Eleonora made sure that there was enough soup and bread to keep everyone sustained.

Donna Cristina had retreated to her chambers immediately after hearing the news of Niccolò's death and would not see anyone. It was eventually Eleonora herself who managed to persuade Cristina to let her in. She even took some soup, although hardly enough to nourish her.

"Why did it happen, Eleonora? Why my Niccolò?" she pleaded, as if the cook held all the answers.

"There is no reason, *Madonna*. Nobody can explain the wickedness in men's hearts. To do such a thing inside the house of God...and during Mass. It is beyond understanding or explanation. We just have to grieve for those we have lost and pray that God has welcomed them into His arms."

Cristina nodded and dissolved into more tears. "Poor Gino!" she sobbed. "He is so young to have lost his father. What are we to tell him?"

"Children always surprise us, *Madonna*. He will always remember his father, and we will always remind him what a wonderful man he was, but Gino will not suffer from this. He has a family who love him very much, and he will grow into a young man Signor Niccolò would have been proud of. This will be a difficult time for everyone, but it will pass, as with all things."

Cristina held Eleonora's hand and looked at her through her tears. "How would we ever manage without you, Eleonora? Sometimes, I believe that you hold this household together."

"*Madonna*, I was not lucky enough to have a husband and family of my own, but I remember my own childhood, my own family, and I remember how happy it was. I have found that happiness here, and I am grateful to be a part of it. You are my family now...if it is permitted for me to say so."

Cristina drew the woman into her arms, and the women embraced warmly, taking comfort from each other.

Eventually, Cristina asked, "How goes it with the rest of the staff? Is everyone well?"

"Everyone is stunned to have heard the news about Signor Niccolò. We prayed together for his soul. It has been such a shock.

"Matteo has a dreadful headache, but he is alive and well, and we all give thanks to God for that. Gianetta is still worried about the bump to his head, but she is relieved to have him near her."

Cristina nodded. Gianetta…something stirred in the back of her mind. What was it? "No matter," she thought to herself. "It will come to me."

"What about the rest of the staff? Are they well?"

"Lucia is well but beside herself with worry."

"How so?"

"She and Antonio had been becoming closer, if you understand me. Personally, I think Antonio was just having some fun, but Lucia was hoping that it would lead to something more permanent. The problem is that Antonio hasn't returned."

"Hasn't returned? Returned from where?"

"Yesterday, he went to watch the parade before Mass. We all went together, but we became separated in the crowds. This was before that dreadful business in the *Duomo*. We haven't seen him since. It is unusual for him to disappear. He has probably gone to check that his family are all well, but Lucia fears the worst and is inconsolable."

"I'm so sorry, Eleonora. Please tell Lucia that I am praying for his safe return."

"Thank you, *Madonna*. She will appreciate that very much."

In his study, Francesco sat at his desk, looking at but not seeing the papers on his desk. He had been sitting in the same position for some time, not really knowing what to do. He looked up as Matteo came through the door with a tray of drinks and bowls of steaming soup. His head was bandaged, but otherwise he appeared fit and healthy. Francesco smiled. "How are you feeling, boy?" he asked.

"My hand is sore," as he glanced at his heavily bandaged hand.

"And I have a headache, but I am very well, thank you *ser*." He put the tray on the desk and shuffled his feet uncomfortably. "Signor Francesco," he began. "I heard what happened to Signor Niccolò. I mean, I just wanted to say how sorry I am…and if perhaps I didn't do my duty to protect him…" He began to fumble his words, until Francesco raised his hand to stop him.

"It is not your fault, Matteo. The only people to bear any blame are those who took their knives into God's house with evil in their hearts. May God forgive them, because I'm sure Signor Lorenzo certainly won't."

Matteo looked to be on the verge of tears but composed himself and placed the soup and drink in front of Francesco. He picked up the tray and turned to Luigi's desk. The desk was empty.

"Signor Francesco? I thought Luigi was here. I have brought his soup."

Francesco frowned. "You're right. I was expecting him here this morning. It is unlike Luigi. In all the years that he has worked for me, I have never known him to take a day off unless I have insisted. I admit that I am concerned. Leave the soup here. Let's hope that he is just a little late."

Matteo did as he was instructed and left Francesco to his papers and grief.

Tessa was sitting alone in her chambers. Gino had left to look for food and the companionship of his friends in the kitchen. Tessa did not blame him. She wasn't much company for the little boy. She had been sitting, looking out of her window for some hours, thinking back over the last eight years of her life.

Her family was not wealthy but was respectable. Her father was a notary in Florence and had taught her to read at a very young age.

In his company, she had learned to explore any books and texts that were available. He had encouraged her thoughtful and inquisitive mind. She knew that it would have been more convenient if she had been born a boy, able to step into her father's shoes and continue his business. However, her father had never made her feel inferior for being a girl and taught her all he could, while she had absorbed it all. She remembered the hours that she had spent in his study. He would explain the intricacies of a particular case to her, and they would work through the texts together to arrive at a solution. They had been happy, stimulating and contented hours. So, when her father suggested a marriage for her, she was devastated.

"Father, I just want to sit and work with you. I don't want to get married and provide endless children for some ugly brute who drinks too much and is too free with his fists."

Her father had smiled at her and said, "Not all men are like the ones we deal with in our courts. I assure you that Niccolò Rosini is a fine man, and he will make an exceptional husband. You must trust that I would only choose the very best for my Contessa."

She knew that he had used his pet name for her to win her over. In truth, she had known in her heart that this day would eventually come. As a woman, it was her duty to marry well, if it could be arranged.

Her father had dealt with some of the more complex contracts of Francesco's textile business, and the two men had developed a respect and a certain affection for each other. The marriage negotiations had not been difficult.

Although Francesco could have hoped for a bigger dowry from a prospective bride, he had considered it more important to find someone that he believed could make his son happy. He had met Tessa on a few occasions and considered her to be honest, kind and intelligent, traits that had been rare in other brides he had considered.

Tessa, too, had learned to respect Francesco, even to like him, and had hoped that his son was cut from the same cloth.

After their first few meetings, Tessa and Niccolò had been relieved to discover that they could be a very good fit for each other. Niccolò had found Tessa to be stimulating conversation, with a pretty smile that did not rely on hours in front of the looking glass. Tessa had also been surprised to find Niccolò to be a gentle man, who respected her contributions to conversation and had wit enough to make her laugh. Yes, she knew that her father had chosen well for her, and she would always be grateful for that.

They had married in the *Chiesa di Ognissanti* and returned to Palazzo Rosini to make their home. Their love for each other had grown, and within a year, Tessa had given birth to Gino, making Niccolò the proudest man in Italy. Tessa loved her son unconditionally, and he'd soon become the darling of the Palazzo, his joyfulness and charm winning every heart.

Tessa, however, had found it difficult to fit into her role in society. She had known that Niccolò loved her and was proud of her, but she had also known that some of the other ladies in society looked down on her for not being as fashionable or as elegant as their trends dictated. She had no interest in their jewellery or gowns, and they had no interest in her intellectual conversation. Eventually, it had seemed easier to retreat into her role as mother of the eventual heir of the Rosini family home and business.

Only recently, Cristina had tried to encourage her to support Niccolò in his business dealings. She had always encouraged her with love, and Tessa had never felt inadequate in her presence, but she had been right. Tessa had not played her role as she should have, and now Niccolò was gone. What was she to do? She put her head into her hands and sobbed.

When the tide of grief had subsided, Tessa looked around at her books, thinking of her father. "Papà, you taught me so much," she said aloud. "There must be a reason. I must be able to put it to use somehow." And she started thinking. Perhaps she could not support the family business as a society hostess, but perhaps she could put her mind to work. Perhaps...

CHAPTER 14

Thursday after Easter

Several days later, the grief at the loss of Niccolò was still palpable, but death in Italy was an integral part of life and was accepted as such. Lorenzo's men who had identified Niccolò's body in the cathedral had returned it home to his family. As was the custom, he had been tended to by the women in the household.

Cristina and Tessa had worked silently together to clean and dress him, pausing to pray together when they reached his fatal wound. Now, he lay silently as friends and colleagues came to pay their respects and share condolences with the family.

While the family business now encompassed trade in many textiles, Francesco's ancestors had been founding members of the *Arte della Lana*, the Wool Guild, one of the seven major guilds in Florence. Francesco and Niccolò had remained active and respected members of the Guild. Now, in his time of need, Francesco knew that he could rely on them as they prepared for Niccolò's funeral. When the time came, members of the Guild would carry Niccolò to the church and then on to his place of burial. Francesco was grateful for his fraternity of brothers, silent but supportive.

Donna Cristina had emerged from her chambers, and while she and Tessa were often seen with red, bleary eyes from crying, they began to resume some of their day-to-day activities. Tessa considered herself lucky that she had Gino to occupy her time and provide her with company, and they spent many hours at the spinet or walking in the park.

Gino was quiet. He missed his Papà, especially the games they used to play at bedtime. His Mamma always got cross when they ran too fast or laughed too loudly, but he somehow knew that his Mamma would like to see that now. He was very sad, and he could see that she was too.

There was still a strong undercurrent of anxiety, as neither Antonio nor Luigi had returned to their duties in the Palazzo, nor had anyone had word of their whereabouts.

Eleonora had to use every weapon in her arsenal to get Lucia to do any work. She persuaded, she cajoled, and she bullied. She was sympathetic to Lucia's plight but felt that she needed to encourage her to engage in life. There was a dreadful feeling in the pit of Eleonora's stomach that the news, when it eventually came, would not be good.

Matteo and Gianetta worked hard. Such was their gratitude at being alive and together that they felt they needed to repay it somehow. They didn't know where the focus of this gratitude should lie, but they did know that they were very fortunate.

"Matteo, I will always thank God for returning you to me. It's as if He wanted you to stay and care for me and our baby. He was certainly protecting you in the *Duomo*."

"I told you that I never shirk my responsibilities," replied Matteo with a smile. "I also promised you that we would marry before Pentecost. I still plan to keep that promise."

"We can't discuss plans for a wedding, Matteo. The household is grieving. It would be too insensitive."

"We can wait until after the funeral," he said, "but believe me, everyone will be very happy for us. It will be something to look forward to, and the household needs that right now."

"We can speak to the priest, I suppose. There would be no harm in that."

However, that would have to wait a little while. Today, she had shopping to do. During the last few days, the streets had not been considered safe for law-abiding citizens, and certainly not safe for a young girl out shopping. There had been pockets of resistance, still trying to push for an overthrow of Medici rule, while also trying to escape capture and punishment, but they could not withstand the strength and number of the soldiers of the *Signoria*. A semblance of law and order had returned, and Eleonora was running short of provisions. So, Gianetta gathered her basket and left the Palazzo.

Meanwhile, Francesco was sifting through papers in his study. He never did enjoy the administrative side of his business, much preferring face-to-face negotiations and the hands-on feel of the textiles that he sold. There was little he didn't know about velvets, silks and brocades, but when it came to the fine detail of a contract, he preferred to leave it to Luigi. Luigi always arranged the necessary paperwork. Prompt payment to suppliers and delivery of orders to customers ensured that the Rosini reputation was never questioned. This in turn encouraged customers to pay their bills on time. The penalty clauses that Luigi included within contracts added a further incentive for timely payments.

"Ah, Luigi," whispered Francesco, running his hands through his hair. "Where are you, *mio amico*?"

"I worry about him, too," said Cristina from the doorway. "It's not like him to disappear. We should try to contact his family."

"Yes. Yes, we should." After a pause, he asked "How are you, *cara*? You look a little better today."

"I am a little better, but when do you ever recover from the loss of your son? There will always be an emptiness in my heart that nothing will ever fill."

Francesco walked around the desk and drew his wife into an embrace and a silence that comforted them both.

Cristina eventually broke the silence. "Something has been bothering me, Francesco. I can't quite pin it down, but I had to speak to you about it. There is something about Gianetta that is…well, not disturbing, as such, but…something about her is making me unsettled.

"Don't misunderstand me. She is a lovely girl. She does her work well and is always a pleasure to be around but, there's just something about her…"

Francesco looked at her closely, thinking back a few days to when Gianetta had comforted him on hearing of Niccolò's death. Something had struck him at the time, but he dismissed it as grief and not thought of it since. Perhaps there was something…

"Does she remind you of someone?" he asked, quietly.

"Yes, I think she does." Cristina nodded now, as the mental pictures started to fly through her mind.

"All those years ago. The girl in Fiesole?"

Cristina nodded, as she realised the implications of where this train of thought was taking them.

They were silent with their own thoughts for a moment, then they looked at each other and said in unison, "Nonna!"

Nonna would have the answers. A few years ago, just after Gino had been born, they had been looking for another pair of hands to help in the household. Nonna had been the one to suggest Gianetta. She knew her mother, she had said.

Francesco knocked gently on Nonna's door. She had spent the last few days either at prayer or asleep, and he was afraid of waking her.

"Nonna? Are you awake? May we speak with you?"

"*Sì, entra!*" Nonna's voice sounded strong and alert.

They found Nonna sitting up in bed, a rosary wrapped around her hands and an empty glass on her bedside table. Francesco rightly assumed it to be one of Eleonora's sleeping draughts. If she had just taken it, they may have only a short time to speak to her before she became drowsy, so they sat down alongside the bed and Francesco came straight to the point.

"Nonna, Cristina and I have some questions which we think you may be able to answer."

"*Sì...* Gianetta, *si?*" Nonna was nodding as she spoke.

Francesco and Cristina were open-mouthed. "Nonna, you never cease to amaze me. I don't know how you do it. How did you know that we wanted to ask about Gianetta?"

"I saw you looking at her in the study, on that dreadful day. I saw you looking at her, and I knew the day was coming when you would ask what you have come to ask. Well, *giovane*, ask it."

Francesco paused a beat before asking, "Do you know anything of her family? Cristina and I are reminded of a young girl in Fiesole, many years ago. Please, Nonna, tell us what you know."

Nonna looked at them each in turn, as if deciding which path to follow, then nodded to herself. "It is time.

"You are correct. The girl who you see so well in Gianetta is Clara, her mother. She was a maid in the Villa Medici in Fiesole. I was not fortunate to meet her, but I understand that she was a fine girl; hard-working, kind and beautiful. Just like Gianetta, in fact."

Francesco and Cristina were captivated. In their hearts, they knew where this story would lead.

Nonna continued, "As you know, Niccolò spent some months there, and they met and fell in love. The heart does not follow the rules that govern our society. Neither Niccolò nor Clara would have chosen their path, but when love is found, there can be no reason. Love is the joy of the good, the wonder of the wise and the amazement of the gods." She smiled at Francesco.

"Plato again, Nonna? Please, continue."

"The girl became pregnant. It happens. Niccolò struggled with his conscience for a very long time, but he had decided to marry the girl. His greatest fear was of letting down you and the family."

Francesco and Cristina spoke at the same time.

"How do you know all of this?"

"What happened to Clara?"

"Sometimes, God has a way of working that none of us understands. Gianetta came safely into the world, but sadly, Clara died while giving birth to her. Niccolò was young, afraid and heartbroken. He made a decision that I believe he regretted for the rest of his life. He left Gianetta to be cared for by Sofia, Clara's mother. Sofia became her mother and raised her as if she were her own child, rather than her grandchild."

"How do you know what Niccolò was thinking? How do you know that he was her father? All this could be just speculation." Cristina was beginning to be defensive of her much-loved, departed son.

"Niccolò told me himself. When Gianetta arrived here, he also saw the resemblance between her and Clara. He knew it to be true when he recognised the small pink birth mark behind her ear. He said he remembered touching it before he left her in the care of Sofia. He came to me, as you have, and asked how she came to be here."

They all pictured Gianetta's face…and the small pink birth mark. They knew Nonna's story to be true.

Cristina said quietly, "Then God has given us another grandchild. Gianetta is our granddaughter."

"Well, the meaning of Gianetta is God's gracious gift," said Nonna, beginning to sound a little sleepy.

"…and He has truly given us a gift at a time when everything is so bleak." Cristina gave a weak smile.

"Nonna," said Francesco. "Thank you for your honesty. We can see that you are getting tired, but please answer one more question. How did you know all this? How did Gianetta come to be here?"

Nonna concentrated as she fought the effects of Eleonora's sleeping draught. "Sofia is my sister. We correspond regularly, although I have not seen her for many years. When Gianetta was old enough to leave home to work, she wrote and asked me if we could take her. She said that she knew Clara would want her child to be near her father. It was just at the time that you were looking for extra help, so the timing was very convenient. I could not tell what I knew. It was not my secret to tell. But I watched. I watched as Niccolò watched Gianetta. He loved her very much and was very protective of her. He would do anything for her."

Francesco felt that a veil had been lifted, and he was able to make sense of it all. Francesco thought about how Niccolò behaved whenever Matteo was near. It was not simple animosity. He was a protective father. He thought of Niccolò's reluctance to have Matteo at the Easter Mass, and how much he knew the boy meant to Gianetta. Suddenly, he understood his son. "Ah, *mio figlio*, my son." He shook his head sadly. "I wish you had been able to speak to me about this."

Cristina took Francesco's hands in hers. "He was a proud man, *tesoro*. All we can do now is take care of his daughter as he would want us to do."

"Thank you, Nonna," she said, but Nonna was fast asleep. There would be no waking her for the next few hours, so they left, closing the door quietly behind them.

"We should speak to Tessa," said Cristina.

Francesco agreed. "It isn't a conversation that I look forward to, but I will speak to her."

CONTORNI

On its own, the main dish risks becoming one-dimensional. Our palate for food and stories requires some complexity, a little more flavour to bring the Secondi Piatti alive. With the Bistecca alla Fiorentina, we have had a substantial portion of meat to sink our teeth into, as well as little tenderness from the fillet of the same cut. This Contorni, or side dish, provides some contrast and a little spice and bitterness to complement the main event.

Spinacci con Aglio e Peperoncino
(Serves 2)

- *75ml olive oil*
- *3 large garlic cloves, peeled and crushed, then chopped*
- *1-2 chilli peppers (depending on taste), chopped finely*
- *1 large bunch of spinach, washed and chopped*

In a large heavy pan, gently heat the oil, garlic and chilli pepper for about 5 minutes. Do not allow to boil or brown. Add the spinach and stir the oil mixture through the leaves at it wilts. Season with salt and freshly ground pepper and serve immediately.

CHAPTER 15

Friday after Easter

There had been no rain to clean the streets of Florence since that fateful Sunday, and the evidence of the terrible bloodshed remained throughout the city. People walked around the blood stains on the cobbles and avoided the corpses of those who had died in the fray but had no family to claim them. Like most Italian cities, Florence had a confraternity of men who would collect and bury the indigent dead outside the city walls, but it had been unsafe for even this work to be carried out. Their work would need to resume as a matter of urgency. It had been several days since these men had died and with temperatures rising in the late spring, the stench would soon be overpowering. The plague which had claimed so many lives across Europe was still very much in the minds of the people, so any death and decay was to be feared and dealt with cleanly and swiftly.

Gianetta, who normally relished her morning walk through the streets, struggled to complete her errands. Feeling the effects of her pregnancy and the demands of the child growing inside her, she had become sensitive to strong smells, and there were plenty of unpleasant sights and smells that morning. She fought her nausea, until she had to duck down a small alleyway, where she vomited up the meagre breakfast that she had forced herself to eat. Still feeling a little unsteady, she continued her shopping trip. She had collected vegetables and cheeses from the market, and now had one more stop to make. The *macelleria* near *Santa Croce* church sold the finest nduja sausages in Florence, and Eleonora would not settle for anything less. It was a little way out of her usual route, but Gianetta felt that the walk would do her good. This walk took her past the *Bargello*, the seat of the city's highest magistrate, who ensured that justice was carried out according to local laws.

As she approached the building, Gianetta began to feel some unease. Crowds had gathered around the building to gawp at the corpses of those who had taken part in the atrocities of just a few days before. They still swung from the high windows, beginning to rot now in the sunshine. Their bloated faces and swollen tongues had taken on a greenish hue. Some had already lost their eyes to passing birds. Their clothing was stained, either with blood from their fighting, or from the moment they realised their fate and soiled themselves. Unlike many of the people of Florence, Gianetta had no wish to linger in the area and quickened her step. She manoeuvred around a group of women, who had paused their daily tasks to gossip and pass judgement on the culprits.

"*Vai all'inferno!*" shouted one, as if the dead were not already in Hell.

"Not so brave now, are you, *bastardo*?" called another.

"*Figlio di puttana!*"

As the profanities fell from their lips, they crossed themselves piously. A group of small boys entertained themselves by throwing stones at the corpses, cheering riotously when one hit its mark, making it swing. Gianetta kept her gaze firmly to the ground, until she almost tripped over a young man. She recognised him as an acquaintance of Signor Sandro's, an artist from the small town of Vinci in the hills of Tuscany. She had served him during a Rosini family banquet and remembered thinking that he had intelligent eyes.

"Signor Leonardo! *Buongiorno*!" She gave a small curtsey, as the well-dressed young man rose from his seat on the road.

"*Buongiorno,*" he replied, with a bow of his head. "Surely this is no place for a member of the Rosini household?"

"No, *ser*," replied Gianetta. "I had to pass here to reach the *macelleria*. I do not intend to stay any longer than is necessary." She started to move past him, but then her eye caught sight of a paper in his hand.

He saw her looking at his work and lifted it to show her more clearly. He had been making an ink drawing of one of the hanged men.

Gianetta looked horrified. "I don't understand, Signor Leonardo. This is not the art that you create. Yours is beautiful. This is…ugly. Death is ugly."

"*Certo*!" he agreed. "Death is ugly, but our life is made by the death of others. It is only by understanding this that we can learn and grow."

Gianetta looked uncertain, but Leonardo said, "The noblest pleasure is the joy of understanding. I am here to simply understand. That is all."

Gianetta looked at his drawing, then back at the man with intelligent eyes. Her own eyes then slowly turned towards the walls of the *Bargello* and upwards, to the hanged men. What she saw hit her in the pit of her stomach, so much so that she gasped out loud and staggered backward.

Leonardo caught her and helped her to sit on his small seat. "What is it?" he asked.

It took some moments for her to find her voice. "Antonio!" she whispered.

"*Scusi?*" Leonardo looked confused.

"It's Antonio. Next to the man you were drawing. See? The man with the blue top? That's Antonio. He served you that night you visited Palazzo Rosini. Oh, but there must have been a dreadful mistake. Poor Antonio!" Gianetta was crying now in despair.

"I don't think there was a mistake, my dear," said Leonardo, gently. "All the men here were caught in the act of attacking the Medici or their men or taking part in the riots in the streets afterwards. There was no doubt. I'm so sorry, my dear."

Gianetta was silent, as she let the information sink in. "It was Antonio? All this time, it was Antonio? I don't believe it. He was the one to push the stone that night? He tried to poison Signor Lorenzo? Oh Antonio, what made you do such a thing?"

Leonardo held her hand. "I am so very sorry that you had to see this. There is no knowing how the seed of evil is planted and grown. You may never know what drove him to his actions. You look shocked, my dear. You should make your way home. Can you manage?"

"Home…yes. Yes, I can manage, thank you." After a short pause, she cried "Lucia! What am I going to tell Lucia? Oh, *mio Dio*!" She covered her face with her hands and wept.

Leonardo sat beside her until her tears subsided, then he helped her to her feet. "Are you sure that you can make your way home without my help?"

"Yes, *ser*," she replied. "You have been very kind. *Grazie… grazie mille. Vai con Dio.*" Before Leonardo could reply, Gianetta disappeared into the crowds, heading back to Palazzo Rosini, without a second thought for nduja sausage.

While Gianetta had been talking with Leonardo, Tessa had made her way to Francesco's study. The seeds of an idea were beginning to germinate in her mind, and she needed to discuss it with her father-in-law. When she arrived, the study was empty, so she started to browse through some of the papers scattered across Francesco's large desk. There had been no secrets about the business within the family, so she did not feel that she was snooping.

She was beginning to get a sense of the business's current affairs when Francesco walked in.

"*Buongiorno*, Tessa. *Come stai?* How are you today?"

"I am well, Papà. Gino is beginning to sleep a little better, so that means that I sleep well too." After a short pause, she said, "I miss Niccolò so much. I can't imagine what our life will be like without him...but we must try, mustn't we?" She attempted a sad smile.

"Yes," he replied. "Yes, we must. For the sake of the family, we must try." He cleared his throat and ran his fingers through his hair, as he was wont to do when he was nervous.

"Tessa, I'm glad that you're here. I need to speak to you on a matter of some...delicacy."

Tessa looked up, curious.

"It concerns Niccolò. It's something that Cristina and I knew nothing about until just recently, and we felt it right to share this knowledge with you. I'm sorry that it might be rather distressing for you."

They both sat down, facing each other across the desk, Francesco gathering his strength for the task at hand, and Tessa, her face impassive.

"Yes...umm...as I said, it concerns Niccolò and something that happened many years ago, when he was a young man. Well, you see, young men being what they are, their heart is given freely. He spent some time in Fiesole, in the Villa Medici. He was there to learn some aspects of business management…not that this is relevant. I'm sorry, my dear. This is very hard for me."

Tessa said nothing.

"Niccolò fell in love with a young girl in Fiesole, and she had a baby. I truly believe that Niccolò would have done what was right. He was an honourable man, but the girl died in childbirth, leaving the child to be cared for in Fiesole. We have since discovered that the child, Niccolò's daughter is…"

"…Gianetta." Tessa looked at Francesco as she finished his tale.

Francesco looked up sharply. "You knew?"

"Yes, Papà. I knew. Niccolò told me about it soon after she arrived here. He said that our marriage was too important to keep such a secret." She smiled. "I loved him for that. He told me about his time in Fiesole, how he met and fell in love with Clara, and how he struggled for a long time, trying to decide what to do for the best. He didn't want to let you down, you know. He knew it wasn't what was expected of him in the family, but he had made his mind up to do the right thing. He loved her and would have married her and taken the consequences.

"When Clara died, he was heartbroken. Then he made a decision that he felt was right at the time. He left the child in the care of the woman who had brought her into the world, her grandmother. As he grew up, he realised what a dreadful mistake he had made. He considered it cowardly, but he didn't know what else to do. When Gianetta arrived at the Palazzo, he felt that he had been given another opportunity, although he didn't speak to her about it. He thought that he could help protect her from afar, and in his way, he did, didn't he?"

Francesco nodded. "You didn't mind?" he asked, looking at her curiously.

"How could I mind? It happened so long ago. I loved Niccolò

unconditionally, and I knew that he loved me. Gianetta did not change that. Are you going to tell her?"

A deep sigh escaped Francesco's lips. "I think we must," he replied. "It is what he would have wanted, that we look after her. Gino is his legitimate heir. Nothing will change that, but we should do our best for the girl."

Tessa nodded her agreement.

"Thank you, my dear. You made a difficult job so much easier for this old man." He smiled warmly at her. "But tell me, you were here as I came in. Did you want to speak to me?"

"Yes, I did, Papà. I have been thinking about the business. Niccolò is gone, and we don't know when Luigi will return. How will you manage?"

Looking at the papers scattered on his desk, and then across at Luigi's neat, organised desk, he shrugged. "I really don't know."

"I believe I have a solution," she said carefully. "I know how unusual it is to have a woman take an active part in business dealings, but I have knowledge and experience which would help you. You know how my father taught me. I could take care of the administrative side of the business, organise the paperwork. When Luigi returns, we can work together. He is very like my father, you know. I am sure we could work well together."

Francesco cast a worried look across at Luigi's desk.

Tessa continued. "I can deal with contracts, while you deal with suppliers and customers. It's what you do best. As Gino grows up, we can teach him together. What do you think?" She held her breath as she waited for his response.

Francesco got up and paced round the room. He paused at Luigi's desk and admired the man's sense of order. He returned to his own desk and picked up a sheet of paper that contained so much legal language that it might have been written in ancient Greek. He handed it to Tessa. "What do you think of this?"

She read it briefly and handed it back. "It's a standard sale contract for silk brocade, but they are trying to include loopholes in the agreement to stop you enforcing your penalty clauses should they default their payments. I would not sign that."

Francesco laughed, loudly. "That's precisely what Luigi told me. Yes. Yes, I think your idea is a good one. It is truly a family business." He looked as if a great weight had been lifted from his shoulders.

Tessa sighed, as she slowly felt a sense of purpose returning to her life.

CHAPTER 16

Eleonora tested the sponge with the tip of her finger. Yes, it was cooked and ready to be cut up to line the dome-shaped mould. She had all the utensils and other ingredients laid out on the table. The bottle of alchermes liqueur stood proudly, waiting to play its part. She unstopped the bottle and took a hefty sniff. "Ahh, *delizioso*," she said to herself. The liqueur had been new to her when she had arrived from Pistoia but was a favourite among Florentines, and it had become a central flavour in this recipe. Her *zuccotto*, like many of her recipes, was legendary. She had just started to slice the sponge into finger shapes when she felt a tug on her skirts.

"What are we making, Eli?" said a little voice.

"Ah, Gino. I haven't seen you all morning. I was beginning to think that you weren't hungry!"

"I'm always hungry, Eli. Can I help?" By this, Eleonora took his meaning to be, "Can I eat the bits that fall off?"

She lifted the little boy up, sat him on the table near her and put the *zuccotto* mould near him.

"Now, as I cut this cake into fingers, I want you to press them into the mould, like this…" Gino nodded seriously, as he watched her. "I need the whole mould to be covered, with no holes. When it's turned out, it will be like the dome of *Santa Maria del Fiore*. We wouldn't want to have holes in that roof, would we?"

"No, Eli. Don't worry. I can do it." And he set about his task with concentration.

Meanwhile, Eleonora set about mixing the cream and candied fruit for the filling. With the dome now completely covered with sponge, apart from the few pieces that found their way to Gino's mouth, she soaked the lining with the alchermes liqueur.

"What's that, Eli? Can I have some?"

"No, this isn't for hungry little boys. This has got medicine in it for the grown-up people." She wasn't exactly lying. Alchermes featured in a number of her remedies, as well as her *zuccotto*. She had just finished filling and topping the dome when Gianetta returned from her shopping trip.

"Eleonora, where is Lucia?" She glanced nervously at Gino.

As if she could read her mind, Eleonora lifted Gino from the table and gave him a handful of leftover cake and fruit. "Off you go now, *piccolino*. I have to unpack the shopping with Gianetta."

Gino, very satisfied with the wages from his work, trotted out of the kitchen with a smile. "*Ciao*, Gianetta!" sang the happy little boy.

"Antonio?" asked Eleonora, and Gianetta nodded.

Several minutes later, after Eleonora had heard the whole story, Lucia returned to the kitchen, having taken a tray to Nonna.

"Sit down, *cara*," said Eleonora. "Gianetta has news." The three women sat together around the kitchen table, while Gianetta recounted her story from the *Bargello*.

"It isn't true! I don't believe it! You were mistaken, Gianetta. You saw someone who looks like him, that's all." Lucia's voice was rising in panic, as she shook her head in disbelief. She stood up and backed away from the table. Her hand went to her mouth and then to her head. She looked one way, then another, and turned back to Gianetta. "Why would you say such a thing? Are you jealous of Antonio and me? Is that what it is?" She was almost screaming now.

"No, of course not." Gianetta tried to keep her tone soothing. She knew how difficult this was for Lucia to hear.

"Of course it is! You're jealous!" she cried, and she picked up a clay pitcher and hurled it across the room in Gianetta's direction. Luckily, in her despair, her aim was poor, and the pitcher smashed on the floor near the fireplace.

Eleonora jumped up and took a firm hold of Lucia's shoulders.

"*Basta!* Enough!" she said firmly, almost shaking the hysterical girl. "You know that Gianetta would never make up such a story. She made sure of her facts before coming here to tell you this." In a gentler tone, she continued, "We don't know what happened to Antonio to make him do such things. We may never know. Come here, child." And she drew Lucia into her comforting embrace, while she sobbed.

"Eleonora," said Gianetta, quietly. "Should I go to speak to Donna Cristina? She will want to know what's happened."

"Yes, good idea. I expect Signor Francesco will have some more questions, but that can wait. You go and speak with her now. I think she is in the *sala.*"

Gianetta knocked gently on the door of the *sala.*

"*Entra!*" Donna Cristina's soft voice encouraged Gianetta, as she entered.

She had always respected her mistress and even felt a kind of affection for her. She knew she could share her story without fear of judgement or doubt. Little did she know that there was another story waiting for her behind that door.

"*Madonna*, I have news of Antonio," she said.

"Come and sit down, child. I need to speak to you, but first tell me what you know of our Antonio."

Glancing at Signor Francesco, sitting quietly in the corner of the room, Gianetta took a chair near Cristina and recounted her story, including her conversation with Signor Leonardo and how he assured her there had been no mistake.

Cristina nodded sadly. "Thank you, child. That can't have been easy for you, but I am relieved to know that the mystery in this house has been solved. I assume that there is no doubt that he was the one to push the stone that night?"

"I think there is no doubt, *Madonna*. The only people it could have been were Antonio, Luigi or Signor Niccolò. Has there been any news about Luigi, may I ask?"

"No news, I'm afraid," replied Cristina. "Signor Francesco has been asking around, and there is nobody who can give us any news. We don't know where his family live. As you know, he was a very private man. I don't know what else we can do."

The conversation seemed to come to an end as Cristina gazed out of the window, so Gianetta stood up to go but then remembered what Cristina had said when she first entered. She turned back to Cristina. "You said you wanted to speak to me, *Madonna*?"

Cristina came to her senses and said, "Yes! Yes, I did. I'm sorry that the news about Antonio threw my mind into a bit of a whirl. I'm afraid that I might just do the same to you now. Please sit back down, child, and I will tell you our news."

Curious now, Gianetta slowly sat back in the chair facing Cristina. "What is it, *Madonna*?"

"Gianetta." She paused, not really knowing how best to approach this delicate subject. She decided that the direct approach would be the best, leaving no misunderstanding.

"Gianetta, we have just found out who your father is."

"My father?" Gianetta was confused. "I don't even know who my father is, where he came from…or indeed anything. How could you know…if you don't mind me asking, *Madonna*?" In her shock, she almost forgot her manners.

Slowly, and in as much detail as she could, Cristina told her the story of how she and Francesco were reminded of Niccolò's lost love in Fiesole, how they had spoken with Nonna and discovered the truth.

"So, you see, my dear," she said, watching her granddaughter's face closely, "we are…family."

"That makes you…my grandmother?" Gianetta's mind whirled until she was dizzy. She thought of all the times that Niccolò had been kind to her, and she knew that she was hearing the truth.

"Yes, child. Yes, it does." Cristina knew that this news was a lot to take in for the young girl, so she gave her some time to let her work through everything she had heard. In the silence of their thoughts, they each came to terms with the fact that their lives would never be the same again.

Eventually, Gianetta said, "I'm not sure what this means, exactly, *Madonna*. Can I…can I still work here? Or is it too…difficult for you?" She wondered if it might be a source of shame for the family to have their son's illegitimate child in the same house. Would she have to leave? Where would she go? What about Matteo? Matteo! Suddenly, all the difficult encounters between Matteo and Signor Niccolò made sense. She smiled and thought to herself "My father was protecting me!" Then her thoughts turned to that Easter Sunday morning, and her eyes filled with tears. Her breath left her lungs, and her throat tightened, and she let the great teardrops fall down her cheeks. So much sadness. How could anyone bear it?

Cristina watched, following the girl's thought processes. She had already been through the same emotions, and she answered her question. "No. No, you won't be working here anymore, Gianetta."

Gianetta nodded and rose to leave. "I will collect my things and leave immediately, *Madonna*."

"That's not what I meant at all. You are a part of our family, as much as Tessa and Gino, so we will take care of you, as Niccolò would have wanted us to."

"I don't understand, *Madonna*. What do you mean?"

"I mean that you will now live as part of our family. There will be no more shopping, cleaning, dressing and serving. We will help you become part of our society. You will want for nothing. My Niccolò is not here, but he would want us to do our best for you."

Gianetta flopped back into the chair, her mind reeling with all the revelations and discoveries of the day, her polite protocols forgotten.

"But I'm not part of this world. Cooking, cleaning, organising the household...it's what I know. I don't know how to speak to the ladies of society...or how to behave..." Her eyes darted back and forth as she began to panic.

"We will teach you, my dear." Cristina was beginning to look puzzled, as she had imagined the girl would be delighted at the news.

"What about Matteo?"

"I'm sure Matteo will be delighted for you."

"But...*Madonna*, we are going to be married. We were planning to tell you, after Signor Niccolò's funeral. We..." Gianetta cast her eyes downwards. "We're going to have a baby," she almost whispered.

Cristina was silent as she thought about the news...of a great-grandchild. With a bright smile, she said, "That's even more of a reason that we should care for you. Don't you worry about Matteo. He is a bright young lad, and he will see that this is for the best."

"But we love each other! Surely, that's what is best?"

Cristina was now totally flummoxed. Did the girl hear her correctly? Did she realise the life that she was offering her? Cristina really didn't see what the problem was. She sat upright, hands folded in her lap, and her facial expression brooking no argument. "Giving birth and raising a child is no simple matter. It is hard work, child. You will need a great deal of support. No matter how much Matteo says he loves you, it is not something that he can provide."

As if she hadn't heard her, Gianetta stood up. "I must speak with Matteo," she said, as if to herself.

Just remembering herself in time, she turned at the door, bobbed a small curtsey and was gone, leaving Cristina dumbfounded.

"Well," said Francesco, rising from his chair and pacing around the room. "That rather complicates matters."

"Hmm," replied Cristina, lost in thought.

"What to do now…"

"What do you mean?" asked Cristina, now back in the present.

"You heard the girl. She's pregnant! We can't have her living here as a member of our family, unmarried and with a fatherless child. I know she is our blood, but what are we to do? Should we speak to Padre Cristoforo? A convent, perhaps...?"

"I don't think it will come to that," said Cristina, calmly.

"I don't understand, Cristina. How are we going to resolve this?"

"I've just remembered a conversation I had with Maria Conti a little while ago. Leave it with me." And with a mysterious smile, she left the room.

"Have you seen Matteo?" Gianetta asked Eleonora, who was taking a rare opportunity to sit and rest in the kitchen.

"Not for some time, child," she replied. Seeing Gianetta's face, she asked, "What is wrong?"

As if she hadn't heard her, Gianetta muttered that she would check his bedroom and left the kitchen.

Eleonora was worried. Never had she seen or heard such disruption in a household in such a short time. What worried her more was that she had a feeling that it hadn't ended yet, and her feelings were rarely wrong.

Gianetta knocked on Matteo's bedroom door. "Matteo? Matteo! I must speak with you."

Matteo opened the door with a welcoming smile. In this house of mourning, he always felt guilty for feeling the sheer joy of being with Gianetta. He grasped her by the hand and drew her to him, kissing her passionately, but Gianetta pushed him away. "What..?" He looked confused, wondering what he had done wrong.

"I'm sorry, Matteo," said Gianetta. "This is important." He looked at her with growing concern, wondering what would make his bright, lively Gianetta look so serious. They sat down on his bed, and she recounted the story of Niccolò and Clara. "Matteo, I'm Signor Niccolò's daughter."

After a pause, Matteo threw back his head and laughed. "You can't be! You're my Gianetta...from Fiesole. Signorina Gianetta? That is funny."

"Matteo, don't laugh. It's true. Donna Cristina explained how he spent his time in Fiesole, and how he left...me...and how much he regretted it. Nonna confirmed it all. She was the one who arranged for me to come here. She is my Mamma's sister!"

Matteo put his bandaged hand to his head, trying to make sense of everything he had heard. "But what does this mean for us? Do we have to leave?"

Gianetta lowered her eyes. "Donna Cristina wants me to stay as part of the family." Feeling Matteo stiffen next to her, she rushed on. "Oh, but I don't want to do that! I must be with you. Matteo, what are we to do?" Gianetta had always considered herself to be a strong woman who knew her own mind, but right now, she felt fragile and confused.

They sat in a sad silence as they pondered the implications of their situation.

Several miserable minutes later, there was a knock on the bedroom door. Matteo got up to answer it, looking straight into the green eyes of Cesare Conti. He sighed, wearily, too burdened as he was to observe the niceties of society.

"Signor Conti," he said. "If you've come to make a pass at me, you are wasting your time," and he opened the door to show Gianetta sitting on his bed.

Cesare raised an amused eyebrow as he looked at them both. "I hope I'm not interrupting...?"

"No," said Matteo, remembering his manners. "Please, come in. What brings you to this part of the Palazzo? I didn't think you'd know..."

But Cesare interrupted him. "Oh, I've had cause to use the back stairs before now," he said, smiling at his own wit. "I have actually come to help you, boy. To repay a favour, as it were." He glanced at Gianetta, wondering how much she knew about his nocturnal activities. "You saved me from a ...er... difficult situation, and now I am in a position to do the same for you."

As if the afternoon hadn't thrown enough at him, Matteo now looked thoroughly bewildered.

Cesare went to the end of the bed, sat down and made himself comfortable, while Gianetta drew up her legs, hugging them to herself.

Matteo crossed his arms and looked directly at Cesare. He was in no mood to be toyed with.

Sensing that it was time to get down to business, Cesare began. "How much do you remember about the Easter Sunday Mass?" he asked.

"Not much," replied Matteo. "I remember the start of the attack. I remember lots of fighting, screaming…and I remember someone making for Signor Francesco with a knife. I know I wanted to stop him, but I don't know what happened then. I remember nothing until I woke up back here, in the kitchen." He looked suspiciously across at Cesare. "Why do you ask?"

Cesare looked down at his clasped hands and sighed. "I'm afraid that I saw rather more than that. I also saw the man heading for Francesco. My friend, Niccolò was next to Francesco. To give you credit, I saw you try to stop the man attacking Francesco, but what happened next…" His breath shuddered before he continued. "What happened next was that you grasped that blade and plunged it into Niccolò's chest." In the stunned silence, each of them looked at Matteo's bandaged hand.

Matteo shook his head slowly in disbelief. "No," he said. "No, I would never…"

"I know you would never do that intentionally," said Cesare, soothingly. "I know that it was an accident. You can have a clear conscience on that score."

Seeing that Matteo could not comprehend all that he had heard, Gianetta asked, "Why?"

Cesare turned to her. "Why what, my dear?"

"You have known about this since it happened. Why have you not told anyone? Why tell us now?"

Cesare looked intently at Matteo as he answered Gianetta. "As Matteo knows, I am indebted to him for a previous…good turn. I felt that it would benefit no one to share what I knew. However, it seems that I am not the only one who saw what happened that day."

Matteo looked up sharply.

"Yes, that's right," he continued. "It seems that someone else also saw what happened but saw it in a different light, as it were. I don't know this person, but he is telling people that you killed Niccolò intentionally. This came to me through a third party, of course."

Now Matteo and Gianetta were on their feet, looking down at Cesare in sheer panic. "They can't believe that I…"

"Wait!" said Gianetta. "Who is this person? Where is he?"

"I have no idea who or where he is, my dear. I only know what I heard. I also heard that he is planning to tell the authorities. He intends to see you hang."

Gianetta clung to Matteo. "This is craziness! Nobody would believe it!"

"Wouldn't they? The word of a servant boy? There is no such thing as a fair trial these days. Anyone involved in the attack is being rounded up and hanged. I wouldn't give much for your chances, boy."

Matteo and Gianetta looked at each other, knowing that what Cesare said was right. Whether it was an accident or not, if he had put the blade into Niccolò's chest, he would hang.

"We'll leave," said Gianetta. "We'll pack up and leave right now."

"You can't run away with me. It's too dangerous," said Matteo. "I don't know where I'll go or what I'll need to do to stay safe, but I can't ask you to do that with me. Think of the baby."

Cesare looked sharply at Gianetta, raising an eyebrow at the news. "Your young man is right, my dear," he said. "He should run. He should find a safe place to hide until this all blows over. I can help there. I know of a place where he can stay and not be discovered. Everything will turn out for the best. I promise you."

Gianetta nodded in resignation. "You are right. Thank you, *ser*." She turned to Matteo. "Will you send for me?"

"Of course I will! As soon as the danger is over, and I have a place for us, I will send word. Until then, take your place here. Look after yourself and our baby and remember…I love you. I will always love you."

Gianetta held on to him tightly, not wanting to ever let go, but Cesare said, "We must hurry. I don't know when they will come looking for you."

Matteo stepped away and reached for a small sack, put in the few clothes that he owned and stood at the door with Cesare at his side.

Gianetta could not bear to tear her eyes away from him until the door closed behind them. Burying her face into Matteo's pillow, she wept until she fell into a fitful sleep.

CHAPTER 17

One week after Easter

The hours came and went in a haze for Gianetta. She had told the family that Matteo had been called to see his father urgently, and they had accepted the story, hoping that it was nothing serious and that he would return soon. As much as she hated lying to the family, she felt that she had no choice if she was to save Matteo's life. She did, however, confide in Eleonora. She felt that she had to tell someone the truth and share the weight of the situation.

Eleonora had held Gianetta close as she told her what had happened. She made soothing noises, comforting the young girl who was in such distress, but she kept her true thoughts to herself.

Cristina had arranged for Gianetta to be moved to one of the family rooms. It was large and bright, with a comfortable bed and luxurious furnishings.

Gianetta was familiar with the room, as it was often used as a guest room. She had cleaned it and changed bedding here many times, but now it was her own. How strange! She sat on the edge of the bed, running her hand over the rich fabric bedcover. She examined the texture, the colour, the design, the needlework. It was beautiful, but it didn't feel real, not when she was used to a simple woollen blanket on her bed. Would she ever get used to it?

There was a knock at the door, and Tessa's head popped round. "May I come in?" she asked.

She was pushed aside by a small whirlwind, who ran into the room and jumped on the bed.

"Gino!" cried his mother. "You must always wait to be invited into someone else's room, and we do not jump on their bed!"

Gino looked shamefaced, crawled off the bed and went to stand by his mother. "Sorry, Mamma," he whispered.

"*Va bene!* It's fine!" said Gianetta, laughing. "Of course you can both come in. It's lovely to see you. Come on, Gino. You can sit up here next to me."

The little boy looked up at his mother for permission, before leaping up and sitting next to Gianetta. Tessa indicated a chair next to the bed.

Gianetta looked a little confused before she realised what she was being asked. "I'm sorry, Tessa. Yes, please sit down. I'm really not used to being asked to give permission for someone to take a seat. In fact, I'm really out of my depth here."

Tessa looked at the girl with sympathy. "I quite understand. It takes some getting used to. I remember feeling much the same when Niccolò and I first married. Francesco and Cristina are very kind, but they have a very different way of life."

Gianetta nodded, then tears filled her eyes. "I know they are trying to be so kind, and I do appreciate it. I really do…but I miss my Matteo. He loved me, and I loved him. We were to be married, did you know?"

Tessa nodded, sadly. "Yes, I did."

"But then all this changed everything." She lifted a pretty handkerchief to her face, as the tears spilled over her lashes.

"Don't cry, Gianetta. We love you." Gino stood on the bed beside her and wrapped his little arms around her neck.

"Oh, Gino. I love you too," she replied, smiling through her tears and hugging him back. "Your Mamma is so lucky to have such a kind young man to look after her."

Gino looked serious for a moment. "I think I could look after you, too, if you like."

"I would like that very much. Thank you."

With that matter settled, Gino hopped down from the bed and wandered to the window, where he could play with his toy on the windowsill and watch the people below.

"I'm sorry, Tessa. I haven't asked how you are. The funeral is tomorrow. You must be finding it all so difficult."

"I'm doing…well, thank you. I loved Niccolò so much, and I can't imagine what our life will be like without him, but Gino helps. He really does."

Gianetta put a hand to her tummy and wondered if her baby would comfort her while she was missing Matteo.

"It's really the funeral I came to speak to you about," continued Tessa, pretending not to notice the gesture. They discussed the arrangements for a little while; how the brothers of the Guild would come to escort Niccolò's coffin to the church, their local *Chiesa di Ognissanti*. The Mass would be attended by many of his friends and colleagues, and probably some people from the locality, who were just curious.

"I have decided that you will walk with me and Gino," said Tessa.

Gianetta looked at her but said nothing.

"I'm sure you realise that the gossip has already started, and everyone will want to see this new family member. I want to make them all see that we are one family. We stand by each other, and we support each other. You are Niccolò's daughter, and we are proud of you. I have spoken with Francesco and Cristina, and they are in agreement."

"My Papà was your Papà, too?" said a small voice from the window.

The two women looked at each other, having forgotten that Gino was still there.

"Does that mean you're my sister?"

"Well." Gianetta swallowed nervously, knowing that her response was important to the child. "I am your half-sister. Your Mamma is just your Mamma."

Gino was quiet as he processed this, then said, "You're a bit old for a sister, but I expect that's alright." He shrugged and turned back to the window. Gianetta and Tessa breathed a collective sigh of relief.

The next day, the morning of the funeral was warm and sunny. Gianetta looked at her wardrobe. Cristina's seamstress had been busy making a whole new selection of clothes for her, starting with a gown for the funeral. She knew how to put these gowns on, but only on somebody else. She had no idea where to start dressing herself. There was a knock at the door, and a young girl came in.

"Who are you?" Gianetta asked. The girl could only have been fifteen or sixteen, but she was well grown and apparently wearing one of Gianetta's old dresses and aprons.

"I'm Benedetta. I'm new here, but I know you. You used to visit my father's stall in the market. Eleonora asked me to come and help out."

Gianetta remembered her. She was always polite and didn't try to offload her old vegetables into the shopping, sometimes even throwing in some extras. She smiled to herself, thinking Eleonora had chosen well. Then she frowned, thinking of her old life and how it would never be the same again. The space in her heart for Matteo ached even stronger. "Where's Lucia?" she asked.

Benedetta blushed a little, avoiding her eyes. "She's busy…helping in the kitchen," she replied.

Gianetta sighed. Lucia had been avoiding her since that day of revelations. Whether it was because she still didn't believe the story she told of Antonio, or whether she was resentful of Gianetta's new life, who was to know? Gianetta regretted the loss of her friendship. She really needed it right now.

She allowed Benedetta to help her dress and prepare her hair. When she looked at herself in the looking glass, she didn't recognise the person staring back.

"So, this is my life now," she said to herself. For all the finery and luxury surrounding her, she couldn't help feeling despair.

Niccolò's funeral was large and well-attended. Everyone from the *Arte della Lana*, the Wool Guild, was there. Usually, just one or two representatives would attend the funeral of one of their members, but it was testament to Niccolò's reputation and regard that every member wanted to be there. There were, no doubt, some who had come to gaze at the servant who had become rich overnight, but mostly, people were there to pay their respects to a much-loved man. Lorenzo de' Medici did not attend, as he was still recovering from his injuries and was grieving for his lost brother, Giuliano.

The church was full: full of people, full of candlelight, full of incense smoke and full of quiet dignified tears. Padre Cristoforo conducted the Mass with sensitivity and genuine emotion. He had conducted Niccolò's baptism and wedding and had not expected to conduct his funeral.

From her position next to Tessa and Cristina, Gianetta marvelled at the Rosini women, the picture of calm and elegance, with no trace of the hysteria that she had witnessed at other funerals. Consequently, the other female guests followed suit and restrained their loud mourning.

Gino sat next to his mother, holding her hand and desperately trying to put on a brave face, but seeing his bottom lip quivering, Gianetta thought her heart would break for the little man. At the end of the requiem Mass, after Niccolò's coffin had been borne out on the shoulders of his fellow guildsmen, Gianetta watched and listened as people approached Francesco and Cristina, speaking to them of their sorrow at such a tragedy.

Cristina turned to speak to a woman accompanied by her young son, a dark-haired, serious boy, who appeared to be watching everyone.

"Donna Cristina, I am so sorry for your sad loss," she said, with feeling. "Your son was a fine man, and he will be a great loss to Florence. As you know, I named my own son after him. I hope he can be half the man that your son was."

"Ah, Signora Machiavelli, you are so kind. Thank you for such lovely words. I am sure that your son will make you very proud." She looked at the boy's intense gaze. He must have been about nine years old. "Curious," she thought to herself. "Such a solemn young man."

The family continued to meet and converse with everyone who had attended. Gianetta was amazed at their resilience. At a time when they must be feeling at their lowest, they still managed to give their time to others. She would have much preferred to retreat to her room, pull the curtains closed and hide under the bedcovers. There was still so much for her to work out in her mind: the loss of a man that she hardly knew on a personal level; the discovery that this man was actually her father; the loss of her old life; the realisation that she needed to make a new life; the loss of Matteo. Oh, Matteo! She took a great gulp of air to stop the avalanche of grief that threatened to overwhelm her. A little hand slipped into her palm, and she looked down into Gino's eyes, dark, like his father's and her own.

"It will be alright, Gianetta," he said. "I will look after you." And at that moment, she knew that he would.

CHAPTER 18

Several days later, the household was gradually returning to its old rhythm. While there was still an emptiness and an aura of grief over everyone, they continued their daily chores, and the family business was restarting.

Gianetta still spent most of her day either alone in her room, playing with Gino or talking to Nonna. Since discovering that Nonna was Mamma Sofia's sister, she found great comfort in their long conversations, learning about their early life in Fiesole. Somehow, it made her feel still connected with her old life.

Tessa was familiarising herself with the details of the Rosini textile business. She had learned what orders had been fulfilled and paid for; what payments were still due, and what orders had to be delivered and when. She knew who their suppliers were and who their major customers were.

Francesco made sure that he introduced them to her personally. Niccolò had been known as an efficient and fair businessman, and Francesco wanted to let everyone know that Tessa was not to be underestimated. They could expect the same service and treatment from the Rosini business, and the Rosini business expected the same from their customers and suppliers. There were some raised eyebrows and some lewd comments when Tessa was introduced, but she gave them short shrift and soon put them in their place, while maintaining a pleasant and professional demeanour. Francesco was beginning to see what an asset she was going to be to their business and silently cursed himself for not including her before.

There was much paperwork to be dealt with, and in the absence of Luigi, it took Tessa some time to make sense of it. Without his logical orderliness, however, it could have taken her much longer. They were poring over a particularly tricky contract when Eleonora knocked the door and entered the study.

"*Scusi*, Signor," she said. "I have something that I think you need to hear."

"What is it, Eleonora?" said Francesco, putting down his pen. It was not often that the cook ventured into the study, so this was to be taken seriously. "Come, sit down."

"Oh no, Signor," she replied. "I just wanted to check that you were free. I sometimes have a visit from Carlo, the foreman at Signor Sandro's workshop." She blushed slightly but carried on. "After I heard what he had to say, I sent him to get the boy himself."

Thoroughly confused by now, Francesco just waited.

Tessa asked, "Should I fetch Cristina?"

Francesco looked at Eleonora who nodded.

A few minutes later, Francesco, Cristina and Tessa were sitting in the study, as Eleonora showed in Carlo, who dragged a snivelling boy by the ear. Francesco stood up. "What...?"

Carlo gave a small bow, then smacked the boy, who bowed while wiping his nose on his sleeve.

"What is this? What is going on?"

"I am sorry for this intrusion, Signor," said Carlo. "I have just discovered the truth about this boy, who I am ashamed to say, works in the Maestro's workshop as an apprentice. His name is Marco, and he has something important to tell you."

"From the workshop, you say? Is it about my commission?"

"No, *ser*. It's about Antonio…and Luigi."

"Luigi!" Francesco sat down in his chair with a thump. "Let's hear what you have to say, boy."

Marco continued to cry, tears and mucus running down his face.

He took another hefty whack from Carlo. "Speak, boy!"

Tessa stood up and gave Marco a clean handkerchief. He blew his nose noisily and copiously into it and offered it back to her. That earned him another clip across the ear from Carlo.

"I thought…I thought it was going to be alright. I thought we were brave, and what we were doing was right. I just went to the meetings. I didn't do anything!" His voice was rising in panic. Another whack.

"*Basta*, Carlo," said Francesco. "That isn't helping. Enough babbling, boy. Just tell us what you know."

With much snivelling and crying, the boy told his story, which started several months ago.

"Well, *ser*, I met Antonio sometime last year…probably in the summer. The weather was good, I know that. I know it because it was a warm day when I was resting in the alleyway behind the studio." He glanced up at Carlo.

"Shirking again?" Carlo shook his head in frustration.

"I…I know I shouldn't have been there, but it was just so hot, and I was so tired…"

"Let's get to the point, shall we?" said Francesco firmly.

Marco, still looking at his feet, nodded. "I'd been there a few times, at the same time of day." He flinched, expecting another beating from Carlo, but none came. "I'd noticed that Antonio came past at about the same time on the same day. I recognised him as someone who worked here at the Palazzo, so I said hello. We chatted...mostly about nothing important. What we did in our jobs during the day. The bits we enjoyed, and the bits we didn't enjoy so much. His work seemed so glamorous compared with mine. He worked in a big Palazzo, with grand people, who were kind to their staff." He glanced up at Francesco, who acknowledged the compliment, then nodded his head to encourage him to continue.

"He said their food was better than anywhere in Florence." Behind him, Eleonora blushed. "He told me about one of the pretty maids. He..." Marco stopped and reconsidered the indelicate comment he was about to share.

"After a few weeks, I asked him where he went every week at the same time, but he didn't seem keen to tell me at first. He said he just went to meet some friends. I wanted to go with him, but he said no. He told me it was more of a political gathering. That made me want to go even more. I..." Marco broke off nervously, wondering how much to share.

Francesco saw that he needed to encourage him if he wanted to get the full story. "Your political views are of no consequence under the circumstances, don't you think? Be frank, boy. Tell it as it is."

Marco looked up and continued with a hint of defiance. "I was fed up of seeing my friends and family struggle and starve, while people like the Medici lived in luxury. I wanted to see a change in Florence. It seemed that Antonio's group of friends felt the same way. Eventually, he said I could join him, but I had to understand that the group intended to get rid of the Medici, and I had to agree that I would do what they asked. It sounded so exciting..." He tailed off, twisting his tunic between his fingers.

"I went to their meetings. There was a lot of wine and a lot of talk, but to me, it seemed that that's all it was. A lot of men complaining about life and politics and so on. Somebody said that the group was backed by a powerful family, but nobody knew who it was, so I just thought it was more talk. I could see that Antonio hated the Medici, though…and I mean really hated them, particularly the older one… the one in the *Signoria*."

"Signor Lorenzo?" asked Francesco.

Marco nodded. "Yes. He killed Antonio's brother!"

"He killed Antonio's brother?" repeated Francesco. "I can't believe that."

"That's what he told me, *ser*."

"If I may, *ser*?" Carlo jumped in. "When Marco first told me this, I went to speak with a friend of mine. He works in the kitchens at *Palazzo Medici*. I think I know what happened."

Francesco waved him on.

"Antonio's brother also used to work in the kitchens at the Palazzo. This was just a couple of years ago. He wasn't a particularly good worker, a bit lazy, often drunk, but not enough to get rid of him. One Christmas though, he was caught stealing a brace of pheasants, so Signor Lorenzo sacked him."

"But he didn't kill him?" Francesco wanted to make sure he understood what happened.

"No, *ser*, he didn't kill him. He listened to the boy's pleas but wouldn't be swayed. He gave him a week's salary and told him to leave immediately, which he did. He took that salary straight to the local tavern. He got very drunk and on his way home, slipped, fell into the river and drowned."

"…and that is why Antonio believed Lorenzo killed his brother…"

Francesco shook his head, understanding, but still incredulous. "*E cosi,* now we know about Antonio, but I want the full story, Marco." Francesco spoke directly to the boy, who was still twisting his tunic in his hands, looking a mixture of defiant and terrified. He nodded.

"The meetings seemed to change. The leaders had messages delivered to them often."

"Who delivered these messages?"

"I don't know. He didn't seem to want to stay, just delivered the messages and went."

"What did he look like?"

Marco shrugged. "I don't know. Just ordinary…apart from the fox's tail on his belt. A bit strange if you ask me."

"*Non importa.* Carry on."

"We were told it was going to happen on Easter Sunday. They told us that we'd all be going to the *Duomo*, we'd be given a dagger, and we should simply attack anyone in Medici colours. I'd never held a dagger before…and I worried what my Nonna would think…"

"Your Nonna is the least of your worries now, boy," said Carlo, but Francesco shook his head at him.

"What was the plan?"

"We were split into groups. I was with Antonio. We were told to wait by the South Door, so we waited. It was busy, but there was nothing special going on. I remember thinking that nothing was going to happen, and we'd be home soon for lunch. Then the screaming started…"

The room was silent. Everyone absorbed in their own painful memories of that day.

"People started to rush out of the doors. The South Door, where we were waiting burst open and people flooded out, crying, hurt… I couldn't stop looking at them, but Antonio… Antonio was in the thick of it, stabbing people as they ran out and swinging his dagger at anyone who passed. I was so scared…" A big teardrop escaped and ran down his cheek. He brushed it away impatiently. "When…when it was finished, Antonio was covered in blood. I don't think any of it was his. He grabbed me, and we ran."

"Where did you go?"

"We went to our meeting place. We met in a room underneath a stonemason's *bottega*. It was a good hiding place. I think it was a storeroom. Nobody would know it was there, unless you knew…if you know what I mean." He paused and looked up.

"The room was full of men from our group. Some had been wounded and were wrapping their cuts. Some of the men, though…" His eyes widened, as he remembered them. "Some of them looked crazy, *pazzo*… They loved it. They paced round the room like caged dogs, shouting about the things they had done. Antonio was one of them. I tried to hide behind some of the sacks. I just wanted them all to go, so I could get home," he said, sadly. "There are little windows at the top of the room. They open out onto the street. Just big enough to let some light in. I saw some feet running, and I just knew they were coming for us. I was so frightened…so frightened… They ran into the room. They were soldiers of the *Signoria*, I could tell, but one of them wasn't. I recognised him, but I didn't know who he was. Antonio knew him, though, because he stopped and faced him. All he said was "Luigi!""

"Luigi…" Cristina spoke softly.

"They argued. Luigi said that he knew Antonio was up to something but was shocked at what he'd done. Antonio said…some horrible things." Marco looked embarrassed.

"Some things about his…personal life."

Cristina looked confused, but Francesco nodded.

"He said he hoped all the Medici were dead and wished he could have done it himself. Then he pointed his dagger at Luigi." Marco looked confused, his brow furrowed as he continued. "Luigi didn't seem scared, though. He seemed more…angry. He shouted at Antonio, about how he didn't know how lucky he was; that he had a good home and worked for a good family, and that he should be ashamed of himself for bringing dishonour to the family. That seemed to make sense to me. In the early days, when we just chatted, Antonio had told me that he worked for a good family. I thought Antonio remembered it too because he seemed to pause. I thought he was going to drop the dagger, but then he changed his mind again and pointed it at Luigi again. Luigi had a knife in his hand too, but he didn't seem to know what to do with it. One of the other soldiers pulled his sword out and made Antonio put his dagger on the floor, which he did. The soldier got some rope from his belt, and I thought Antonio had given in. He put his hands behind his back…but he had another dagger hidden in the back of his trousers. I was behind him, so I could see what he was going to do, but I had no voice." Marco looked around the room, pleading with his audience. "I swear, signor. I swear that I couldn't do anything to help."

"What happened, Marco?" Francesco asked, quietly.

"Antonio rushed at the soldier and pushed him out of the way, but he pushed his dagger into Luigi's chest. He dropped his own knife and as he fell to the floor, he looked straight me. I watched Luigi die…I've never seen anyone die before…"

All eyes were on Marco, as his chest heaved with the weight of all that he had experienced.

"The soldiers took Antonio?"

"*Sì*, signor. They tied him up and took him away. More soldiers were there by that time, and they took everyone else. Nobody discovered me hiding. I waited until it was dark before I left, and then I came straight back to the workshop." His face was the picture of misery.

The studio was silent. Each of them with their own thoughts, saying a silent prayer for their lost friend.

Eventually, it was Francesco who broke the silence. "What happened to Luigi's body?"

"I don't know, *ser*. I didn't want to go back there."

Carlo spoke up. "I made him take me there, Signor Francesco. There was no sign of his body, but there was enough blood to confirm the boy's story. Also, I picked up this knife. Marco thinks it was the one Luigi had."

He held out a knife, and Eleonora moved forward to look. She nodded. "Yes, that's my knife. It went missing sometime before Easter. Luigi must have known what was going to happen…or at least suspected it."

"What would have happened to Luigi's body, Carlo?" asked Francesco.

"It was probably either left in the street to be collected or dumped in the river."

Cristina let out a cry. "How cruel! Not to allow him the dignity of a Christian burial. His soul will be in torment."

"We will have Masses offered for his eternal soul," said Francesco, not taking his eyes off Marco. "What do we do with you now, boy?" he said to the room in general.

"I haven't spoken with the Maestro yet, *ser*, but I am sure he will do whatever you think best," said Carlo.

Marco stood shaking and crying even more now that his story had been told. He waited for his punishment.

"He's Sandro's boy. It should be his decision. Carlo, if he doesn't want him…and I totally understand if that is the case…he will come here. We need extra hands, and we will teach him how to be a true Florentine." He stood up, put his hands behind his back and walked around the boy. "You will work, and you will learn. You will rise at dawn and sleep at sundown. You will not leave this house without my express permission. You will see how the Medici run the city and make it a safe and prosperous place to live.

"Carlo, as you leave here, take this boy home via the *Bargello*. I want him to stand and look on those hanging there. I want him to think about how he could so easily have been one of them. When you think he understands, take him home to the Maestro and let him decide what to do with him." Francesco turned his back, and the meeting was over.

Carlo left the room, followed by a very contrite Marco.

As expected, Signor Sandro wanted Marco gone. He said that he couldn't create beauty when there was so much ugliness to distract him, and he certainly did not want it in his own workshop. Carlo repeated the conversation that he had had with Signor Francesco, and with a theatrical flourish of dismissal, Marco's fate was decided. True to his word, that same night, Francesco took the boy in and put him to work, under the supervision of Eleonora and Lucia.

CHAPTER 19

In the study the next morning, Francesco and Tessa were poring over a ream of documents, discussing the finer points of a new contract for the delivery of the best linen and silk to a particular seamstress. They assumed, correctly, that one of the members of the *Signoria* had acquired a new mistress and had promised her a new wardrobe. Who were they to judge? A timid knock on the door caused them to look up.

"Yes, Benedetta?"

"*Signor, Madonna.*" The young girl nervously curtsied. "Signor Conti is here to see you."

"Piero?" Francesco stood up from his desk.

"No, *ser*. The younger one."

At that, Cesare pushed past the girl and strode into the room with his arms open wide. "*Zio* Francesco! *Come stai*? I have been so worried about you and all the events of these past days." He shook his head, sadly.

"*Buongiorno*, Cesare. Thank you. It has indeed been a very difficult time for us all."

"I'm afraid that I am going to add to your troubles, *Zio*." He always referred to Francesco as his uncle, and Francesco had always held the boy in some affection, while secretly glad that he didn't have to deal with some of his indiscretions and drunken tomfooleries.

"What is it?" asked Francesco, looking as if he couldn't take any more bad news.

Behind him, Tessa sat down quietly.

"Your boy…Matteo?"

"Matteo? Yes, he's visiting his father, but he's been gone longer than I expected. Unlike him. He's a trustworthy boy, a reliable sort. Do you know something of this?"

"I do." Cesare nodded his head, stroking his small, neat beard. "I understand that he has been hanged."

Francesco looked at Cesare, wondering if he had heard correctly. "How? Why?" He reached for his chair and slowly lowered himself into it.

"I don't know how best to put this… *Zio*, Matteo was the one who stabbed Niccolò."

Tessa gasped.

Francesco looked as though he had been hit in the stomach. "How many more blows can a man take?" he thought to himself, his elbows on his knees, and his head hanging low. "Tell me everything," he whispered.

"I heard it all from a man in…" He paused. "Well, never mind that. I heard it from a reliable source. On Easter Sunday, at the *Duomo*, during…everything that happened, someone saw Matteo take hold of another man's blade and stab Niccolò in the chest. It has taken this long to identify and find Matteo but find him they did…and he hanged yesterday."

"I can hardly believe it. First Antonio and now Matteo. How did I not see this?"

"Antonio?" asked Cesare, raising an eyebrow.

"Yes, the other servant boy. You know him. I saw you looking at him, Cesare." Francesco sounded weary, as though he had the weight of the world on his shoulders.

"Ah, yes. I think I know the one you mean." Cesare spoke lightly, as if it was no matter.

"Well, it seems that he was the one to push the stone from the balustrade at our dinner that night…was it really only a few weeks ago? So much has happened. So much has changed.

"Anyway, it seems that he was also involved in that Easter Sunday plot. He was found and hanged almost the same day."

Cesare took a deep breath but said nothing.

The room was silent, each with their own thoughts.

Eventually, Francesco said, "Gianetta will be upset, but we will help her."

"Gianetta?" Cesare's ears pricked up. "The servant girl?"

"She is more than that, Cesare. She is Niccolò's daughter."

Now it was Cesare's turn to look shocked. "Niccolò's daughter? Are you sure?"

"Yes. Absolutely sure. Why?"

"I…I just wanted to make sure that she will not take advantage of you. You are a very rich and very generous man…" Cesare spoke carefully, but his eyes flicked from left to right as his thoughts raced through his head. "She was betrothed to Matteo?" he asked.

Francesco nodded. "They planned to marry. I understand that she is with child." As he became more distressed, he ran his fingers through his hair, as though trying to disentangle his thoughts. Looking up, he said, "I'm sorry, Cesare. That is not your worry. We will manage this."

Cesare, who had also been deep in thought, bowed to Francesco and to Tessa, who was weeping quietly at the desk. "I am sorry to have disturbed you, *Zio*. I will bid you a good day. No need to send for the maid. I know my way out." And with that, he was gone.

The atmosphere with the staff was strained, as they had heard the full story of Marco's involvement with the group responsible for the attack in the *Duomo* from Francesco himself.

Lucia was hard on the boy, making him repeat his chores if they did not come up to her standards, and even when they did, she found fault. She made him scrub the floor tiles in the kitchen until his fingers bled. She gave him the job of cleaning the chamber pots and disposing of the rotten vegetable peelings.

Marco took it all quietly and with resignation.

For a few hours, Eleonora allowed her the freedom to mete out her punishments, but that afternoon, she decided that it was time to call a halt. "Lucia, sit with me," she said. The two women sat near the window, as the summer sun was beginning to make its presence felt. "Lucia, what happened to Antonio was not Marco's fault. It was his own choice. Yes, Marco was wrong to have been mixed up with it all, but he didn't cause Antonio's fate. He knows he did wrong, and he knows how lucky he is to have found a place here, with us.

"I think we can make something of the boy. He has an intelligent mind, if sometimes misguided, and he can work hard when he puts his mind to it. Given the right encouragement and teaching, we could make a good man out of Marco." She paused and looked at Lucia, who was picking at her nails in her lap.

"I have been hard on him, haven't I?" she said.

"Yes, child, you have." Eleonora continued. "I think he understands, but now it's time to move on and start teaching him properly. Signor Francesco wants him to learn what it means to be a real Florentine, and we must play our part."

Lucia nodded. She looked up at Eleonora with tears in her eyes.

"I was such a fool, Eleonora. I really thought Antonio loved me. I thought we would be married. When he used to go out on his evening off, if he wasn't with me, I thought he was visiting his mother, not plotting a revolution. How blind I must have been!"

"Love makes fools of us all, *cara*," said the cook.

"I can't imagine anyone making a fool of you, Eleonora."

"I have learnt from bitter experience, child. I was also going to be married many years ago."

Lucia looked up at Eleonora. She had never heard her speak of her past, apart from her father's work. Before Eleonora could say any more, they were interrupted by a knock on the big front door.

"So much coming and going today!" said Eleonora. "You'd better see who it is, Lucia."

A few moments later, Lucia returned. "It was the Conti family...all of them! Signor Cesare only left an hour or so ago. I wonder what's going on there."

"I'm sure we'll find out eventually," said Eleonora, getting up to start preparing the pile of vegetables waiting for her on the table. "I'm in no rush to hear any more gossip." And she continued chopping her vegetables with renewed vigour.

"Eleonora?" Lucia ventured. "You were going to tell me about your young man...?"

Eleonora looked up from her chores. "Yes, I was, wasn't I?" She carefully put down her knife, left the table and resumed her seat by the window with Lucia.

"I was going to be married to a very handsome man... Alfredo. After my father died, I had little money, but Alfredo persuaded me to sell everything I had. He promised to buy us a little house here in Florence, and when it was all arranged, I would follow him, and we would get married straight away." Her eyes misted over, as she returned to her memories.

"Well, I waited for him, but when I had no word, I managed to get a ride from Pistoia into Florence. I had no idea where his home was, but I remembered him speaking of a particular tavern. *Il Cane Nero.* I remember it to this day. So loud and busy…and smelly. I got talking to one of the waitresses, who seemed kind, and explained who I was looking for. She knew him. It seemed everyone knew Alfredo. Full of charm and big stories. That sounded like Alfredo. It turned out that he gambled. He gambled heavily and was often in debt. This time, it seemed that he was in debt to the wrong people, and Alfredo was found floating in the Arno."

Lucia was holding Eleonora's hands, hanging off her every word.

"I will never know if he really loved me, or if he just wanted my money to pay off his debts. So, you see, child, I know how you feel. You can't let the experience make you bitter, or it will eat away at you your whole life."

Lucia nodded in agreement. "I think Antonio did love me, you know," she said, "but he must have been so consumed with hate for the Medici that I took second place…and I'm worth more than second place." She sat up a bit straighter and pulled her shoulders back.

"That's the way," said Eleonora. "Someday, someone will be worthy of you. Until then, you hold your head up high."

"How did you come to work here?" asked Lucia, curious now to know more.

"That night, I had nowhere to go, nothing to eat, not even a crust of bread. The waitress was actually the owner of *Il Cane Nero* and let me sleep on the floor for a few days. I started to help out, cooking for the customers…not that they appreciated my food. Eventually, I worked through a number of jobs, always learning new techniques in the kitchen, until one day Signor Francesco came to one of the dinners that I had cooked. He was in need of a new cook. I think

Nonna Isabetta was trying to help out in the kitchen, and they'd had a few disasters! Anyway, here I am. I have always been happy here, and the family appreciate my work. I have good friends. What more could I ask?"

"Someone to love?" ventured Lucia.

"Ha! Well, who knows what the Good Lord has in store for me! Now, enough chatting. We must get on. The dinners won't make themselves."

"I must speak to Gianetta," said Lucia, suddenly. "I'm afraid Marco isn't the only one I've been making life difficult for. I've hardly spoken to her lately."

"Yes, it's time to make peace. Go now but be back soon. We have dinner to prepare, and there is much to be done."

Lucia went to speak to Gianetta in her room. It was a fair assumption that she would find her there, as she rarely ventured from it. However, the bedroom was empty. Hoping that Gianetta was beginning to emerge from her despair, she promised herself that she would return later and apologise for her behaviour. She left feeling a little more positive.

Gianetta had been invited to join Francesco, Cristina and Nonna in the *sala*. As it was a direct invitation, Gianetta did not feel that she could refuse. However she felt about her situation, she did not forget her manners. As she entered, Francesco was sitting in his chair, steepling his fingers, Nonna was snoozing in the corner, and Cristina was pacing the room. They were not the only people in the room. The whole Conti family were there too. There was an air of anticipation which made Gianetta uncomfortable.

"*Buona sera*," she said, with a small curtsey. She found it hard to dispense with the habit.

"Come in, child!" Cristina rushed to her side and taking her by the hand, led her to a comfortable chair near the window. "Sit! Tell me, how are you feeling? Are you and your child well?" She glanced at Gianetta's tummy, which was beginning to show signs of her pregnancy. As an automatic gesture, Gianetta placed a protective hand around her baby.

"We are well, thank you, *Madonna*." She would never be able to call her Cristina, or even Grandmother. She glanced nervously at their guests, assuming that they now knew of her condition.

"We have news for you, child," said Cristina.

Nonna was now wide awake and watching closely, wondering how this would be handled. She knew this conversation was going to be very difficult. Looking around, it seemed that only Cesare looked relaxed and…yes, pleased with himself. He looked pleased with himself. Nonna snorted to herself and turned her attention back to Gianetta.

Holding both Gianetta's hands in hers, Cristina took a deep breath. "Gianetta," she said. "Gianetta, I am afraid that Matteo is dead."

Gianetta snatched her hands away. "No! No, this can't be." She shook her head forcefully.

"I'm sorry, my dear, but I'm afraid it is."

"But…how…?" She glanced across the room at Cesare, who was looking intently out of the window.

"He has been hanged," said Cristina. "He was hanged with the other members of the group who carried out the attack in the *Duomo*. He was responsible for…the death of an innocent man." Cristina spoke flatly, desperate to keep the emotion out of her voice.

"It's not true," cried Gianetta. "Signor Conti, tell them it's not true! You know it's not true!"

Cesare Conti looked pityingly at the girl and said in a sad voice.

"I'm afraid it is true. There were witnesses to his crime."

Gianetta looked around the room, shaking her head. "No! Poor Matteo! He would never… What am I to do? How will I…?"

Cristina held her hand, gently. "We have other news for you, child, better news for you."

Gianetta's ashen face looked blankly at Cristina, then at Francesco. What more could there be?

Francesco began, nervously. "Well, my dear, as you know, we have been delighted to welcome you into our family. To have another living reminder of Niccolò is a blessing which we could not have imagined before. The fact that you are carrying his grandchild makes it even more special."

"It may be his grandchild, but it is my child," Gianetta thought to herself.

"However," continued Francesco, "the child makes it a little more…difficult…for you."

Gianetta was not sure where this conversation was leading, but even in her distress, she felt that things were going to get worse.

"In normal circumstances, we would have had time to search for a suitable husband for you."

Gianetta thought of Matteo and her throat constricted. Matteo was the only husband she would ever want.

"These are not normal circumstances, though, with…err…the baby." Francesco was now beginning to look more uncomfortable, but he continued bravely on. "That is why our news is such good news."

Gianetta's heart was thumping in her chest. She was now thoroughly nervous. She just knew that she was not going to like what was to come.

"You have met our family friends, the Contis, and their son, Cesare?"

She looked across at them. Signor Piero looked serious; Donna Maria looked a little uncomfortable but with a tinge of excitement; Cesare looked like a cat with a mouse. "Oh no!" she thought. "This can't possibly be happening!"

"Well, Cesare has offered to take you as his wife! He knows about the baby and has agreed that it should be brought up as his own son or daughter. Signor Piero and I have discussed the matter, and the wedding will be held in just three weeks' time. Isn't that...good news?"

Gianetta felt her head spin. She did not have the words to respond or breath enough in her body to even cry out. She thought of Cesare Conti and how he had promised to look after Matteo. She thought of how he had made vulgar comments to her, looked at her with greed in his eyes and even stroked her bottom when he thought nobody could see. She closed her eyes to shut out the images in her mind, but still they flew into her vision. She put her hand to her mouth as she felt herself gag. This was not the reaction that the family was expecting, but they seemed not to notice.

Cristina looked at her with encouragement. "A wedding! Think of it, child. Such a joyous occasion after the sorrow that we have all endured! It will be held in our *Chiesa di Ognissanti*, and we will host a special party here. There will be no expense spared. And your gown! Oh, child, your gown will be spectacular. It will be made from the finest silk brocade that Francesco can find, and my seamstress will begin work on it immediately. You will look divine!" She tried to ignore the silence from Gianetta.

"Gianetta?" The quiet voice came from Nonna. They all looked at the young girl.

She was staring into the distance, not seeing or hearing anything in this room, until she let out a sob and fled from the room.

Francesco looked at Nonna for wisdom, as he always did. Nonna heaved a weary sigh.

"The poor child has had her whole world turned upside down in these last weeks. She doesn't know whether she's in Florence or France, or even if the sun will rise tomorrow. She has just lost her young man. Don't expect her to be delighted at this."

Cristina was stunned. "What else could we have done? She is in such a mess, but we have done everything we can. She will never want for anything in her life."

"It's not her life now, though, is it?" Nonna replied. "She recognises nothing of her life, the places, the people, but she is a good girl. She knows you are doing your best for her, but it doesn't make it any easier for her. Give her time."

"She doesn't have time, Nonna! Her belly is already beginning to swell. It is good of Cesare to make the offer of marriage." She smiled across at him, and he bowed his head modestly.

Francesco looked at his friend, Piero, who was perched uncomfortably on the edge of a chair. "Piero? What are your thoughts?"

Piero was hesitant, as he chose his words carefully. "In truth? I am unhappy about this arrangement. I had hoped for better for our only son." He held a hand up. "I'm sorry, Francesco, but I must share my true feelings."

Francesco nodded his head.

"If it had been any other family but yours, I would have forbidden it, but I can see what a difficult situation it is for you, *amico*." Glancing across at his son, he continued, "And Cesare seems set on the idea. He is very taken with the girl. I suppose I should be happy that he is willing to marry at all."

Cesare's face was impassive. Eventually, straightening himself up, he said, "She is a fine girl. If I can help the daughter of my friend,

Niccolò, God rest his soul, and join our families together, then I am honoured to do so."

Donna Maria's eyes welled up with pride, but Piero simply raised an eyebrow at his son.

"Yes, well…" he cleared his throat. "It seems that the agreement has been made, and we should make the best of it. A dinner here to mark the occasion? Tomorrow?"

Francesco also cleared his throat. "Yes! Yes, of course. A celebration, eh?"

Piero stood up. "Hmm. Until tomorrow, then." And he left the room, closely followed by his wife.

Cesare stood up and unhurriedly left the room behind his parents.

Francesco ran his hands through his hair. That had not gone as he had expected at all. He slumped into his chair, put his head in his hands and wondered how life could get so complicated.

CHAPTER 20

The next day

Gianetta was lying on her bed, exhausted. She thought she had
cried enough tears in the last few days to last her whole life,
but no. After yesterday's news, she found that there were plenty more
tears, and she had shed them copiously into her pillow. Now, she
found herself in the grip of hopeless despair, with no idea what would
happen to her. She couldn't possibly marry Cesare, but what else was
she to do? She had no other choice. Her need for Matteo to hold her
was a physical ache with no possibility of relief.

Lucia knocked the door and let herself in.

Seeing her friend at last, Gianetta rushed into her arms and sobbed
all over again.

Lucia was grateful that she had appeared to be forgiven for her
behaviour, but the sight of her friend's pale face and shrunken features
alarmed her. Benedetta had told her that Gianetta was refusing to eat
all her meals, but the effect shocked her.

"Oh, Gianetta! *Amica mia!* What have you done to yourself?
Are you ill? Can I get you something? One of Eleonora's tonics?
Anything?"

"Lucia, have you heard about Matteo?" she asked, ignoring her questions.

"Yes, I have heard the news. I am so, so sorry. Perhaps we both chose our partners poorly."

"But Matteo did nothing! He would never have killed Niccolò. It was all a big mistake. Oh, how did everything go so badly wrong? And now…" Gianetta was distraught.

Lucia looked at her carefully. "This is more than just Matteo, isn't it? What is wrong?"

"Oh, Lucia!" She started to sob again. Once she had control over her emotions, she continued. "I'm to be married. To Cesare Conti!"

Lucia did not know how to react. She knew Gianetta's feelings for the son of the Conti family and secretly thought that a life in a convent might be preferable to marrying the brute, charming though he may appear to be. However, she also knew that Gianetta was soon to bring a child into the world and needed security for them both. There was no doubt that Signor Francesco and Donna Cristina were trying to do their very best for her. Oh, what a mess! Erring on the side of caution, she replied, "I'm sure he'll make a fine husband for you. The Contis are a kind family."

"Is that what you really think, Lucia?" She searched her friend's face.

"I… I just think that you have to do what is best for you and your baby. It is a good offer…" She tailed off, uncertain how to deal with the dilemma. She looked at Gianetta's empty eyes and decided to take a more practical approach. "Let me dress you for dinner," she said. "Eleonora and I have been cooking up a frenzy in the kitchen. I'd love to know how it tastes. You will have to tell me all about it, afterwards."

Gianetta was compliant as Lucia dressed her and arranged her hair, but there was no more conversation. It was as if she were in a trance.

"Is Nonna ready for dinner?" she asked.

Lucia gave a tentative laugh. "Nonna, as you know, is always ready for dinner!"

With no acknowledgement of the joke, Gianetta nodded and turned away.

Realising that their conversation, such as it was, was at an end, Lucia left the room and returned to the kitchen, extremely worried.

Gianetta sat in the small chair in Nonna's chambers.

Nonna was watching the young girl's face with concern.

"What am I to do, Nonna?" she said, wearily. "I know the family are just doing what they think is best, and they have been so kind to me...so very kind. They could have had me thrown into the street when they heard that I was Niccolò's daughter. They have accepted me into their family and treated me as such. I want for nothing: clothes, food, shelter...and now, even a husband. But I had a man who was going to be my husband. We loved each other...at least, I still love him. I will always love him."

"I know, child. I know," said Nonna, soothingly, as she patted her hands. "Women must grieve in their own time, and grieve you will, but now you must be practical. You must think of your baby."

"Oh, Nonna!" Once again, Gianetta found herself drowning in her own tears.

When the tide had ebbed somewhat, Nonna asked, "Is it so terrible, this marriage that they are proposing for you?"

"Yes, Nonna. Yes, it is! I could never be happy with that man. He is very charming to everyone, but I have seen what he can be like. My life would be so miserable."

They sat in silence for some moments, each with their own thoughts.

Nonna looked up with sadness at the young girl in such torment. "Sometimes," she said. "Our path is chosen for us…sometimes, we have to make our own path."

Gianetta looked at her closely and nodded.

"God will guide you, child. Put yourself in His hands."

Getting up from her chair, Gianetta leaned into the old woman and embraced her, kissing her paper-like cheeks. "I will, Nonna. I will," and she left.

Nonna blessed herself with the sign of the cross, clasped her hands, closed her eyes and began to pray.

An hour or two later, the dining room was prepared and waiting for its guests. It was a sunny evening, and the curtains and windows were open, letting in air and bright sunshine. As expected, Eleonora and Lucia had created a sumptuous spread, fit for a celebratory dinner. The *credenza* was creaking with delicacies and sweet treats, flanked by jugs of wine. Nonna had already made her way to the dining room and was casting her eye over the dishes as both the Rosini and Conti families entered.

Maria Conti had linked arms with Cristina and was gushing with excitement. "To think we have been friends all these years, and now we are going to be family! We will have such a time planning the wedding. What colour will you wear? You must let me share Agnese, our cook. Eleonora will be grateful for the skilled hands, I'm sure."

Cristina was rather doubtful about that, but she let Maria continue. She was also excited at the prospect of a wedding to join the two families, but after the conversation earlier that afternoon, she felt that it might not be a smooth process. She looked around, hoping to see Gianetta, but the girl had not arrived yet.

Tessa was talking to Gino, who was surreptitiously trying to get a head start on the sweet biscuits.

Piero and Francesco were deep in conversation, no doubt discussing the finer details of the wedding contract. Dowries, dates and duties were serious business when it came to matrimony in Florence. There was no room for the fripperies of romance.

Standing near the door, looking uncharacteristically nervous, was the groom-to-be, Cesare Conti. He had clearly gone to a lot of trouble with his appearance for the occasion. His hair was freshly washed and brushed; his beard was neatly trimmed; he was wearing his best doublet and hose in a rich green, which he believed enhanced the colour of his eyes. Those green eyes were darting back and fore to the door, eagerly awaiting to feast his eyes on the woman who was to be his wife. He knew that the situation was less than ideal, but oh! Gianetta was to be his! He thought of the times that they had met in this house before. He could smell her clean hair. He thought of her deep dark eyes. Now they would be gazing into his own eyes, not that young tramp who used to work here and was now long gone. He pictured her tiny waist and the shape of her hips below it. He was beginning to perspire. He remembered how her soft, generous breasts peeped from above the apron she wore as she served their food. He shifted, uncomfortably, as he began to harden at the thought of nights to come. Yes, she would soon be his, and he was about to join a very rich family. He smiled greedily.

"So, where is our bride?" asked Piero, looking around the room.

"I expect she is taking extra care with her preparations, wanting to make an entrance, Piero," replied his wife, who was also looking at the door expectantly.

Francesco and Cristina looked at each other nervously. They looked at Nonna, who was avoiding their gaze and concentrating hard on the offerings on the *credenza*.

"We shall have some wine!" announced Francesco, cheerily. "Marco, will you serve, please?"

Marco jumped to attention, eager to please his master, and started to pour the wine into the guests' goblets. He had not met the Contis before but was struck by a flash of recognition as he served. Dismissing the thought, he carried on his duties with concentration. It would not do to spill some of this expensive wine over the family's honoured guests.

Lucia and Benedetta stood to the side, waiting for Gianetta to arrive and take her place at table so that they could start to serve. Over a goblet of wine or two, the conversation continued for a while, until the atmosphere began to get a little strained. All eyes flicked towards the door whenever there was a slight noise, but Gianetta still did not appear.

Cesare was now beginning to look openly annoyed. He would not stand for this behaviour when they were married, and he looked forward to teaching her that lesson.

"Lucia!" Cristina quietly called her over. "Run to her chambers, please, and see what is keeping her. Tell her that our guests are waiting." Lucia nodded and left. Cristina then asked Benedetta to hand around plates of small bites to stave off her guests' hunger. She noticed Cesare push the plate away impatiently and wondered if he might not be the charming young man she had always thought him to be.

Conversation was now quite stilted, and even Maria had ceased her wedding chatter.

Eventually, Lucia returned to the dining room. "*Madonna*," she said with a curtsey. "She will not come. Her door is locked, and she says she is at prayer."

Cesare exploded with rage. "What is this? Are you trying to make a fool of me?! I'm offering to take this bastard off your hands, and her bastard child into the bargain, and this is how you treat me?"

"Cesare, please!" said his mother, blushing with embarrassment. "I'm sure it's just a misunderstanding." She looked pleadingly at Cristina, then Francesco, who both looked at Nonna. Nonna said nothing but watched with interest. Francesco ran his fingers through his hair.

Cristina was the first to find her voice. "Gianetta has been unwell of late. Her pregnancy, you understand..."

"I think it's best if we postpone this dinner, Francesco," said Piero, in a business-like tone. "This is not quite the celebration that we had planned. Perhaps we can rearrange it...if circumstances allow..." Both men cleared their throats and nodded in their discomfort. Maria and Cristina embraced briefly. Cesare pushed back his chair and stormed out of the dining room, closely followed by his parents.

There was an awkward silence before a little voice piped up, "Can we have a slice of cake now, please?"

After a moment of silence, Nonna said, "I think that is a very good idea, young man," and Gino beamed.

Cristina agreed. "There is nothing we can do about this evening, so we might as well eat. Benedetta, take some plates to the kitchen so that you and the staff can enjoy some food too."

Benedetta bobbed in acknowledgement and left with some of the plates.

"Lucia, before you go," Francesco stopped her leaving. "Did Gianetta say anything else to you?"

"Not really, *ser*," she replied. "Only that she was at prayer and was not to be disturbed by anyone. She did add that she had to consider her path...whatever that means."

In the silence that followed, appetites suddenly disappeared, and Nonna closed her eyes as she offered a silent prayer.

CHAPTER 21

The early morning air was cool and fresh when Gianetta stepped into the silent street. She shivered, but she wasn't sure if it was because of the chill or the uncertainty of her future. Turning around, she gently pulled the door closed and gazed up at the grand house which had been her home for so long. The faces of Eleonora and Lucia appeared in her mind's eye: friends, good friends whom she would miss dearly. She thought of the Rosini family and especially little Gino, and she smiled sadly. She so wished that she could see the little boy grow into the man that she knew he would become. Naturally, she also thought of Matteo. She remembered the day that they first met, after he had been given work and lodging at the Palazzo. She remembered that he had been asked to bring some deliveries up to the kitchen. She remembered how he had pushed the heavy kitchen door open and caught sight of her, how he had become flustered and dropped the basket of vegetables over Eleonora's clean kitchen floor. She remembered being captivated by his bright blue eyes and his slow, easy smile. Before she remembered to breathe again, she saw him mouth the words, *"Ciao, Bellissima!"*

True to form, Eleonora had much to say about bruised peaches and dirty carrots, but Matteo hardly heard a word, as Gianetta rushed to help him pick up the vegetables. It didn't take long for their love to grow, and her heart ached when she remembered the first time that she lay in his arms in her small room at the top of the Palazzo. She remembered how he had stroked her cheek, how he had lifted her hair and kissed the small pink birth mark behind her ear and told her that he loved her.

Biting back the tears, she took a deep breath and looked up and down *Via Porta Rossa*, before turning to her left and striding out towards the River Arno.

Her confident stride gradually slowed as she approached the river. She walked along the riverbank for a few minutes before stopping at the edge, lost in thought. She gazed into the deep waters, the eddying current reflecting her thoughts and emotions. How had she got to this? She raised her eyes to the heavens. What was left for her now? Her gaze returned to the turbulent water.

While Gianetta spent several hours gazing into the water, contemplating her fate, La Volpe sat alone in his favourite tavern, gazing into his cup of wine. His mind had been troubled for several days. In the weeks leading up to Easter, he had been busy. He had been busier than he ever had before, transporting secret messages to boarding houses, meeting rooms and grand *palazzi*. He was grateful for the work, of course, but he hadn't given it much thought. It didn't do to dwell on the contents of the messages he delivered. That was a lesson he had learned over the years of his career. His lack of curiosity had made him a discreet and reliable courier of delicate messages. He knew that mostly he delivered the secret love notes of those involved in illicit affairs, business secrets of rivals and anonymous reports of illegal nocturnal activities. For the most part, what he did didn't bother him.

It wasn't his business, so why should it? This time, though, things were different.

On Easter Sunday, he had woken from his hangover, sitting in the doorway of the Baptistry, to carnage. He closed his eyes as remembered the scene. The noise had hit him first and dragged him from his sleep. Screams of hysterical women…and men; shouts of panic from those trying to escape; clashing of metal on metal, as blades continued to fight. As he'd looked around, he'd seen blood, so much blood. One man sat next to him, deathly pale and still, while the red pool around him spread across the paving stones, the gash on his thigh still bleeding but slowly now. A young boy, no more than six years old, had stood in the middle of the piazza, crying and looking around for his parents. Sitting on the steps of the *Duomo*, he had seen a woman sitting still, her hair escaping from its net, her sleeves and skirt torn and bloody. She held a young man in her arms. He was clearly dead. The emptiness in the woman's eyes would haunt his dreams forever.

Taking a gulp of his wine, he shook his head. How much had he been responsible for this? He knew he had delivered many messages in the weeks leading up to Easter, but he hadn't questioned it. He was grateful for the extra business, but was that enough? Should he have asked more questions? No. He shook his head. That wasn't how to do this job. If he hadn't done it, then someone else would. But…did he deliver the instructions to the group responsible for this mess? Was this all down to him?

Marina, the whore from upstairs, came and sat next to him and poured herself a cup of wine from his jug. She moved up close and put her hand between his legs, but he pushed her away. Without a word, she shrugged and moved away to another table, leaving him with his thoughts.

Sitting on the next table were two men. La Volpe had seen them here before, but he hadn't taken much notice of them. Their heads were close together, but their voices were still raised, partly to be heard over the din of the tavern, partly due to the wine they had already consumed. La Volpe noticed them now, though. His ears were attuned to surreptitious conversations. He had conducted many of his own and recognised the signs. He shook his head at the foolishness of conducting their private business under the influence of wine. Wine should always come after business. He was about to turn his attention back to his own wine, when he heard one of the men say, "Mandragora…"

"Mandragora? The poison?" he thought to himself. He'd heard of it being used before, and it had never ended well. He glanced across just as one man handed the other a packet under the table. "So that's what's happening," he thought. "Someone is in for a tough time."

"I thought the first dose would finish him off," said one, "but he's clearly stronger than I thought. I'd better do the job properly this time or I'll be in trouble."

"Why not just stick a blade between his ribs?" The man who had handed over the packet laughed. He'd received his payment and didn't really care what happened next.

"The boss didn't want any mess, but if this doesn't work, I might have to make a quick job of it. I just want this done now. He's not a nice man to work for, let me tell you."

"Who is the poor fellow?"

"I don't know. Some young lad. Seemed a decent enough boy. Completely oblivious to what I was giving him to drink though. Seemed quite grateful, in fact!" They both barked with laughter, slapping each other on the shoulders, as if they'd been part of a great joke.

La Volpe's stomach churned, and he pushed away his wine. Hadn't Florence had enough death lately? He didn't want to be part of that anymore. Perhaps he would just follow the man with the package. Perhaps he would just see where he was going. No more than that. The two men drained their cups and pushed their chairs back as they got up unsteadily and left the tavern. They were too wrapped up in their own world to notice the man with the fox's tail slip out behind them.

Gianetta had spent a tortured morning walking up and down the riverbank, wrestling with her thoughts. The water had always calmed her and helped clear her head, but nothing seemed to be helping. She'd had to fend off unwanted attentions from a group of river workers when she had strayed too far into their territory. Tormenting cat calls from the women in the windows of the bordellos brought her back to reality. She needed to turn back. Turn back? To where? She was becoming despondent, and tears threatened to overwhelm her. Perhaps she should just put her fate into the hands of the River Arno and jump. She retraced her steps along the river and as she continued walking, the river path opened into a small piazza. Of course! The *Chiesa di Ognissanti*...her church. The place where she had always felt welcome, where she could always go for comfort. She needed to pray. For guidance, for inspiration? She didn't know what to pray for, but she knew she needed to pray.

The outside façade of the church was awe-inspiring. Not in the same way as Florence's *Duomo*, but it always made her feel the power of God. She pushed open the small front door and entered the main body of the church. A single small step, and she felt arms of comfort wrapping around her. Nonna was right. God would guide her. He had guided her here this morning, and He would guide her next steps. She sighed gently and put herself in His care.

She walked up the main aisle, slowly, careful not to make a noise. One or two of the faithful were in the church, kneeling, head bowed, sending their prayers and petitions to Heaven. As she reached the front, she genuflected, made the sign of the cross and took a seat to her left. Before kneeling to pray, she looked up at the great crucifix. She remembered overhearing Signor Francesco and Maestro Sandro talking about its painter, someone called Giotto. She didn't know who he was, but never had she seen such skill. He had portrayed the pain of the crucified Christ in a way that tore at her soul. She gazed up at His suffering face and felt such despair that she thought her heart would break.

Shuffling footsteps made her look behind her. Padre Cristoforo had been the priest of *Ognissanti* for many years. Some said that he had been there for over a century and was expected to be there still in the next century. Looking at the old man, Gianetta could almost believe the stories.

He was bent with age and had a slow, unsteady gait. He had wild curly hair, greying now, and gnarled fingers, which always clutched a handkerchief. His eyes, though, held a twinkle and a brightness that showed a sharp, intelligent mind. His face was full of kindness and love. God had truly blessed the people of Florence when He gave this man to care for them.

"Am I interrupting your prayers, child?" he asked Gianetta.

"No, Padre," she replied. "I am glad to see you."

Padre Cristoforo eased himself onto the bench next to her with a heavy sigh. "The Lord has given me many blessings, but some days, I wish He would give me a new back." He smiled and looked at Gianetta carefully. "What troubles you, Gianetta?"

The dam that had held back Gianetta's tears finally burst, and she sobbed, while Padre Cristoforo sat silently next to her.

"I'm so sorry, Padre," she said. "That was unforgiveable."

"Nothing is unforgiveable, child. You know that."

Gianetta nodded, and they sat in silence for several minutes. Then Gianetta turned to him and told him the whole story.

Eventually, Padre Cristoforo said, "The Rosini are kind, good-hearted people. Can you not speak to them about your troubles?"

Gianetta shook her head. "I cannot," she said. "You're right. They have shown me every kindness in so many ways, but I have refused the man they wanted me to marry. I have publicly embarrassed them. I can't possibly return to them. It would be unfair and unkind. I don't know where to turn, Padre."

"You can always turn to God and His church, child." He held up his old, crooked hand before continuing. "I know! That is not what you wanted to hear, although the convent is very welcoming." He paused. "But who do we turn to in times of trouble? Family."

They looked at each other for a long moment, until Padre Cristoforo nodded and painfully stood up.

"May God be with you and your child, Gianetta. I'm sure we will meet again soon," and he left Gianetta deep in thought.

By early afternoon, Gianetta had managed to find something to eat and was beginning to feel a little more positive about her situation, having finally come to a decision. It was clear that she needed to trust her instincts. Her instincts told her that it would be a great mistake to marry Cesare Conti and distressing though it was to leave her home and the people she loved, she knew that she couldn't stay with the Rosini family any longer. Indeed, she didn't know whether they would still accept her after the way she had embarrassed them in front of their friends. She thought of Matteo. Her lungs constricted, and she felt a painful stab of sorrow that she would never see him again, and that he would never meet his baby. She held her growing belly with a protective hand, before turning her steps towards the market.

The market wasn't as busy as in the early morning, and the produce on sale was not as fresh. There were still customers milling around the stalls, though. Those who were looking for a bargain or could not afford the best quality fruit, vegetables, meat or fish could be seen looking carefully at what was left or haggling with the stall holders, who were tired after a long day's trading. Gianetta kept her head bent low. Most of her friends and acquaintances did their shopping in the early morning, but she did not want to be recognised by any of the stallholders.

She was looking for Alessandro, hoping that he had not yet left with his deliveries.

Alessandro was well-known to everyone in Palazzo Rosini, as he delivered the best Chianti wine from the Tuscan vineyards to the richest families and houses in Florence and the surrounding areas. Signor Francesco entertained many of his clients at home and had a mutually beneficial arrangement with some of the vineyards, meaning that Alessandro was a regular visitor to Palazzo Rosini. He was a gruff-looking character, with a large belly, presumably from sampling the wares that he transported. His stained moustache supported the truth of the theory. His demeanour didn't encourage social chat, especially as his favourite topic was complaining about his domineering wife and the demands of his five children. However, if he was caught in the right mood, he would be happy to do a favour for his friends and customers.

Gianetta hoped that today would be such a day. She made her way to Alessandro's yard, not far from the market. The big doors were closed, and her heart sank. As she neared the yard, though, she could hear Alessandro talking to his horses, and she breathed a great sigh of relief.

"Now to hope that he is in the mood to help!" she said to herself and stepped forward to knock hard on the gates. Muffled curses ricocheted around the yard, and heavy footsteps made their way toward the gate before it was flung open. A large belly, covered in a worn leather apron, and an unkempt moustache peered into the street.

"*Chi è?* Who is it?" he barked. "Oh, it's you! What do you want? I'm busy." And he turned away, back to his horses. They were harnessed to a great cart, already loaded with barrels to be delivered to his customers. Alessandro returned to his task of checking the ropes, making sure that they were secure.

Gianetta took a deep breath. This wasn't going to be as easy as she had hoped. She followed him into the yard. "Alessandro, I need your help."

"Ha! *Le donne!* Women! You're all the same. You always need something from Alessandro. My wife wants me to fix the roof. My daughters want me to provide them with husbands. They all want my wages. Well, there is nothing left to give. I work all day, every day, and there is nothing left for Alessandro. What makes you think I will give you anything?"

"I don't want you to give me anything, Alessandro." She explained what she wanted from him and waited while he thought.

Eventually, he nodded with a grunt and carried on with his preparations.

Across the Arno, La Volpe followed the two men until they went their separate ways. He stayed with the man carrying the package, as he stumbled along the road, taking them further into the poorest area at the edge of the city. The roads became narrower, as the houses got closer together. La Volpe stepped over piles of human excrement that had been emptied from windows above. His work took him to all levels of society, but even he had rarely ventured into this part of Florence. He kept the man in his sights but made sure to stay well enough behind so as not to be noticed.

Eventually, the man stopped at what looked like an animal pen or a storage shed. The door was old and warped, but it was held in place with a shiny lock. The man fumbled about in his trouser pocket until he brought out a key. Letting himself in, he closed the door behind him, as La Volpe slipped into the tiny alleyway opposite. The man was only inside for a few moments before he re-emerged. He stopped at the doorway, looking back inside. He seemed to nod in satisfaction before locking the door and heading back down the road.

When he had disappeared from view, La Volpe ran from the alleyway straight at the door of the shed. It was so rotten that it gave way easily. He stood in the doorway for a moment, letting his eyes adjust to the darkness, while covering his nose and mouth from the stench of excrement, sweat and vomit. A movement in the corner of the room caught his eye. A figure crouched on a dirty, makeshift bed. The figure hadn't seemed to notice the intrusion, as he raised a cup to his lips. In one bound, La Volpe strode across the room and knocked the cup from his hand, sending its contents flying against the wall. Turning back to the figure on the bed, he saw that he was a young man, tall, probably, although it was difficult to tell as he was curled up on the bed. His black hair was plastered to his face with sweat and vomit.

Still dazed from the mandragora in his system, Matteo looked up at his saviour. "Are you Botticelli?" he asked, slurring his words. "You look like Botticelli...except taller...and thinner... I expect I'm late for work. Am I late for work? Can I grind the colours today? I've always wanted to grind the colours, and I've seen so many colours in this room."

La Volpe looked around at the dank, dark shed and couldn't

imagine any colour making an appearance in this wretched place. "It's the mandragora," he said, turning back to Matteo, who was heaving what little remained in his stomach onto the floor.

"Come on. Let's get you out of this place." He hauled Matteo up off the bed, hoisted his arm over his shoulder and grasped him around the waist. Throwing his cloak around them both, he dragged Matteo to the door. The alleyway was dull. The houses were so close together and so miserable that little sunlight was able to penetrate it, and yet Matteo still squinted at the bright light. With no plan of what to do with the boy, La Volpe knew that he had to get him as far away from this place as possible.

The people they passed paid no attention to them, assuming that Matteo was just another drunk being dragged home, but as they got closer to the river and into the main part of the city, this changed. Passers-by started to give them a wide berth, some looking disgusted, some looking amused, most covering their nose and mouth from the smell.

Matteo was still suffering the effects of the drugged drink. He'd shouted that the Arno was running purple, and he stopped to have a conversation with a cat called Gianetta.

La Volpe knew that he had to do something with the boy...but he couldn't just dump him in the street. "Botticelli," he thought. "He must work for someone called Botticelli. Botticelli...Botticelli..." He racked his brains to place the vaguely familiar name, until he remembered who he was talking about. "The painter! Yes!" He had a rough idea where the painter had his workshop, and it wasn't too far away, thankfully. The boy was getting heavy.

They crossed the river and made their way along the bank, until they reached the *Chiesa di Ognissanti,* where they turned into the road leading away from the river. Eventually, the painter's workshop could be seen at the end of the road, and La Volpe breathed an exhausted sigh of relief.

CHAPTER 22

It was just half an hour earlier when Carlo, Sandro's foreman, returned to the painter's workshop from Palazzo Rosini, having delivered Signor Francesco's commissioned painting. The family had seemed somewhat distracted but were pleased with the painting. He marvelled to himself, as he always did, at the skill of the Maestro and the images he created. He entered the workshop on the *Via Nuova*, where the bright spring sunshine lit the spacious working area.

The air was thick with dust as one of the apprentices, Dino, prepared a large panel in readiness for the Maestro's next commission. It was at the very beginning of its journey to become a masterpiece of art. Made of poplar wood, Dino had collected it from Giacomo, the carpenter, who had prepared the thin layers of wood in readiness for painting. Dino was now sanding it to a smooth finish, after which, he would apply several layers of gesso, a thick mixture of gypsum and animal glue. The final layer of gesso would then be highly polished in readiness for the application of the Maestro's strokes of genius.

Carlo nodded an acknowledgement to Dino and moved on.

Behind a curtain, in a separate room and away from the dust, Lapo was preparing pigments for the tempera paint favoured by the Maestro. Some of the materials used in this process were very rare and expensive and could only be handled by his most trusted and experienced apprentices. This afternoon, Lapo was washing and grinding azurite, a heavenly blue which would create the perfect veil for the Virgin Mary in a future work of art. It would hang in a chapel or dining room for many years to come, depending on who wanted to pay most to assuage their sins. Lapo had been working on this task for most of the day, and it was hard work. His face was streaked with shades of azurite blue, vermillion red and the yellow of orpiment, where he had wiped away the sweat from his brow.

Carlo stepped from behind the curtain and stopped to check Lapo's work and the quality of the materials.

"This is a good batch, Signor Carlo," said Lapo. "It grinds well, and the colour is rich."

"Yes," replied Carlo. "Now I have delivered his latest commission to Palazzo Rosini, the Maestro will be keen to flourish his paintbrushes again soon! Good work, Lapo." And he patted him on the back and went to the stairs in the corner of the room.

Lapo stretched his neck, shrugged his aching shoulders and continued his work.

Upstairs, Carlo found the Maestro, Signor Sandro, making notes and sketches at his desk. His head was bowed low, and he was muttering, scribbling and scratching out his work. Carlo knew better than to distract him. When Signor Sandro was frustrated and waiting for his creative mood to appear, only the ignorant or the foolish would dare to interrupt him. Carlo took the bag of money from his pocket and the papers of receipt recently signed by Signor Francesco, and deposited them in the strong box, carefully locking it and storing the key in his pocket.

As he made his way back downstairs, he heard an urgent knocking on the workshop door. Somebody was hammering on the door loud enough to wake the dead. "*Madonna Santa!* Who needs a painting this urgently?" He opened the door, ready to share some choice words with whoever was making such a racket, but instead, he felt a heavy weight fall onto his feet.

"Matteo? Is that you? It can't be!" He kneeled next to the slumped figure in the doorway, recoiling slightly from the smell. The boy looked drunk. Carlo looked exasperated. "Dino! DINO! I need help."

The young apprentice ran out to the door, stopping in shock when he saw who was on the floor by his foreman. "But he's dead! He was hanged! Everyone knows that!"

"Well, like the Messiah, he has risen. He's clearly not dead. He's drunk. Now, help me get him inside."

Carlo lifted Matteo's shoulders, while Dino picked up his feet, and they took him into the main room of the workshop, laying him on a pile of dust sheets.

"Matteo!" he said, kicking his feet to wake him. "MATTEO! Wake up, boy!"

Matteo stirred and tried to focus on the source of the voice. "I'm awake...I'm awake!" he said. He didn't see Carlo had picked up a bucket of cold water until it hit him in the face. After several minutes of cursing that would have brought blushes to the bordellos of the Oltrarno, Matteo sat up cold and wet, yet still dazed and confused. He gazed at Carlo with a puzzled look on his face. "I know you. Don't I know you?"

Carlo looked at Dino. "He's either very, very drunk, or..."

"Mangra...dor," said Matteo.

"What?"

"Mangra...dora...mandragora. He told me to tell you mandragora."

"Who told you?"

"The man."

"What man?

"Just…the man." Matteo settled back on the dust sheets as if it was a feather bed and drifted off to sleep.

Carlo sat back on his heels and looked with concern at the sleeping boy. "Dino, run to Palazzo Rosini and fetch the cook, Eleonora. She'll know what to do"

Dino ran from the room, and Carlo made himself comfortable next to Matteo, hoping that Eleonora would be quick.

Matteo stirred. "Did I tell you she is carrying my child?" he said.

"Who? Gianetta? Yes, I know that, Matteo," Carlo replied, gently.

"I dreamt of her last night, you know. A beautiful vivid dream. I could have been there, it was so real. She was in a forest of orange trees, but not just orange trees. There were flowers of so many kinds there, impossible to count, but so beautiful..." He sighed before continuing. "At one side, there was Zephyrus."

"Who?" asked Carlo.

"Zephyrus," replied Matteo. "An old Greek god, I think. I remember someone saying something about him being responsible for the March wind. He looked like he was trying to catch hold of a woman with leaves around her. Next to her was a young girl in a floral dress, and she was scattering flowers around her, as if there weren't already enough! Further out to the side, was another group of young girls, all in floaty gowns and dancing with each other. But in the centre, oh, in the centre was my beautiful Gianetta. She was dressed in rich clothing…as I assume she always will be now." Matteo paused, sniffed and wiped his nose on his filthy sleeve. "Yes, a rich white gown that showed her swollen belly. Such a wondrous sight, don't you think? A red cloak draped over her shoulder and around her belly. There isn't a sight as wondrous as a beautiful woman who is with-child, don't you think?"

Carlo nodded with a smile.

Matteo continued. "Did I say there were flowers? So many flowers. I suppose it must have been spring...*primavera*."

Neither of them noticed the Maestro, who had come to see what the hubbub was about and was now nodding and scribbling furiously.

As if he hadn't spoken, Matteo lay back and slept again. Carlo shook his head.

"What has happened to you, boy? Who has done this to you?"

"Will the boy be well?" asked Signor Sandro.

"I hope so. I have sent for help."

The Maestro nodded, turned and went back to his room.

Several minutes later, Dino came running into the workshop, closely followed by a puffing Eleonora.

Carlo jumped up at the sight of her. "Eleonora! I'm so glad to see you. That is...I mean... It's Matteo. He needs help. I think he's been drugged with mandragora. Can you help him?"

Even in such a serious situation, Eleonora had the power to make Carlo tongue-tied. She went straight to Matteo and knelt beside him. "His heart is racing," she said, with her hand on his chest. "Has he been hallucinating?"

"Hallucinating?"

"Yes," she said, impatiently. "Has he been seeing things? Things that are not there?"

"Yes. When he hasn't been sleeping like this, he has been saying some very strange things."

"Hmm. Has he vomited?"

"Judging by the smell, I would say yes."

"Good." Eleonora nodded. "I think he will be ok. We just have to keep a close eye on him, give him water and wait for him to wake up.

I think you're right, but what made you say mandragora?"

"Matteo said it. He said the man told him to say mandragora." He shrugged as Eleonora looked up at him, quizzically. "I don't know what man. It's just what he said. I assume Matteo has a guardian angel."

Eleonora snorted. "It was no guardian angel that did this to him. We thought he had been hanged. At least that's what Signor Cesare said…" She tailed off, biting her lip. Snapping her attention back to Carlo, she said, "I have to go and prepare dinner, but I shall come back later. I won't mention this back at the Palazzo just yet. I need to think. Try to listen to anything he says. It might be a mumble or sound like nonsense, but it might be useful. We need to know how he came to be in this state. Oh, and don't tell him about Gianetta."

"Gianetta? What about her?"

"She's gone."

"Gone?"

Eleonora huffed, impatiently. "Yes, Carlo. Gone. Disappeared. Run away."

Carlo put his hand to his forehead. "Oh no! What happened?" he whispered.

"It's a long story, with, I think, a little treachery."

"Matteo will be devastated."

"Yes." She put her hands on her hips and looked at the sleeping boy with sadness. "Yes, he will, and after all he has been through, we will have to be careful how he hears the news. Wait until I return this evening, and I will explain it all."

"*Sì. Grazie,* Eleonora. *Grazie.*"

Eleonora closed the door quietly as she left, and Carlo settled himself on the floor next to Matteo.

As the afternoon wore on, Matteo began to show signs of recovery, waking to take a drink of water, recognising Carlo and his surroundings but not questioning why he was there. He was still very sleepy. By evening, the sun had set, and Carlo had lit some lanterns, but he still sat with Matteo.

He was recovering quite quickly now and was beginning to ask questions. "What am I doing here, Carlo? My head feels as though it's stuffed with straw, and I can't quite think straight. Everything is such a muddle." Then he sat bolt upright. "Gianetta! Where is Gianetta? Is she safe? Where is she?"

Carlo put his hands on the boy's shoulders to calm him. "*Calmati! Calmati!* As far as I know, Gianetta is fine. Things have been a bit… eventful around here, lately, but Eleonora knows more than I. She will be here soon, and then we will know."

Matteo seemed to accept this, and after a thoughtful silence, asked what Carlo had been up to that day.

"Well," began Carlo. "This morning, I delivered Signor Sandro's latest commission to Signor Francesco and Donna Cristina at Palazzo Rosini. Such a wonderful painting. Nobody prepares tempera like our Lapo, and the brush strokes of the Maestro? Simply genius! The figures are so life-like, I almost expected them to speak to me. The Rosini are so very lucky to be able to look at such work every day. They were so delighted, they begged me to take some refreshments in the kitchen before I left. Of course, Eleonora's cooking is legendary, so how could I refuse such an invitation? How lucky was I? Eleonora had just prepared her famous *zuccotto*. When she brought it out from the cold room, my eyes almost popped out of my head. Such a magnificent dome of a cake! It could almost rival Signor Brunelleschi's dome atop our beloved *Duomo*. She cut a generous slice for me, and the aroma! Oh Matteo, the aroma of that alchermes liqueur is heavenly.

No wonder the Medici buy so much of it."

Matteo smiled as he watched and listened to Carlo talking about Eleonora. He was right. Her cooking was second to none, but he had a feeling it was not just her culinary skills that Carlo admired. They carried on talking about the Maestro's painting and Eleonora's cooking until they heard a knock at the door.

"Carlo? It's me."

Recognising Eleonora's voice, Carlo jumped up and opened the door.

Eleonora came in with her arms full, and Carlo helped relieve her of her packages. "I've brought some food. I doubt either of you have eaten all day."

Carlo's eyes lit up. He was indeed very hungry, and he knew that whatever may be in those packages, it would surely be delicious.

"But first, let's clean you up, Matteo. You look a mess, and you smell worse. Carlo, fetch some water. I've brought some clean clothes from Antonio's room." There was an uncomfortable silence, as they thought of Antonio's fate. "You look better, though, Matteo," said Eleonora. "How are you feeling?"

"Yes, better," he replied. "I still have a dreadful headache, and my thoughts are a big jumble, but I am feeling much better. Eleonora, what's been happening? Please tell me."

Looking at the desperation in his eyes, Eleonora thought her heart would break with the news she had to share. "I will, child, but first, clean yourself up and let us have some food."

A short while later, Matteo was looking and feeling more like himself, and Carlo was patting his stomach in satisfaction.

"Now, Eleonora," said Matteo. "Tell me. How is Gianetta? Can I come back with you to see her?"

"It's…not quite as simple as that, Matteo," she replied. Wondering how best to tell the story, she decided to go back…was it really only a few days? "You know that she had recently discovered Signor Niccolò was her father?"

Matteo nodded. Carlo kept quiet and watched. There had been talk of little else since the news came out before Signor Niccolò's funeral.

"Well, after you left…" Matteo opened his mouth to speak, but Eleonora raised her hand. "I'm sure you had good reason, but we will come to that soon enough. After you left, Donna Cristina had Gianetta moved into one of the guest rooms as part of the family."

Matteo nodded. He knew that this is what Donna Cristina had wanted for Gianetta.

"Of course, she wasn't pleased, but she did as she was asked. She worried about you constantly. A few days later, the Contis came to visit. They came to…" Eleonora paused. "They came to arrange the betrothal between Gianetta and Signor Cesare."

"WHAT?" Matteo jumped up from the bed, spilling his cup of water over the floor.

"Sit down, Matteo," said Eleonora, quietly. "There's more."

Matteo swayed slightly, then sat down on the wet dustsheets, staring into space.

"Matteo, Signor Cesare told the family…and Gianetta… that someone had seen you kill Signor Niccolò."

Matteo looked as though all the breath had left his body. "No! No, that can't be. He told me that he believed it was an accident. He told me that nobody would ever know. He told me that he would protect me. He…" Matteo looked up at Eleonora and Carlo. "He planned this all along!"

"Perhaps it's time for you to tell us your story," said Carlo.

"Yes, what happened to you, child? Maybe we can make sense of all this."

"The day that Gianetta found out about Signor Niccolò being her father, she came to my room. She was upset, because the family wanted her to be part of their family now, but we wanted to be together. We planned to get married. You know that she is carrying my baby?"

Eleonora smiled and nodded. "Yes, I know."

"Anyway, we were in my room, wondering what we could do, when Signor Cesare came to my room. I thought he had come to make a pass at me."

Whatever they had been expecting, neither Carlo nor Eleonora expected that.

"He knew I had seen him coming from...well...coming from a sodomite house. I'd seen him more than once, often when I was running errands for Signor Francesco or you, Eleonora, but only once he saw me. He spoke to me about it on the night of the dinner with Signori Lorenzo and Giuliano, the night the stone nearly killed Signor Giuliano. He said he was grateful to me. That he would remember the good turn I had done by not reporting him. He made it sound as though he would do me a favour one day, but it felt more like a threat.

"When he came to my room, I was mistaken. He wasn't there to make a pass at me. He was there to protect me, he said. He said that he saw me grasp the blade that killed Signor Niccolò, and he saw me stab him. He said he knew it was an accident but nobody else would believe it. If I didn't run, somebody would find me, and I would hang for it." He looked at Eleonora with desperation in his eyes. "You have to believe me. I didn't do it. At least, I don't think I did." He glanced at the wound on his hand, which had almost completely healed by now. "So, it seemed that he had come to do me a favour, after all. He promised that he knew where I could hide out until it was all over, and then I could send for Gianetta."

"What about Signor Francesco and Donna Cristina? What would

they think when Gianetta left them without a word?"

"I think we thought we would be helping them. We thought it would be better for the family not to have to worry about her or the baby."

Eleonora said nothing but waited for him to continue.

"So, I left. He said he had a safe place but first, we would stop for a drink. We went across the river to a tavern. It was rough. I was surprised that he knew about such a place, but it seemed he'd been there before, because he spoke with some of the men there. We sat, and we drank…and that's the last I remember until I woke up here."

"Do you remember how you got here?" asked Carlo.

Matteo frowned. "Not really. I seem to remember being supported by a man. He reminded me of a fox, but I can't remember why." He shook his head. "No, I'm sorry. I don't remember anything. Can we go to see Gianetta now? They won't expect her to marry Cesare now that I'm back, will they?"

"Matteo, I still haven't told you everything. When Signor Cesare came with his parents to offer marriage to Gianetta, he also brought more news. He told them that you had been caught and hanged."

"Why would he do that? It doesn't make sense."

"Of course it makes sense, boy" said Carlo. "Your mind still isn't right, because you would have worked it out, like I have. That was his plan all along. Getting rid of you (because that was obviously his intention from the start) was of great benefit to him. You held a secret about him that could easily cause him a lot of trouble with his family and the society that he inhabits. He didn't know if he could rely on you to keep that secret. The additional benefit of your absence would be that Gianetta would be free to marry. Like all of us, he must have heard that Signor Niccolò was her father. It would be a very convenient way into a very rich and powerful family."

"He's already very rich!"

"For a man like Cesare Conti, there is never enough wealth in the coffers. An alliance with a family like the Rosini would ensure that he could continue his lifestyle for many years to come. Finding out that Gianetta is pregnant just played into his hands. He would be seen as a saviour to the Rosini, helping them out of a difficult situation. I'm afraid you just had to go. I'm guessing that whoever was hired to finish you off with the mandragora drink didn't do their job properly. It could easily have killed you, but it can't have been strong enough. Am I right, Eleonora?"

Eleonora nodded. "I think you have it quite right, Carlo."

"Then we can just go back to the Palazzo and tell them everything." Matteo was on his feet again, making for the door.

"Matteo…Gianetta is missing."

Matteo's head spun round to look at Eleonora, his eyes wide in terror. "Missing?"

"There was a dinner last night, to celebrate the betrothal. The whole family and the Contis were there, but Gianetta didn't come. Lucia went to her room, but she wouldn't come out. She said she was praying. Signor Cesare was furious," she said with a hint of a smile. "The next morning, this morning, she had gone. Her room was empty. Signor Francesco has been out all day, looking for her, but he came back this evening with no news. We are all so very worried about her. I'm afraid that she might have…that she might have done something terrible."

"We must go back to the Palazzo. We must go now."

"They believe you killed Signor Niccolò," said Carlo with warning in his voice. "They think you've been hanged. They might very well send for the authorities so that you do hang."

"What does that matter? Gianetta and the baby are in danger. I have to do something!" Matteo flung the door open and headed out into the street.

DOLCE

When we have taken our fill of all that the previous courses had to offer, we start to crave something a little sweeter, something to ease the heaviness that has gone before. The final course, the Dolce, provides this sweetness, a little indulgence that will bring a smile and round off the story and the meal with satisfaction.

Torta della Nonna (Nonna/Grandma's Cake)

Pastry:
450g plain flour/00 flour • 200g butter • 160g caster sugar
2 eggs • Grated zest of 1 lemon • Pinch salt

Custard:
750ml full fat milk • 2 tablespoons plain flour/00 flour
2 tablespoons cornflour • 3 eggs + 1 egg yolk
225g caster sugar • Peeled zest of 1 lemon

Topping:
25g pine nuts (soaked) • Icing sugar

Make the shortcrust pastry by rubbing the butter into the flour until the mixture resembles breadcrumbs, then stir in the sugar, salt and finally mix in the eggs and lemon zest. Wrap the pastry and refrigerate for about 1hr.

Make the custard by gently heating the milk with the lemon peel. In a separate bowl, mix the eggs, yolk and sugar. Sift flours and mix into egg mixture. Remove lemon peel from milk and pour a small amount into the egg/flour mixture. Once mixed, return to the pan and cook slowly, stirring, until it thickens. Remove from heat and cool.

Line a 10" pie dish with half of the pastry, pricking the bottom. Fill with the cooled custard, then top with remaining pastry. Prick top, then sprinkle soaked pine nuts over the top.

Cook in a preheated oven (160° fan) for about 40 mins. Cool, then sprinkle with icing sugar.

CHAPTER 23

It was by now late evening, and most of the family had retired to bed. All except Francesco. His dear friend, Lorenzo, had arrived unannounced after dinner. They had not seen each other since the dreadful events of Easter Sunday and had much to catch up on. Francesco found Marco completing his final chores before heading to Antonio's room, where he now lived.

"Marco, we need wine," he said. "Fetch two cups and a jug of wine and bring them to the *sala*. Then you can go to bed."

Marco bowed and quickly ran to the kitchen. He still felt that he had to prove his worth to his new master and was keen to impress.

Francesco and Lorenzo settled themselves in the comfortable chairs of the *sala*. After Francesco had been reassured that Lorenzo's injury was healing well, their conversation turned to the aftermath of the attack in the *Duomo*.

"I saw them all hang, Francesco," said Lorenzo, clutching his cup, still seething with anger and grief at his brother's death. "I watched every one of them dangle by their necks. Even those Pazzi bastards. We got them, too, you know. Jacopo ran. So much for being the head of a dynasty. He ran, like the coward he is, but we got him. They found him in Castagno and brought him back. After some time in our dungeons, he was thrown out of the window of the *Palazzo della Signoria*, where he dangled next to Salviati, that other traitor."

"He was tortured?"

"He was given time to think about what he had done... Their death was too quick a punishment for their deeds, but if God is just, they will be in Hell's torment for eternity."

Francesco nodded, thinking of how Matteo had taken his son from him so violently. "It doesn't take the pain away, though, does it?"

"Francesco, *mio amico*. I am so sorry! I have been so wrapped up in my own troubles that I forgot you're grieving too. Please forgive me."

"Nothing to forgive," said Francesco with a sad smile. "We are both grieving, but you also have to worry about Florence and its people. It's a difficult time for us all."

"How are Cristina and Tessa coping?"

"They are devastated of course but coping surprisingly well. They are strong women. Gino keeps Tessa busy, and we have Gianetta to think about now, too."

"Gianetta? I'm afraid you have lost me."

"Of course, you won't have heard what has been going on here." Francesco proceeded to tell Lorenzo about how they had recognised a likeness in Gianetta and discovered that she was Niccolò's daughter.

"So! You have a granddaughter?"

"More than that, I am to be a great-grandfather!"

Lorenzo laughed loudly, for what felt like the first time in a very long time. "Ah, my friend, how time passes, and age catches up with us all. So, the girl is with-child, eh? Do you know who the father is?"

Francesco's face clouded over. "I do. Matteo. The boy who was part of your staff that day."

Lorenzo nodded. "Tall boy. Black hair. He seems a decent enough boy. I assume you'll pay him off?"

"No, I won't be paying him off. He was one of those you saw hanged."

Lorenzo sat forward on his seat, looking at Francesco in shock. "Hanged? Was he part of it? I must say, that shocks me. I thought I was a good judge of character, and I would have considered him an honest, loyal boy. Are you sure?"

"I agree with you, Lorenzo. I thought the same as you, but the worst part of it is that he was the one to kill Niccolò."

"Where did you get that idea?" Lorenzo looked horrified.

"The Conti boy, Cesare. He saw it all." The muscle in Francesco jaw pulsed with anger.

Lorenzo opened his mouth to speak but was interrupted by an urgent knocking on the door.

In one large stride, still feeling the anger and betrayal of Niccolò's death, Francesco pulled the door open to look straight into the eyes of Matteo. All the pent-up emotions of the last days overflowed from every pore of Francesco's being, and he launched himself at Matteo, grabbing him by the collar of his tunic and pulling him into the room. Throwing him up against the wall, his face inches away from Matteo's, he grasped Matteo's throat and snarled through gritted teeth.

"How dare you! How dare you show your face here! I know what you did to my son. I know that you killed my Niccolò. I thought you had hanged already, but by God, you will hang before tomorrow is out."

Lorenzo forced his way between them, peeling Francesco's fingers from Matteo's throat. "Enough, Francesco," he said, pushing Matteo into a chair, while Francesco paced the room, simmering with rage.

"*Ser*, I am sorry, but you are mistaken," said Matteo. He was shaken, but his words came out with a confidence neither of them expected. "*Ser*, I did not kill Signor Niccolò. By the blood of all the saints and our holy Mother Mary, I swear to you that I did not kill him."

"Boy, you were seen. Cesare Conti saw you do it. He told me he saw you stab my son."

"The boy is right, Francesco. He didn't stab Niccolò," said Lorenzo, bringing a shocked silence to the room.

Matteo looked at Lorenzo with relief and gratitude. He knew that he was going to have a difficult time convincing everyone that he didn't kill Niccolò, but here was a man, a very powerful man, who believed him.

"But Cesare saw him," Francesco spluttered. "He said he saw him plunge the blade into his chest. Are you saying he was mistaken?"

"I am saying the boy didn't do it," said Lorenzo firmly. "It's one of the few memories I have of that day. Someone was coming at you with a knife, and young Matteo here was coming to your defence, when someone knocked him on the head, and he went down, out cold. After that, someone else jumped over one of the benches and stabbed Niccolò. I don't know who he was. I'd never seen him before, but he was caught and killed by one of my men. After that, everything is a bit hazy for me, but that is something I remember clearly."

"But, Cesare… He saw him…" Francesco was looking more and more confused.

"That would be some feat. I saw the young Conti boy leave through the side door at the start of Mass. I would only assume that he knew there was going to be trouble."

Francesco sat in his chair, eyes flitting around the room, hands shaking, as he tried to make sense of everything that he had learned.

Matteo sat quietly but breathing deeply, as he recovered from

Francesco's outburst.

Lorenzo filled Francesco's cup with wine and handed his own to Matteo, who took it gratefully.

After several minutes of silence, Francesco turned to Matteo. "Please accept my apologies. I hope you are not hurt."

"No, *ser*. I'm fine. I half expected it. We figured out what was going on."

"We?"

"Yes, me, Eleonora, Carlo...Carlo looked after me."

"I don't understand. I think you'd better tell me everything. This evening just keeps getting stranger."

So, Matteo recounted the story again, this time including his discussion with Carlo and Eleonora and how they worked out what Cesare had been up to.

"Signor Francesco," finished Matteo, standing up. "I must look for Gianetta. I just have to find her. Florence is not safe for a woman on her own." He turned to Lorenzo. "You must know this."

Lorenzo, not used to being addressed with such informality from a servant, nevertheless understood the seriousness of the situation and nodded. As he was standing, Matteo felt the room spin and his feet and fingers become cold and sweaty.

Francesco caught him before he hit the floor, and the two men managed to carry the young servant to the long sofa. "Clearly, the drug is not out of his system yet. You're not going anywhere tonight, boy," he said to the unconscious Matteo. Turning to Lorenzo, he said, "The boy is right, though. A young girl is not safe on her own in Florence at night."

"I pray that one day soon, anyone will be safe to walk the streets of our beloved city, but until that time, we must do what we can to protect our citizens...and she is one of our citizens." Standing up, he made for the door. "I will get some of my men to continue looking overnight. If she is in Florence, I swear we will find her." And he left, closing the door behind him.

Earlier that afternoon, Alessandro had led the horses around his delivery route and was now heading out of Florence, encouraging them to draw the heavy load up the steep hills into the mountains. It was a long and uncomfortable journey, and Alessandro was not the best conversationalist, but that suited Gianetta. It meant that she could be alone with her thoughts, as the horses drew the laden cart through the streets of Florence. They had stopped at two large houses so far, and the time it took to unload a barrel of wine at each stop seemed interminable to Gianetta. She needed to get to her destination soon. She needed to know that she had made the right choice. Shaking herself out of this train of thought, she said to herself, "We will get there when we get there."

The journey, if anything, seemed to get slower and slower, but Gianetta was now resigned to the speed and was simply grateful that she was nearly there.

Finally, Alessandro pulled the cart to a stop. They were standing in the main square of Fiesole, alongside the old Cathedral of San Romolo.

Gianetta climbed down from the cart slowly, stretching her painful limbs after the journey. "Thank you, Alessandro. I'm so grateful for your help," she said.

Alessandro looked at her kindly and said, "God be with you, child." He flicked the reins, and the cart trundled off further into the town.

Gianetta looked up at the façade of the old cathedral. It wasn't the same as her *Chiesa di Ognissanti*, but there was a childhood familiarity to the building that comforted her. Offering up a little prayer, she turned her steps to a small road that led downhill and out of the main town. On her way, she passed the Villa Medici, and she paused to look through the gates. The gardens had always fascinated her, with beautiful trees and flowers and a wonderful view across the valley.

"Time to see Mamma, now," she said to herself, as she left the gates and carried on down the narrow road towards the farmhouse, where she had spent a happy childhood with Mamma Sofia. She realised how much they had to talk about: her life in the Palazzo; her friends; Nonna Isabetta…her father… She wondered if she should be angry that the secret had been kept from her, but then realised that there was little point in futile recriminations now. Mamma Sofia had done what she thought best for her, just as she had always done. How could she possibly argue with that? "Best to look forward now," she thought to herself. "I have more pressing concerns to deal with."

She thought about her future. She would spend it with Mamma Sofia. She would tend the garden; she would help with the sewing tasks that came in from the village; she would cook and clean, just like at the Palazzo, and she would look after her child with Mamma's help. Although she knew that Mamma Sofia was actually her grandmother, she would always consider her as her mother. Nobody could have given her more love throughout her childhood. There would always be a hole in her life, left by Matteo, but what could she do? She promised that her little one would know everything about their father, how he had loved her and how he had wanted to meet his child so much. Her child would know that they were loved by both parents and that he had been taken from them by a cruel trick of fate. She brushed away a tear. She vowed that her child would know love and not be fuelled by the hatred that had filled the hearts of so many in Florence. Fiesole was a good place to bring up a child. She was sorry that the baby would miss the love of their paternal great-grandparents, Eleonora, Lucia...oh, and their cousin, little Gino. She smiled as she thought of the games they could have played, but it was not to be. So be it. Gianetta was not given to pointless sentiment. By this time, she had reached the end of the track and come across the entrance to the farm.

She rested her hand on the warm wood of the gate, feeling its familiar smoothness and knowing exactly when it would creak as she opened it. Walking up the path, she looked at the house, old and homely...her home. She felt like a child again, returning from the market. Just as she did then, she called out, "Mamma? Mamma, I'm home!"

The door opened, slowly at first, two dark brown eyes peering through the gap. Then the eyes widened, and the door was flung open. "Gianetta! *Oh, mia bambina! Sei a casa!* You have come home!" The frail-looking woman took hold of Gianetta and hugged her with all the strength of her youth. When she finally let go, she held her at arm's length and looked closely at her, tears coursing down the furrows of her weather-beaten skin.

Gianetta thought that the smile on her grandmother's face was the most beautiful thing she had ever seen. "Mamma, I..."

"Not a word, child. There is enough time for talk later. Come inside and have some food and water. You look as though you need it...both of you."

Gianetta smiled and rested her hand on her small bump. Mamma never missed much. She followed her inside, the old sights and smells wrapping themselves round her, comforting her like a warm blanket. She let Mamma fuss over her, making sure she was comfortable, had enough to eat and had drunk plenty of water. It was so wonderful to be cared for like this again, to be loved and cherished. If only... All the emotions of the last few days crashed over her and broke like a tidal wave from her. As she sobbed, Mamma put her gentle arms around her and rocked her like she did when she was a child.

"Mamma is here, *bambina*. All is well. Whatever it is, we can work it out."

"Oh, Mamma, we can't. Nothing will ever be the same again."

"Tell me everything, child. Start at the beginning."

Gianetta started by tell her about the events in the *Duomo* on Easter Sunday.

Mamma Sofia nodded. "I had heard of this from Tommaso. He had been into the city to get some supplies. Such blasphemy during Mass!" She crossed herself, bristling with anger.

"One of the men who died was Signor Niccolò, Signor Francesco's son." She looked carefully at the old woman, who met her gaze and nodded.

"You know?"

"Yes, Mamma, I know now, but only after he had died. Why didn't you tell me before I left for Palazzo Rosini?" She didn't feel angry about this anymore, just curious.

"I wasn't sure if I should tell you, child, but Isabetta…Nonna Isabetta… advised me to keep the secret. She said it was for Signor Niccolò to reveal it himself. I'm sorry that he didn't get the chance to do that."

"Nonna said that he recognised me."

"You are very much like your mother," she said softly, gently tucking a dark curl of hair behind Gianetta's ear.

"She said that he didn't know what to do for the best. That he wanted to protect me but was ashamed of having walked away and was afraid I would reject him. He deeply regretted his decision to leave, she said."

"He was a good boy," said Mamma. "He loved Clara very much,

and your mother loved him very much too. I think it was the weakness of youth that made him leave."

"I wish I had had the chance to speak to him, Mamma."

"I know, child… Tell me what else has happened to you to bring you home to me."

Gianetta told her of her love for Matteo and their baby, how Cesare had promised to protect him but had told her that he had been hanged, how the families arranged their betrothal. Then she told her how she had run away, how she contemplated the great Arno River and how easy it would have been to simply jump in. "But then I saw my church. Nonna had told me to put myself in God's hands, so I went in. I knelt and prayed for a while. Then Padre Cristoforo came to speak with me. He talked about family. I think he meant the Rosini family or the church's family, but I knew God meant me to come home to you. So here I am."

Listening to her story, Mamma went through a whole spectrum of emotions. She felt the happiness of Gianetta's love for Matteo and hope for her baby. She felt such rage at Cesare for not keeping his promise of protecting Matteo. She felt the heart-breaking sadness of Gianetta's realisation that she would never see her love again. She felt complete despair, as Gianetta told of how she stared into the depths of the river, but finally she felt the overwhelming relief of her home coming.

"You are here now, child. You are safe here. Know that you will always be safe here. Now, I think you need to sleep. By the look of you, sleep has been something of a stranger to you of late. Your body needs rest. Your baby needs you at full strength, so now is time to sleep. Over to the bed with you. I need to see to the chickens first, and then I will make us some stew for this evening."

Without a word of argument, Gianetta went across the room to the bed, lay on the old covers, rested her head on the straw pillow and fell into a deep, healing sleep.

Taking a blanket from the old wooden chair, Mamma gently lay it across Gianetta's shoulders and said a small prayer for her young family.

CHAPTER 24

Early the next morning, while Gianetta was still sleeping soundly in her childhood home in Fiesole, Matteo, five miles away in Florence, slowly opened his eyes and let them roam around the ceiling above him. He didn't recognise it, and it took several minutes to realise where he was and remember the events and revelations of yesterday. He sat up quickly and grabbed the elaborate bedcovers as his head spun. Grasping his long black hair, he rested his elbows on his raised knees and took deep breaths to steady himself. Eventually, he felt a little more like his old self, lifted his head and looked around the room, realising that this was probably Gianetta's room. He ran his hand over the soft pillow next to him, wishing that he could feel her warmth alongside him, her comforting presence, reassuring him that all would be well. He had to find her.

Flinging back the covers, he swung his long legs over the side of the bed, his toes feeling the silk rug beneath his bare feet. Such luxury. He could imagine Gianetta being uncomfortable here alone. He took a drink from the water beaker alongside the bed. It tasted… Before he had time to decide how it tasted, his stomach lurched and he grasped the bucket that had been placed on the floor. With his head resting on the side, he vomited up the meagre contents of his stomach. As waves of nausea washed over him, he ran a shaky hand over his face, wiping away the sweat. Mandragora! What devil created such a plant? He would be careful what he drank in future.

"How are you feeling?" said a voice from the door.

"Eleonora! I'm so glad to see you. Can you give me something to stop this sickness?"

"My remedy is helping then?"

"You mean you gave me this to drink? This is what's doing this to me?"

"Yes, I did. I always keep a small amount of ipecac root for just this sort of situation. Sometimes, it's better to get rid of everything in the body, especially if it's doing harm, such as the mandragora was doing to you. I knew you'd got rid of most of it yourself, but when you collapsed last night, I knew there was still some poison in your system. I had to get rid of it."

As she spoke, Matteo continued to vomit, his whole body heaving with the effort. Eventually, his body rested, the waves of expulsion dying away. He lay back on the pillow, exhausted. "I have to get up, Eleonora. I need to look for Gianetta."

"Stay where you are, boy. Signor Lorenzo has had his men out all night looking for her. I believe he's just arrived. I heard his voice in the study with Signor Francesco as I passed just now."

Again, Matteo made to get up. This time, he managed to stand upright without spinning or vomiting. As he looked around for his shoes, the door opened and in walked Francesco and Lorenzo, looking serious. "What is it?" he asked, desperately. "Have you found her?"

Lorenzo spoke first. "No, boy. We have not found her." At the look of panic on the young man's face, he raised his hand and continued quickly. "That is not a bad thing. She has not been pulled into any of the brothels, as girls on their own often are. She has not drowned. My men searched the river. They hunted throughout all of Florence, waking up anyone who may have seen her. I don't think she is in Florence, boy. Might she have left the city?"

Matteo slowly looked up and through strands of black hair, his blue eyes met Eleonora's gaze. Their thoughts combined as they nodded.

"How can I help, Matteo?" asked Francesco.

"A horse, *ser*? May I borrow a horse? I may not get back today, but I think I know where she may be."

An hour later, after Matteo had washed, dressed and been persuaded to eat a little bread, he and Francesco arrived at the stables, where the Rosini family kept two horses, for transport and for hunting. The stable boy had jumped to attention when Signor Francesco walked in.

"*Buongiorno, ser.* Shall I saddle your horses?" The boy was eager to please.

"Just one, please, Gio. I'm not going on this trip," replied Francesco. "Will you saddle up Flora, please?" He turned to Matteo. "Flora is swift but steady," he said. "How is your riding?"

Matteo looked at the large, chestnut mare uncertainly. "I used to ride when I was younger, but not for a long time. I'm sure it will come back to me."

Francesco clapped him on the shoulder. "Flora has a beautiful temperament. She'll take care of you."

Flora and Matteo looked at each other, each weighing up the other, until Matteo stroked her nose and mane, and Flora made up her mind.

She would trust this man. He had kind eyes, and she knew he wouldn't whip her. She stood patiently while Gio, the stable boy, saddled her and made her ready for her ride.

Francesco took Matteo to one side and spoke quietly to him. "The most important thing is to find Gianetta and bring her home safely," he said, with emotion in his voice. "We…we made mistakes. Cristina and I made mistakes. We thought that we were doing what was best. It's clear now, that we were wrong. It's not easy for me to admit that, but…well…there we are." He cleared his throat, nervously. "Bring her home, Matteo. We can work it all out, but please bring her home."

Matteo was a little lost for words at Francesco's candour. He could feel his throat beginning to constrict with emotion too, as he realised the importance of the next couple of hours. What if he was wrong? What if she wasn't there? What would he do then? He pushed the thought aside, as Gio approached them.

"She's ready for you, *ser*," he said.

Flora tossed her head, knowing that she was about to run and eager to be off.

Matteo patted her neck as he took the reins and jumped up into the saddle. He felt surprisingly comfortable, as his childhood memories of horse-riding returned to him. His confidence grew a little, and he began to think that it might all turn out well, after all.

"God go with you, Matteo, and may He return you both safely to us," said Francesco, as he tapped Flora's flanks.

Matteo dug his heel into Flora's side, flicked the reins, and they flew out of the stables. The last glimpse that Francesco had was of Flora's chestnut tail and Matteo's black hair flying out behind them, as they headed north. He said a quiet prayer under his breath, thanked Gio with a generous tip and left the stables to return to the Palazzo.

The sun was high in the sky. Gianetta had slept well and woken refreshed and ready to face her new life. She knew that she would have to become accustomed to the empty place in her heart that Matteo would never fill.

Mamma had prepared a bowl of water for her to wash and had taken her dirty clothes, washed them and spread them in the sun across the bushes in the garden. She had found a simple linen dress that one of the village women had given her in payment for some sewing. It was clean and cool and would be loose enough to fall over Gianetta's expanding belly.

Gianetta gratefully took advantage of the bowl of lavender-smelling water, wiping away the grime of the city, finally rinsing the water through her hair. She used mint leaves and water to clean her teeth and mouth, finally feeling as though she could face the world. The linen dress was soft on her skin as she padded, barefoot, to the small garden, where Mamma was feeding the chickens.

"*Madonna Mia!* You look like my Gianetta again. The sleep has transformed you. How are you feeling?"

"Much better, Mamma. You were right. I was very tired. I don't think I realised how exhausted I was. It has been so hard these last days." A tear welled up in her eye and threatened to spill down her cheek, but she brushed it away and lifted her chin. "All will be well, Mamma."

The old woman looked at her in sympathy, then nodded and smiled. "Come, let's eat. I have some fresh cheese from Tommaso's farm, and I made some bread early this morning."

Gianetta's stomach growled, reminding her that she had hardly eaten in the last couple of days. She followed Mamma into the house and sat down at the table, tucking in greedily to the bread and cheese. Mamma had even found some dried figs to share. When she had eaten her fill, Gianetta licked her fingers and breathed a heavy sigh of satisfaction.

"Mamma, that was as good as any banquet at the Palazzo...but never tell Eleonora I said that!" She laughed, but then her smile grew sad as she remembered that she was unlikely to see the cook again.

Following her thoughts, Mamma patted the young girl's hand but said nothing. "*Andiamo.* Come, there is work to do." And with an energy that belied her age, she rose from the table, taking the empty plates with her.

The two women spent a few hours cleaning the house and tending to the garden, feeding the chickens and picking the courgettes that had been ripening in the sun. After a cool drink in the shade, Mamma said, "I have sewing to do. Signora Arezzini wants the sleeves shortened on her dresses. I promised her they would be ready by the end of the week." She tutted and shook her head and headed back to the house.

Gianetta sat for a while, taking in the sights, sounds and smells of the garden. The chickens scratched and clucked around the dirt yard. They each had their own characters and always made Gianetta smile. She looked at the bay tree at the back of the yard. It had been small when she had left for Florence, but now its branches were sending glossy green leaves high into the sky. Eleonora would love it. She used bay often in her cooking and in some of her medicines. Strolling to the end of the yard, Gianetta reached up into the tree and picked one of the bay leaves, rubbing it between her fingers and inhaling the strong, peppery perfume. Closing her eyes, she was back in the kitchen of the Palazzo Rosini, Eleonora's stew bubbling on the fire with a handful of bay leaves floating on the top, filling the kitchen with a heady aroma. Gino was at the table on tiptoes, looking for any unsupervised scraps of cake that he might pilfer. Lucia was at the other end of the table, preparing Nonna's breakfast tray, while the kitchen door opened and in walked Matteo with bagsful of flour, which had just been delivered for Eleonora and the daily bread. "*Ciao Bellissima!*" he would say, as he always did, as he winked at her. Gianetta's stomach turned over, and a tear squeezed through her closed eyelids and dripped from her long, dark lashes.

"Ciao Bellissima!" Oh, what she would give to be able to hear him say that to her again.

"Ciao Bellissima!" She could almost smell him and feel his arms around her.

"Ciao Bellissima!" She felt a presence behind her and heard the words whispered quietly, but that couldn't be…could it? She opened her eyes and turned around.

Leaning casually in the doorway of the house, looking happy and relaxed was Matteo. Gianetta's hand jumped to her mouth as she gasped in disbelief. "Matteo? Is it really you?"

Matteo's mouth broke into a beaming smile, and he nodded. *"Sì, Bellissima.* It is me. I…" He couldn't finish what he was about to say, as Gianetta flew across the yard, scattering the protesting chickens, and jumped into his arms. For several moments, they held each other tightly, not having the words to express their emotions. Eventually, Matteo put Gianetta down, put his hand to his back and said, "Wow, that baby is going to be a big one!"

Gianetta punched him on the shoulder, laughing through her tears. "Matteo, you're…alive! I can't believe it. Cesare Conti said…"

Matteo's face darkened. "Don't believe everything you hear, especially from him. *Bastardo!"*

Gianetta looked shocked, as Matteo was not given to cursing, but guessed that in this case, it was warranted. "Tell me later. That can wait. Just let me look at you." She looked up at him and ran her hand through his long, black hair, then along his cheekbones, his skin rough with stubble. Her fingertips brushed his lips, as she gazed into his deep blue eyes.

Matteo slid a hand under her loose, long hair, reached behind her neck and drew her up to him for the longest, deepest kiss that neither of them wanted to end.

Behind them, Mamma quietly closed the door, shedding a tear of her own.

Over the next few hours and a plate of roasted chicken with salad from the garden, both Gianetta and Matteo told of their experiences of the days that they had been apart, leaving out no detail. When Matteo related his tale of poisoning with mandragora, Gianetta jumped up.

"Bastardo!"

Matteo saw the flash of fire in her eyes and smiled to himself. One of the things he loved most about Gianetta was her strength and determination. The fiery temperament that went with it only occasionally made its presence known. Life with her would certainly never be boring.

The flash of anger subsided when she thought about what Matteo had been through. Looking at him carefully, she said, "And now? Are you recovered?"

"I am," he nodded, with a smile. "Eleonora saw to that!"

"You have been very lucky," said Mamma. "Not many survive mandragora poisoning. Eleonora must be very skilled."

They both nodded fervently. "Skilled in medicines and cooking," said Gianetta. "She is a formidable woman, and we all love her dearly."

Gianetta became serious. She looked across at the man she had thought was dead, the man she thought she would never see again, the man she would love forever, the father of her child. "What are we to do, Matteo? Everything has become such a mess. I thought our lives would be simple, that this sort of complicated life only happened to the nobility. How naïve was I?

"When I thought I had lost you, I didn't know where to turn. I thought my life was over too, but then I came home. I was going to have the baby here and live with Mamma…if she would have us."

"Of course, I would have you here, my child," said Mamma, then paused. "I don't think this is your life, though. What say you, Matteo?"

"Thank you, Mamma Sofia," he said, "but I have been given specific instructions."

Gianetta looked up, confused. "Instructions? From whom?"

"Signor Francesco. They are so very worried about you. I was told I must find you and bring you home."

"They want me to return to the Palazzo? Even after…everything? I embarrassed them in front of their friends…"

He held up his hand and shook his head. "They just want you to return. They are so concerned about you. Little Gino keeps asking when he will see you again, and I can't tell you how worried Eleonora and Lucia are."

Gianetta bowed her head with shame. How could she have done this to her friends? How selfish had she been? "You're right. I must return, even if just to explain myself and ask forgiveness. After that? Who knows? I'm not sure what life has in store for us, Matteo, but if you're with me, I know I can face it."

"Then you will return with me to Palazzo Rosini?"

"Yes, Matteo. Of course, I will return with you."

"Neither of you are going anywhere tonight. The sun is almost down, and the roads between here and Florence are too dangerous after dark. Gianetta, you can share my bed, and I'm sure I can find Matteo a dry comfortable spot in the barn, if you don't mind sharing with some goats."

"After some of my experiences lately, goats will seem like civilised company," he replied with a wry smile.

The next morning, after a breakfast of eggs, fruit and fresh bread,

Matteo went to saddle up Flora, ready for their return to Florence. As she nuzzled into his neck, Matteo whispered to her. "We have to be much gentler on our way home, girl. We have a very precious load, and we need to take care of her."

Flora tossed her head, and Matteo was sure that she understood.

Mamma and Gianetta were saying fond farewells, accompanied by many tears and hugs.

"It has been such a short visit, Mamma. We hardly had any time together."

"Don't fret, child. Promise me that you will send me word as soon as you return. I promise that wherever you are, I will be with you when the time comes for your child to be born."

After a final embrace, Gianetta allowed Matteo to help her up onto Flora's saddle, and Matteo jumped up behind her. Turning Flora's reins to the road, they waved a last goodbye to Mamma and headed off to whatever awaited them in Florence.

CHAPTER 25

On that same morning, the kitchen of Palazzo Rosini was as busy as usual but with a subdued atmosphere. The family still needed to eat. The chores were still to be done. However, the air of trepidation seeped under every door and into every pore. There was no banter between the staff. Indeed, there was very little talking at all. Their minds were too full of their own thoughts, hopes and fears. The number of possible outcomes to this situation seemed endless, and nobody dared to hope that all would be well.

Eleonora was kneading the bread automatically, her eyes focused somewhere in the distance. She didn't even shout at Marco when he spilt flour over the clean floor.

Lucia had returned from the market, having forgotten most of what she went out for.

Gino put his head cautiously through the kitchen door. His family didn't want to play this morning. Nonna, who always had a good story to tell, was at prayer longer than usual. The kitchen was always a good place to find fun and even a few treats, but even the kitchen didn't have the usual welcome. He wished Gianetta were here. She always made him laugh. He wasn't sure why, but he wanted to cry, and so he left the kitchen before the teardrops spilled down his cheeks.

Breakfasts were cleared away. Bedrooms were cleaned. The next job was to start preparing the lunch, and Eleonora went to the cold room to collect some cured meats. As she was closing the door, she heard a noise outside. Putting the meat back on the shelf, she put her head outside the kitchen door. The rumpus was coming from the courtyard. It sounded like screaming...or was it crying? Then she heard "Gianetta!"

Was it really Gianetta? Had she come home? She could hardly allow herself to believe it. Was she hurt, or worse? Calling Lucia, she ran out of the kitchen and onto the top floor balcony, looking over the balustrade. From her birds' eye viewpoint, she couldn't see faces, but there was no mistaking the long dark, curly head of hair. It had to be Gianetta. Oh, and that shock of black hair must belong to Matteo! He had found her and brought her home. Forgetting all points of etiquette, Eleonora and Lucia raced down the stairs to greet their friends.

As they reached the courtyard, they could see Signor Francesco, Donna Cristina, Tessa and little Gino gathered around the two bemused young people. They were all talking at once, excited and clearly pleased to see them. Gino had clung to Gianetta's skirt and obviously had no intention of letting go.

At that point, Gianetta caught sight of her friends and rushed to greet them, taking Gino with her. After several minutes of tears and embraces, they remembered where they were.

"I'm so sorry, Signor Francesco, Donna Cristina," said Eleonora, rather breathlessly. "In the excitement, we forgot ourselves."

As Donna Cristina wiped away her tears, Signor Francesco reassured them. "We are all delighted to see the return of our two friends. It is only natural that you should want to greet them."

He turned to Gianetta and Matteo. "Can I suggest that you take yourselves to the kitchen to get something to eat after your journey? Perhaps we can meet in the *sala* in an hour? We have much to discuss. Eleonora, will you send Marco to me please? He can take Flora back to the stables."

Gianetta and Matteo glanced at each other, but they knew it was a conversation that needed to be had.

Above them all, Nonna had emerged from her room and was looking over the balcony, clutching her rosary and tearfully offering prayers of thanks.

An hour later, having been well fed by Eleonora, Gianetta and Matteo nervously knocked the door of the *sala*.

"Come in," said Francesco. The door opened slowly, and the young couple entered, holding hands firmly. The whole family were sitting in their places: Cristina in her chair by the window, Nonna by the fireplace, Francesco on the couch in the centre of the room, and Tessa in her chair near the spinet. Gino sat on her lap, eagerly looking between the people who made up his whole world. He didn't know why, but he knew this was important.

"*Venite!* Come!" said Francesco. "Please sit." He indicated the couch opposite him, and Gianetta and Matteo made their way to their seats, perching on the edge, as if waiting for sentence to be passed.

"You must think me so ungrateful, after everything that you have done for me," said Gianetta. "That… that night of the banquet with the Contis… I… I didn't know what… I…" She floundered for the right words, all of which escaped her.

Faced with such emotion, Francesco was beginning to look uncomfortable. As he ran his hand through his hair and cleared his throat, Cristina stood up and went to Gianetta, kneeling in front of her and taking her hands in her own.

"Not another word, child," she said. "We all have reason to ask forgiveness, none more so than Francesco and I." At Gianetta's confused frown, she continued. "We should never have arranged that marriage for you. Please believe us when we say that we thought it was for the best."

"We know what sort of man he is…now," said Francesco. He looked at Matteo. "Again, I apologise for believing that you were the one…for believing what he said. I should have believed in you, and I didn't. For that, I am very sorry."

"*Grazie,* Signor Francesco. Thank you for trusting me."

"I must admit that Lorenzo was the one to convince me of the truth. However, we have another testimony." Francesco leaned forward, resting his elbows on his knees, clasped his hands and looked down at his feet.

"Last night, after you had been put to bed, I went back to the studio with Lorenzo. We sat and discussed everything. What a time we have been through! Well, late into the night, Marco knocked the door and asked permission to enter. Thinking that everyone had gone to bed, including the staff, I was taken aback somewhat, but he looked in earnest, so I bade him enter. He told me a story.

"He spoke of the meetings that he used to go to with Antonio, and how much he regretted his actions. He went on a bit about that until I urged him to get to the point. Apparently, while he was serving us during the banquet with the Contis, he thought he recognised one of the faces at our dining table. It was only when Cesare lost his temper that he fully recognised him. He had seen him in the room with Antonio, just after the attack in the *Duomo*. He was one of the members of the group who had carried out the attack. He had been covered in blood and was boasting about how many of his fellow Florentines he had killed."

Francesco stopped and fought with his emotions, biting hard on his clenched fist. "To think that I entertained that man under our very roof…"

"*Ser,* what will happen to Marco?" asked Matteo.

"It was a brave thing for him to do, coming into the same room as the man he had plotted against. After I sent him back to bed, we had a long conversation, Lorenzo and I, but we decided that a Florentine reborn is better than a Florentine hanged. I think Lorenzo was more concerned with bigger offenders. Marco will stay. Eleonora is convinced that he will be a loyal member of our household, and I agree with her."

As if prompted by a cue, a knock on the door revealed Marco to be standing just outside. By his discomfort, it was clear that the boy had heard most of the conversation but tried hard to hide the fact. "*Ser,*" he said, with a bow. "Signor Conti has arrived and asked to speak with you."

"Signor Piero or Signor Cesare?"

"Signor Cesare, *ser.*"

"Where is he?"

"I asked him to wait in your study, *ser.*"

Francesco nodded. He glanced around him at the people sitting with him and knew that he must handle this correctly. There would be no second chances. "Matteo, I don't think that it's wise for him to see you just yet. I am keen to hear what the boy has to say for himself. Go and hide in the room next door until he is in this room with us, and then come and listen at the door. I will let you know when to come in. Gianetta, are you happy to stay in the room with us?"

Gianetta nodded. She also wanted to look this man in the eye after what he had done.

Francesco looked at his grandson.

"Gino, would you like to go to the kitchen and see what Eleonora is preparing for lunch?"

Gino looked as though he knew he would be missing something important, but in the end decided that food was probably more important.

Tessa nodded to Francesco gratefully, took Gino's hand and left the room.

"Now, Marco. I want you to show Signor Cesare in. He is to know nothing about Gianetta and Matteo being here." He looked sternly at the boy, who nodded seriously.

"Then, once he is here, I want you to run to the *Palazzo della Signoria*, tell them that we have one of the traitors in our house and they need to return urgently to arrest him."

Now Marco was looking excited. Surely, this meant that Signor Rosini was beginning to trust him. He had to take this task seriously and perform to the best of his abilities. He was never very good at running, but by all the saints, there would be wings on his feet today. He turned on his heel and made to leave the room.

"*Aspetta!* Wait!" Francesco's voice stopped Marco in his tracks. "Let Matteo leave first." He turned and nodded to Matteo, who left the room and turned right, to hide in the room next door. He was closely followed by Marco, who turned left and headed to the study.

Francesco, Cristina and Gianetta waited nervously for Marco to show Cesare into the room.

Nonna feigned sleep in her chair by the fireplace.

The door opened and Marco came in, bowing and introducing their guest. "*Signori,* Signor Cesare Conti." He closed the door gently behind him as he left, then quietly ran down the stairs and out into the street.

Standing up, Francesco greeted their guest. "Cesare, to what do we owe the honour?"

With a beaming smile, Cesare opened his arms and addressed Francesco and Cristina. He ignored Nonna quietly snoozing. He walked straight past Gianetta, who was sitting in a chair with her back to the door.

"Zio! Zia! Come state?"

"We are well, thank you," replied Francesco. He waited for Cesare to continue.

"I simply came to bring my regards to you, to thank you for your hospitality a few evenings ago and to express my regret at how the situation ended."

Francesco nodded but said nothing. He wanted to see where Cesare was going.

Unperturbed, Cesare continued. "I have been concerned about you all, with all the terrible events that you have suffered lately. I heard that the servant girl ran away. Maybe that was for the best. You must be so worried about your family."

"Here it comes," thought Francesco to himself. "I think we're getting to the point." He simply inclined his head, indicating that Cesare continue.

With the lightness of an innocent question, he asked, "How is Tessa faring? It must be very difficult for her."

"So that's your game!" thought Francesco.

"Tessa is a strong woman, Cesare," he replied. "She is managing very well, considering she has just lost her husband. Why do you ask?"

"She is a strong woman, and a fine woman too. I wondered." He paused, thoughtfully stroking his neat beard. "I wondered if I may visit and pay court to her."

"You forget me so soon, *ser*?"

Cesare's head spun round, and his jaw dropped as he saw Gianetta sitting behind him. Nonna was now wide awake. He opened and closed his mouth several times, looking from Francesco to Gianetta. "You're...here!"

"As you can see, *ser*." Gianetta stood to face him.

"Well..." Cesare spluttered, looking to Francesco for help, which did not come. "Well, I'm glad to see that you are safe and well. I..." Running his finger under his collar, he desperately sought a way of handling the situation.

Gianetta looked at him, enjoying his discomfort. Her thoughts turned to what he had done, how he had tried to kill the man that she loved, the father of her baby and a red mist clouded her vision. In a flash, she crossed the room, and with the strength of all the pain and suffering that this man had inflicted on the people she loved, she clenched her fist and threw it at his face, breaking his fine, straight nose.

Cesare fell back into a chair, clutching his face, blood streaming through his fingers.

Cristina put her hand to her mouth in shock, but Francesco held her. Neither of them moved to help him.

Nonna straightened up and clenched her fists, as though she would also like to join in.

Gianetta stood, glaring down at the bloody face of this hateful man, still seething with fury.

Mopping his nose with a fine linen handkerchief, Cesare caught his breath, then looked up at Gianetta with a fearful rage. He jumped up and raised his fist to strike her, but the door burst open, and Matteo ran in and stood between them, nose to bloody nose with Cesare.

Cesare fell back as though he had been struck again. His face drained of its colour. "You..." he whispered. "You are..."

"I'm supposed to be dead. Is that what you were going to say?"

Before risking any more violence, Francesco decided to step in. "It's over, Cesare. We know everything."

"I don't know what you mean. The boy ran. Surely, you can see that makes him guilty."

"No, Cesare. That's not what happened, is it?"

"You…you don't believe him, do you?" Cesare spluttered, pointing at Matteo. "The word of a servant?"

"I do, actually," said Francesco, calmly. "And even if I didn't, I have the testimony of Lorenzo de' Medici. He saw the man that killed my son, and it wasn't Matteo…or are you suggesting that he was lying too?" He raised an eyebrow, wondering how far Cesare was prepared to go with his story.

Cesare was silent.

"We also have other testimony, which proves you were part of that despicable plot. We know that you also tried to have Matteo killed. You couldn't even do that yourself. What a coward! And now you try to insinuate yourself into my family, first with Gianetta, my granddaughter." He looked across at Gianetta, who smiled at him. "Then, when you believe that wasn't possible, you try your luck again, proposing to court Tessa, Niccolò's widow, when he's not even cold in his grave."

Cesare was beginning to look panicked, eyes darting around like a cornered animal.

"I presume," continued Francesco, "that it was all for the money? Wasn't your own family fortune enough for you?"

"Of course not," Cesare spat. "The old man is too soft with his money. His tenants take advantage of him. They pretend that they don't have enough to eat, so he lets them off their rent. What sort of businessman does that?"

"A charitable one, perhaps?"

"Pah! Foolish, more like! There's change coming to Florence, and it costs money. That fiasco in the *Duomo* was just the beginning. We've got plans…big plans…and I intend to be part of it. Of course, I needed your money." Cesare was now raving, pacing the floor, spittle flying from his mouth with every word. "If it meant that I had to wed that bitch and take on her bastard brat too, then so be it. There are ways of dealing with that afterwards."

Matteo went to lunge forward, but Gianetta put her hand gently on his arm and held him back.

"*Basta*! Enough!" bellowed Francesco. "I won't have you insult me or my family in my house any longer. You have disgraced yourself and your family. Your parents will be so ashamed. I pity them. You have disgraced the people of Florence, and they will mete out their punishment. I'm sorry for you, but it's only what you deserve. As we speak, the guards of the *Signoria* are on their way to arrest you, and may you hang with the rest of the traitors."

Without pausing for breath, Cesare leapt across the room, pushing past Gianetta and Matteo and ran through the door. Outside, the sounds of the guards running up the staircase could be heard, their blades clashing against the walls and Marco shouting directions.

Francesco breathed a sigh of relief, and he pulled Cristina to him, kissing the top of her head. "It's done, *cuore mia*. It's over now." She trembled in his arms, trying to regain her composure.

The first guard ran into the room, his sword drawn. "Where is he?"

"What do you mean?" said Francesco. "He just ran from the room. You must have seen him!"

"We passed no one, *ser*. There are three of us, plus your man. We saw no one."

Francesco put his hand to his head and looked around in confusion.

"I don't understand…"

Matteo spoke up quietly. "The back stairs. He said he'd used the back stairs before. I think he came to meet Antonio. I'm not sure if it was about the plots or…something else." He faltered, embarrassed.

"Run, man!" shouted Francesco to the guard. "You have to catch him."

The guards ran from the room, but Francesco and Matteo looked at each other.

"We've lost him, haven't we?" said Francesco. Matteo nodded. Cristina gasped.

"Don't worry, *cara*. He won't bother us again. He daren't show his face to anyone who knows him. He knows he'll hang if he does."

Finally, Nonna spoke. "*Bastardo!*"

"Indeed, Nonna!"

Later that afternoon, after Eleonora had worked her magic with a chamomile tonic and a light lunch, the family had gathered again the *sala*, with Gianetta and Matteo. They waited for Francesco to return. He had gone to visit his friends Piero and Maria Conti, wanting to be the one to talk to them about their son. It was not a task he'd relished but felt obliged to break the news personally.

Cristina and Tessa were talking quietly by the window, while Gino sat on Gianetta's lap, telling her all about what he'd been doing while she was away.

Matteo crouched next to Nonna, listening to her strong opinions of what should happen to men like Cesare Conti. He smiled and nodded, knowing that she would be quite willing to carry out her punishments given half a chance.

Eventually, Francesco returned, looking weary and sad. He shook his head and sat heavily in his chair.

Cristina stood behind him and put her arms around his shoulders. "How was it? It must have been so hard."

"How do you tell a mother that her son is a murderer? It was the worst thing I have ever had to do. They are devastated, as you can imagine. We sent for Padre Cristoforo for Maria. She will need him, I think. It's as hard as any bereavement, maybe harder. I don't think Piero was very surprised, really. He's an astute man, and I believe he had his suspicions about his son. He will have to deal with the knowledge of what the boy did. I don't know that they will ever get over it."

The room was silent as they thought of the good Conti family and the news that would have changed their lives forever.

Even Gino paused in his storytelling, looking around at everyone, sensing the atmosphere but not really knowing what had happened. He jumped down from Gianetta's lap and went to his grandfather, who lifted him up and hugged him tightly. "*Nonno*," he said, quietly. "Is Gianetta staying with us now?"

Francesco smiled at his grandson. "Let's see, shall we?" He looked across at Cristina, who nodded.

"It seems, my dear, that we have very poor judgement when choosing a husband for you. Far better that we trust your judgement." And her eyes went from Gianetta to Matteo. "I am right? You have chosen your husband?"

"Oh yes, *Madonna*!" cried Gianetta. "With all my heart, I choose Matteo." They clasped each other's hands as if they would never let go.

A voice drifted over from the fireplace. "The family is to have a wedding, after all. *Bene, bene*," and Nonna smiled, closed her eyes and drifted off to sleep again.

Francesco stood up to shake Matteo by the hand.

Donna Cristina and Tessa kissed and embraced Gianetta with genuine warmth.

Not to miss out on the excitement, Gino jumped up onto the sofa next to Gianetta and clambered onto her lap, wrapping his little arms around her neck.

Amid the happiness and excitement, Matteo became serious. Francesco noticed the change in the boy's demeanour. "What is it, Matteo?" he asked.

"I have to ask, *ser*. What are we to do, Gianetta and me? I have to provide for my family, and I can't work at The Maestro's workshop. Would there be room for me on your staff again? I promise you that I will work hard and be loyal to you and the family."

Francesco nodded and said, "I understand. We have already discussed this as a family before you returned from Fiesole... hoping that you would return from Fiesole. We have a proposition. Tessa, would you like to explain?"

Tessa smiled and turned to Gianetta. "Gianetta, you know that since we lost my Niccolò, I have been learning more about the family textile business. It turns out that Luigi took on an enormous amount of work, and I have a lot to do to catch up. We wondered if you might help me out by looking after Gino while I am working." She paused.

Gianetta's eyes gleamed, while Gino jumped up and down with excitement.

"Say yes, Gianetta, please say yes!" said the little boy, clapping his hands.

The two women looked at each other, and Gianetta gave an imperceptible nod and hid a smile. "I'm not sure," she said, with a serious face. "Looking after a little boy is an important job, and I'm going to have a baby of my own to look after."

"That's very true," joined in Cristina. "I think you will need someone to help you when the baby comes. What are we to do?"

By this time, Gino was jumping up and down, fit to explode. "Me! Oh, I can help! Please let me help! Can I, Mamma? Can I help Gianetta when the baby comes?"

"Well, I think we should ask Gianetta what she thinks," she replied.

Gino turned to Gianetta and climbed up on her lap, taking great care to avoid the growing bump. He spoke very quietly. "Gianetta, please may I help you when the baby comes? I'm not a baby anymore, and I can do anything you ask me to, and I promise I'll be good, every day. Well, I'll try really hard. Really, I will."

Gianetta turned to Tessa. "How can I refuse such an offer?" She turned to Gino. "That's settled then. We are to look after each other, while your Mamma helps your grandfather with the business."

Gino nodded seriously, acknowledging the enormity of the undertaking.

Matteo coughed softly. "I'm sorry, *ser*," he addressed Francesco. "I'm very grateful, but I must be able to support my family. I couldn't have my wife working while I remain idle. I have to go where I can work."

Francesco nodded. "I understand, Matteo, and I expected you to feel this way. However, I do have a proposition that would also help me. Previously, there were three of us running this business: myself, Niccolò and Luigi. Now, there is just me and Tessa. I know that Tessa can take care of the legal side of my business, but I need extra hands, strong hands, to help me when I visit customers with samples of my cloth."

Matteo looked unsure.

"This is not a charitable gesture, Matteo," said Francesco, sensing his misgivings. "This is a role I needed to fill, and I had intended to start the search very soon, until the obvious solution was pointed out to me." He glanced at his wife, who looked innocently out of the window. "I need someone reliable, someone strong and someone who will not offend my customers. Matteo, I was foolish not to think of you myself, but I would like you to consider my offer. Your wages will reflect the increased responsibility within the household, and as the husband of my granddaughter, you will share her room."

"My room in the attic?" asked Gianetta.

"Indeed not!" exclaimed Cristina. "You will share the room that you stayed in before...before you left."

Gianetta thought of the large luxurious room that she had hated so much. It had felt like a prison cell. How different it would be to share it with Matteo and their new baby.

Matteo grasped Gianetta's hand and glanced at her before turning to Francesco and saying, "Thank you, *ser*. You are most generous, and we accept your kind offer." He gave a small bow, as Francesco stepped forward to clap him on the shoulder and shake his hand.

"Welcome to the family, young man. At least, you will be part of the family once we have arranged this wedding." Knowing that this was not his field of expertise, he turned to his wife. "Cristina?" He led Matteo out of the room, saying "This is none of our business. We are not needed here...except when it comes to paying the bills!"

CHAPTER 26

Saturday before Pentecost

Palazzo Rosini was silent. There were no business meetings in the study. There was no cleaning in the *sala* or the bedrooms. There was no cooking in the kitchen. There were no shouts from Eleonora, and no sounds of Gino's running feet. The Palazzo was empty.

The dining room, however, was full to bursting with flowers, food and wine. Large floral displays were in each corner, throwing bright splashes of colour into the room, and a heady scent of perfume filled the atmosphere, which almost matched the aroma of the food. The *credenza* was heavily laden with Eleonora and Lucia's best creations. There were cold, cured meats, salmon mousse, stuffed eggs, fresh focaccia bread and salads of every description. There were promising gaps where hot dishes were to be served. For those with a sweet tooth, there were peach crostatas, almond blancmange and fruit pies, interspersed with bowls of sugared almonds. Again, gaps between the platters hinted at more delicacies to come from the cold room, such as *zabaglione* and, of course, Eleonora's *zuccotto*. On a separate side table, an army of wine jugs awaited their call to serve the guests.

The curtains were held open with elaborate swags, and the bright sunshine poured onto the dining table, exquisitely set with shining cutlery, delicate crockery and glittering glassware for guests. The head of the table was set for two, with two grand chairs, each decorated further with flowers to match the displays around the room. This was a dining room poised and eager to celebrate with two guests of honour, and there was love in all the preparations.

The day had finally arrived for Gianetta and Matteo to declare their love for each other in front of God, their family and their friends. Padre Cristoforo was to conduct the ceremony in the family parish church of *Chiesa di Ognissanti*, where many family baptisms, weddings and funerals had taken place over the years.

Just before the ceremony, Matteo had stood at the far side of the small piazza, gazing into the river, just as Gianetta had done not long ago. He was absorbed in his thoughts when a cough behind him made him turn around. "Papà?" He was dumbfounded. He hadn't seen his father since he had been brought by him to Maestro Sandro's workshop to start his apprenticeship. It had been, what? Six years ago? Seven?

"What are you doing here? How did you know? How are you?" He looked with concern at his father, who had aged considerably since he last saw him. Perhaps it was just a trick of his memory, but oh, it didn't matter. His father was here to share the happiest day of his life. Matteo had inherited his blue eyes from both his parents, and he gazed at his father's eyes now, which were turning milky with age. "How did you know?" he repeated.

Clasping Matteo's arms, his father looked at him proudly. "I wouldn't miss this wonderful occasion for all the world, my boy. It seems that your bride-to-be is a formidable woman. She spoke with Maestro Sandro and asked after me. She wrote to me, and well…here I am." His eyes began to fill with tears. "I have brought you something.

It… it may not be as grand as you would like, but… I have brought your mother's wedding ring to give to Gianetta. That is… if you want to…" he faltered.

Matteo's hand slipped to his pocket where he kept the ring that he had planned to give Gianetta. With an advance on his wages from Francesco, he had purchased the ring just days ago. It was expensive and elaborate, just what he thought Gianetta deserved, but then he looked at the plain band that his father held in his hand. This was far more valuable to him, and he knew that it would be just what Gianetta would want too. Unable to speak, he pulled his father to him in an embrace full of emotion. Eventually, he said, "Thank you, Papà. It's just perfect… perfect." They walked arm in arm across the piazza to the church, and as they awaited the arrival of the bride, he introduced his father to his friends.

Gianetta looked dazzling. Francesco and Cristina had wanted to make a statement, showing their acceptance of Gianetta as a true member of the Rosini family, and had presented her with a bolt of rich, rose-coloured brocade. Cristina's skilled seamstress had worked tirelessly to create the wonderful gown that she wore. At the centre of the high waist, the heavy fabric parted to reveal a delicate white silk panel, which flowed gently over her expanding belly. Gianetta's thick, curly hair was dressed with small flowers and held back from her face with a large silver clasp, a gift from Tessa, who had worn the same piece at her wedding to Niccolò.

Matteo was also an impressive sight in a doublet of royal blue velvet, with silver fastenings. His trousers were of the same velvet fabric, finishing at the knees with white stockings. Black shoes of soft leather completed his outfit. On any other day, Matteo would find the ensemble uncomfortable, being so far from his usual attire, but on this special day, he stood tall and proud. He had even managed to tame his wild locks for the ceremony, his shiny black hair brushed back from his face.

Padre Cristoforo stood serenely at the altar, waiting with a smile for the couple he had known that he would one day marry. He looked at the family and friends gathered in the large church and felt the love and happiness in the air, mingling with the incense and candle smoke. The congregation hushed as the bride and groom walked up the aisle hand in hand, ready to begin their journey of married life together.

As Padre Cristoforo conducted the ceremony, there were many happy tears in the congregation. With the religious and legal formalities completed, everyone gathered in the small piazza outside the church to congratulate the couple.

Nonna, sitting on a nearby bench, had the perfect spot. She loved to watch people, what they wore, how they acted. Usually, she would keep her observations to herself and bring them out later to examine them in detail, but on this occasion, she could share them. Sitting alongside her on the bench was Mamma Sofia. It had been so long since the sisters had seen each other, but they soon fell into comfortable familiarity, each commenting who was talking to whom, whether the colour of a gown suited a certain skin tone, or who seemed to be hovering near the wedding party when they had no place being there. Nonna had been delighted to hear that Mamma Sofia would be staying at the Palazzo until Gianetta delivered her baby. Tommaso had brought her from Fiesole, and being such a good friend to Gianetta, had been invited to stay for the celebrations, before returning to care for Mamma Sofia's animals.

"Oh, look," said Nonna, leaning sideways towards her sister. "Here's the Maestro. None other than Signor Sandro."

"The Maestro? Should I know him?"

"He's an artist, Sofia. Everyone speaks very highly of him, and it's true, he does have a way with a paintbrush, but…" She shrugged. "Is he really worthy of the adulation that comes his way? Time will tell, I expect." She turned to her sister and whispered, "They call him Botticelli, you know. His older brother is shaped like a barrel, and so what better name for the little brother? The little barrel!" The sisters put their heads together and giggled as they did when they were children.

Matteo caught sight of the Maestro and headed towards him. "Signor," he bowed to his former employer. "I must thank you for your wedding gift. I know that Signor Lorenzo arranged for the chest and that you decorated it for us. The woman you painted on the main panel…the one with all the orange blossom surrounding her… I recognise her. I'm sure that I dreamt of her once."

Signor Sandro nodded his curly head. "You did. She was born of your imagination, boy. I thought I'd try to bring her to life on one of your panels, but I have plans to make a larger work of her. She holds the promise of great things to come, and that is what I wish for you and your new bride."

As they shook hands, Gianetta joined them to add her thanks.

On the bench, Nonna turned her attention to another group of guests. Carlo, the Maestro's foreman, was paying great attention to Eleonora. They had been talking for some time, and Eleonora seemed to be responding favourably towards him. "In fact," thought Nonna, "one might almost be looking at a young maiden with a suitor." She smiled and nodded to herself.

"What is it?" asked Sofia.

"Eleonora," she replied. "It is time that she had some happiness of her own." And with that comment, their fate was sealed.

"She's not the only one," said Sofia. Following her gaze, Nonna saw Lucia blushing under the gaze of Lapo, the Maestro's senior apprentice.

"Ah, the young," she sighed. "How resilient! How quickly they forget love and loss."

Sofia looked confused.

Nonna patted her hand. "That is a story for another time, *sorella*. Today is for happiness. For now, let us feast. The party is heading to the Palazzo. Come! I am not as quick as I used to be, but I don't want to miss a morsel." And with that, she put on her determined face and headed out of the piazza, with Sofia rushing to catch her up.

The guests left the piazza for the Palazzo, walking in the sunshine and basking in the happiness of the occasion.

Gianetta and Matteo were left alone in the piazza. They held each other's hands and put their heads together.

"I don't want to miss a minute of this," said Gianetta, quietly. "Just a few weeks ago, I thought my life had come to an end." She glanced at the river, remembering her despair. "Now? Now, I can't believe I deserve to be this happy."

"You deserve all this and more, *mia bellissima*," said Matteo. "Remember my promise?"

Gianetta looked up, her brow furrowed, trying to remember.

"Today is the fifth week of Easter," said Matteo. "I promised to marry you before Pentecost."

Gianetta laughed. "So you did! I can never doubt you, ever again!"

Matteo pulled her into an embrace, and as they kissed, the baby between them jumped for joy.

DIGESTIVO

At the end of the journey, whether it is a story or a meal, we want to take time to digest what we have consumed. This is the time to appreciate what has gone before, to think about the ingredients that have been presented to you in such a unique way. A small Digestivo will aid that rumination and make sure that there are no leftovers or loose ends to disturb the digestion.

Select your Digestivo of choice, which is commonly an amari based liqueur or maybe, if you want a slightly different Italian flavour, a local limoncello. Make sure it's cold or served on ice. Sit back and sip the liqueur, allowing the flavours to be savoured on the tongue. Bask in the afterglow of a well-enjoyed repast, knowing that whatever comes next, it will always be a completely new experience.

EPILOGUE

It was a just a few days before Christmas. The weather had turned cold, the skies were dull and grey, and there was the threat of snow in the air. Doors and windows were shut against the chill, but bright lights shone through every window. Market traders were wrapped up heavily, huddling around braziers as they waited for customers. The customers, when they did venture out, were not in the mood for browsing or haggling, so business was slow. Some traders adapted to the conditions and set up on street corners, roasting chestnuts over burning embers. The smell and the smoke drifted throughout the streets.

As ever, the inns were busy. Theirs was a business that prospered at any time of year but especially when the weather was cold. The traders who had suffered since the early hours of the day would gather to thaw out their frozen hands and feet, eat some hot food and enjoy warm wine and company.

Across the river, in the *Oltrarno*, was such an inn. The fire was roaring; the noise from the customers was deafening; the innkeeper and his waitresses were rushing here and there, delivering hot stew and jugs of wine. There was not a spare seat to be found. Tucked away in the corner were two men in deep conversation. One man, with a fox's tail attached to his belt, nodded as he listened to the other.

"Yes," said La Volpe. "Yes, I understand." He looked at the other man, who had kept his hood up. Looking at his soft hands, he could tell that this was a man of refinement, a rich man. At least, he had been a rich man once. His cloak was thick and well-made of the best wool, but it looked a little grubby and was beginning to fray at the edges.

The cloak opened a little at the neck, and he glimpsed a faded green doublet, also a bit worn at the collar.

Seeing La Volpe looking at him, he pulled the cloak tighter around his neck and fixed him with his bright green eyes. "I hope you do understand," he said. "There are very powerful people who are relying on these messages being delivered on time. The people of Florence will…"

La Volpe held up his hand. "I do not need to know any more," he said. "I am paid to deliver messages, and my discretion is guaranteed. It is why my fee is greater than some of the more, shall we say unreliable, messengers that you may find. I do not need to know what is in the messages. Indeed, I find that I sleep better at night not knowing what I am delivering. After what happened in the *Duomo* at Easter, nothing could be bigger than that."

The other man was silent, and La Volpe felt a shiver of apprehension. As the man slid a large bag of coins across the table, he shook off the feeling. He slipped it into his own cloak, patted his breast pocket where he had stored the messages to be delivered and said, "I shall start straight away. I am familiar with the addresses." He stood and wound his way through the crowds to the door, leaving the man with the green doublet and green eyes to finish his wine.

As La Volpe crossed the *Ponte Vecchio*, snow started to fall. Instead of quickening his step, he paused and walked to the edge of the bridge. He looked down into the river. Taking the messages from his pocket, he looked around to make sure nobody was watching. He tore the sheets of paper into small pieces, then let them float, mixing with the snowflakes until they reached the swirling, dark water.

"There may always be treachery, but I don't intend to be a part of it," he whispered to himself.

He stood at the edge of the bridge, watching the river pass, wondering what life would hold for him now. Perhaps God did have something better in store for him. He could but hope. The cold started to seep through to his bones, so he pulled his cloak tightly about him and started to walk back to the centre of Florence. As he walked down *Via Porta Rossa*, he heard the cry of a small baby. He glanced up and recognised the red rose at the door of the Palazzo, remembering that he had visited there once. He smiled.

"Perhaps," he thought. "Perhaps, there is hope for Florence…"

AUTHOR'S NOTE

The Rose of Florence

Thank you for journeying back to Renaissance Florence with me. What a fascinating time it is! The joy of historical fiction is that I can make some changes to historical fact to make it fit my story, and those who know the history of this period will know that I have done this. I hope you will forgive me.

The murder in the cathedral did happen. Without turning this into a history lesson, the facts are that a group of men led by Jacopo Pazzi, opposed to the ruling Medici family, plotted to kill the brothers Lorenzo and Giuliano de' Medici, removing them from power. The Pope (Sixtus IV, whom Lorenzo had also managed to upset), made it quite clear that while he couldn't officially sanction an assassination, he would look kindly on anyone who was able to remove this troublesome family. The attack happened in the Duomo, Florence's Cathedral of Santa Maria del Fiore, during Mass, with some accounts claiming that the first blow was struck at the most solemn part of the Mass, when the priest raises the host. With a shout of "Traitor!", Giuliano was the first to be attacked with an assassin's dagger. He died on the floor of the cathedral, bleeding from nineteen wounds. Lorenzo was also struck in the neck, but luckily, it was just a flesh wound, and he survived. He managed to escape to the safety of the sacristy, where he and some of his supporters locked themselves in until it was safe to come out.

My only adaptation to this event was with the date. The attack occurred on April 26th, 1478, but Easter Sunday of that year was March

31st. The conspirators originally intended to launch the attack during Easter celebrations, but circumstances caused them to postpone their plans on two separate occasions. Eventually, desperation caused them to carry out their plot during Mass. There are reports that following the attack, Lorenzo perpetuated the myth that the attack happened on Easter Sunday, making it appear even more sacrilegious. I decided to keep that myth alive, as it helped with the story's timeline. There are many accounts of what has become known as The Pazzi Conspiracy, the events leading up to it and the characters involved. Some details vary, but such is the nature of working with history that is over five hundred years old.

What of the other historical characters that I've included? Sandro Botticelli did indeed live and work on Via Nuova at the time, and he did have the Vespucci family as his neighbours. Marco Vespucci, who attended that first dinner party at Palazzo Rosini, was a cousin of Amerigo Vespucci, the famous explorer. Marco's wife, Simonetta (who had died two years prior to our story), was a celebrated beauty, and since that time, there have been rumours that she had an affair with Giuliano de' Medici. These rumours have been kept alive in popular writing and TV series, but there does not seem to be any evidence to support this theory.

Leonardo da Vinci made a brief appearance in The Rose of Florence, making a sketch of the hanged corpse of Bernardo di Bandino Baroncelli, one of the first to strike his dagger at Giuliano. Leonardo did make this sketch, and a quick search online will show you his drawing. "The noblest pleasure is to understand" is one of his famous quotes, but of course, I don't know when he said this. I think it unlikely that he said it during his time of sketching the hanged man, but it seemed to fit in his conversation with Gianetta.

Of course, Florence herself has a starring role. Florence was the original inspiration for the novel on one of my first visits to the city, widely given credit as the birthplace of the Renaissance. While the city has evolved over the last five hundred years or more, the landmarks included in my story still stand today. You can visit the Duomo (still a working Cathedral), the Bargello (now a museum), the Palazzo Medici (Palazzo Medici-Riccardo), the Ponte Vecchio over the River Arno (now home to exclusive jewellers' shops, rather than the butcher shops of that time), and the church of Ognissanti (home of Botticelli's tomb). Even Palazzo Rosini is based on a real Palazzo. Palazzo Davanzati is preserved as a 15th century Palazzo and open to visitors. Like Palazzo Rosini, it sits on Via Porta Rossa, between the River Arno and the Duomo. It was Via Porta Rossa in 1478, and it is still Via Porta Rossa today. Walking these old streets of Florence, the walls seem to ooze with tales of years gone by, and it doesn't take a huge leap of imagination to transport oneself back in time.

I hope you enjoyed the journey back to the time of Lorenzo the Magnificent and the characters we met there. It was a time of upheaval and unrest, great art and enlightenment, and we can only wonder what happened to Gianetta, Matteo and their new baby.

Made in the USA
Columbia, SC
03 June 2023

0672468e-c622-45b0-ad66-85804db284f8R01